720 Linden Street

by KC Decker

This is a work of fiction. Names, characters, places, and incidents either are a product of the author's imagination or are used fictitiously. Any resemblance to actual persons; living or dead, businesses, companies, locales, or events is entirely coincidental.

Cover Design by Larch Gallagher
Copyright 2016 By KC DECKER

ISBN 10: 0-692-77876-4
ISBN 13: 978-0-692-77876-0

You cannot discover new oceans unless you have the courage to lose sight of the shore.

— Andre Gide

Chapter One

Work

"Salinger! Are you crazy? What the hell are you doing going to a BDSM club?" I spit out, completely unable to control the shaking of my voice and the weird buzzing between my ears. How can he be so casual? He's not even blushing.

He's just standing there with a huge grin plastered on his face, evidently very satisfied with my reaction. He crosses his arms over his chest, then he puffs up his body with pride and what, achievement maybe? Salinger takes some sick satisfaction in the ability to surprise me. He's obsessed with somehow proving that he is not as conservative as I initially had him pegged.

All I can think about is Salinger and Silas, face to face and the memory of that fateful video chat. Me, naked and spread open for the laptop screen. Silas 2,000 miles away, and Salinger's hand on my bare thigh.

"This is bad Salinger. Silas owns the club! He's going to fucking *kill* you. How many Salingers are there in the world anyway?" I'm speaking in a rapid-fire fashion, lacing my thoughts together with nothing but brittle pauses. Now I jump up and begin pacing in quick

1

fevered strides. Who would win in a fight between them? It would be a dogfight for sure. Neither would win, in fact, all three of us would lose.

"Whoa, hold it right there. Please don't conveniently forget that you, Jessie, suggested I go in the first place." He speaks with a little smirk, clearly loving my unsettled response. "Silas owns the club? That's hilarious. I'll have to introduce myself next time, I didn't happen to catch his name over video chat."

A crude sound anchors tightly in my throat at his idle threat. "So, are you...are you going to go, you know... a lot?" My palms are sweating, and my eyes are bulging in a very disconcerting way. It's one thing to check the place out, but it is a different story if he intends to frequent it, or boldly introduce himself.

"Yes, it was very liberating. You know? Being auctioned off." He laughs at the irony of his words, readjusts his stance, and shrugs. *Cocky bastard.*

"How did that even work anyway?" Curiosity reigns over basic decorum, as I slow my strides and lock on his eyes like a pacing tiger.

"First they stripped us naked, just like I said. Then they put us in shackles and led us out to the stage in front of everyone. All the bright lights glaring down on us made it really hard to see, but there were a ton of people there."

"And then?" I press, sitting on the edge of my desk for a millisecond before getting up to pace again.

"Then people had an hour or so to *preview* us," he says, through a shit-eating grin. He is happy to have me visualize his naked ordeal if his expression is any indication.

"How?" It's a compulsion for me to ask these questions. What I really want to do is drop his key card into my paper shredder, or implant a GPS chip in him to track his whereabouts and then padlock the entrance to the club. I can never let him come into contact with Silas, ever. My jaw aches from clenching my teeth at the mere thought.

"The auctioneer would tell us to do certain things, you know, flex our muscles, spread our legs, bend over, lift our ball sacks, do push-ups, whatever." He even chuckles while he speaks, knowing how unsettled I feel.

"You said they touched and probed you?" Now I'm curious about Salinger's boundaries and how far *he* would let someone go. Suddenly my own introduction to 1462 doesn't seem so lascivious—at least it wasn't in front of a crowd.

"Well, not all of us. We filled out cards about our limits and what all we would consent to. Some said, *'no touching during preview'* or *'no insertion of any kind,'* things like that. So, they separated us into groups based on our different levels of consent. Each group had different times on stage." His explanation is matter of fact, as if he was talking about how to bake a chocolate soufflé, instead of someone probing his dick and spreading his ass cheeks.

"What limits did you give them?" I ask. Now I'm way too curious. In my own naivety with BDSM, the only limits I had given were the ones from the *prohibited edgeplay* section of the paperwork. Back then I didn't know Mrs. Delacroix and Silas were in touch via instant messaging regarding such matters. As I remember it, Silas had taken some bold liberties. I shiver at the erotic memory of bending over in front of him, while he slid my panties down my legs.

Salinger's answer breaks through my ruminations. "Shit, vomit, blood, men, animals, and suspension."

"So you just consented to anything beyond that?" I ask, appalled. Now I don't feel so bad about my own lack of understanding in the beginning. His hard limits are basic; little did he know how far they would push him.

"The whole thing was totally consensual Jessie, it's not like I sold my soul," he says in a relaxed manner. His comfort level with the whole thing shows a stoic indifference, while still offering varying levels of mortification for me. "I was tugged and prodded, licked and stretched. I was hard as an I-beam after about five seconds of very thorough appraisal of my dick." Big grin now, he probably knows I'm sweating from the inside out.

"Who bought you?" I ask. Now the floodgates are open, I want all the details. I point to the chair facing my desk and sit heavily on my own.

He settles in the office chair, his right knee bobbing wildly up and down. His tendency to jiggle his leg is not a sign of distress, it's more of a valve for releasing anxiety he doesn't outwardly feel. I think after active duty, his brain uses the propensity as an outlet to release a world of crap he holds inside.

He answers, "A woman named Mary-Jane and I were both purchased by a very distinguished gentleman." He gives a sly smile, knowing this little tidbit will only lead to further questions.

"Oh God, then what?" He has me now, how could I not want to hear the rest?

"Then we went to a playroom, and he told us what to do, *'lick her pussy' 'slap his cock' 'fuck her in the ass'* that kind of thing." He speaks so calmly, it belies the frank sexual nature of our conversation.

I'm speechless. Salinger and I have always been really open, never having to filter our conversations, but just this once I wish he had. That was a lot of vulgar words in one sentence, and hearing them from such a good looking co-worker is tough…and very, very visual. My focus is on his sexy mouth, and I am trying very hard not to picture it on his fellow slave, tongue bringing her to a squirming orgasm.

I try to lighten the conversation and redirect my own spiraling thoughts, "Salinger, the very poignant image in my head right now is of you on the auction block while someone weighs your balls and fingers your ass," I say, my voice cracking with a suppressed laugh.

"You're welcome," he says with a smirk and a wiggle of his brows.

Chapter Two

Zoo

"Daddy look, you can feed the Giraffes!" Ruby squeals in delight, grabbing my hand and proceeding to drag me behind her like a reckless para-sailer.

Silas laughs as he tugs his phone from the pocket of his jeans and jogs to catch up. "Ruby, be careful. Giraffes are vicious, bloodthirsty creatures."

Ruby stops short, crossing her arms over her chest and rolling her eyes at Silas, clearly used to his sense of humor. "Dad, you are going to scare Jessie," she says, and then shoots me a piteous look, as if apologizing for her disreputable father.

Silas had said she was sassy, and I expected her to be, but the more I get to know Ruby and her relationship with Silas, the more hilarious the dynamic becomes. She is what you would call *an old soul*, and his penchant for sarcasm is pure gold when you factor in her level of seriousness. The scale tends to tip in her favor when weighing the maturity level between the two of them. Sometimes by a lot, but it is all completely entertaining.

After purchasing some lettuce and crackers to feed the gentle giants, I return from the Giraffe Cafe window. Silas and Ruby are leaning back against the exhibits' second story roughly hewn beams, staging their selfie. The dopey faces of three docile giraffes crowd the screen while Silas and Ruby smile into his phone. She pouts her lips and changes poses like a teenager with a selfie stick and a Facebook page. Through the clicks, Silas keeps mostly the same handsome, gritty smile. Until he reaches his tongue up to the base of his nostril then crosses his eyes. His behavior causes Ruby to toss her head back and laugh with glee. She then turns to face the phone's camera with her own crossed eyes, twisted grin, and laughing face.

The zoo had been a long time coming, between first meeting Ruby and Silas' month-long quest for new club real estate. Things had started well enough, seeing as I had only just found out about her, but one apocalyptic video chat derailed the whole *get-to-know her* process.

My own decompensation and wayward expectations, mixed with Silas' brooding lack of communication, had imploded into a totally unnecessary gauntlet of shame and self-loathing.

Now that we are past that whole ugly process, I am definitely warming to the idea that Silas has a kid. She is a little clone of him, and it makes my uterus ache a tiny bit when I see how great he is with her. For someone who never thought he wanted kids, he is a fantastic father. To think of how far he has come since Amber dropped Ruby in his lap is really a testament to his character.

My assumptions about his parenting style were that he must be super regimented and strict, being such a control freak and consummate bachelor. But I couldn't have been more wrong, he is a natural as a dad. His easy grace with parenting is admirable, and he learned it all by being thrown to the wolves.

Despite his status as an amazing father, I am adamant about taking things slow, at least as far as Ruby knows. If it were up to Silas, he would move me right in, and we would have pancakes every Saturday, but I want things to progress at Ruby's pace. My reasoning is that she is not used to sharing her dad with anyone. She's been the Princess *and* the Queen since he took custody of her, and threatening that dynamic would make her turn on me like a rabid dog.

It's a delicate balance, loving Silas and easing Ruby into the logistics of it. But I would rather she be excited for me to come over, instead of anxious for me to leave. So I give her *fun Jessie* in small doses until she forms an attachment. You know, like a drug pusher.

"Jessie, look at their long black tongues!" Ruby squeals, as she backs her head up, just out of range of the thick probing tongue.

"Yes, his girlfriend is very happy," Silas says while leveling his gaze at me, and depositing the phone back into his hip pocket.

My mouth drops open. I'm stunned by the sexual reference right in front of his daughter, but he just winks.

"Because he can reach all the really tall leaves. Right, Ruby?" He says this with a shrug, as if it was my mind in the gutter, and his reference was just as clean and pure as the freshly driven snow.

***

This particular zoo has special private access to feed the Rhinos, and of course, Silas snags the coveted position for his daughter. This fact was never in question because Silas seems to have connections all over the place. It makes me wonder how many of them are nefarious club acquaintances versus more conventional, say, from commercial real estate.

The zookeeper leads us down a winding path, to the back of the pachyderm habitat where a single rhinoceros waits patiently for his 10:45am carrots.

He is cumbersome behind the thick bars but gets excited when he sees the gravy train coming. His small black eyes are somehow wise with the look of many generations of hard-fought battles. They are set deep into thick wrinkles and the puffy eye bags of a lifelong alcoholic. The animal's whole shy demeanor seems to illustrate, *'I'm the gentle one, it's the hippo you should fear.'*

The zookeeper takes a knee in front of the massive beast and calls for Ruby to come join her.

Apprehensive, Ruby takes my hand and leads me down to the fence while Silas remains behind to take pictures.

I stand in solidarity with Ruby as the keeper explains that this is a 5,000-pound white rhinoceros; though actually gray, named Phineas. She explains that a rhino's thick skin forms from layers of collagen. Ruby looks nervous but undeniably interested.

Once the zoo attendant explains to Ruby that rhinos are herbivores that lack teeth in the front of their mouth, and instead use their lips to pluck their food, Ruby warms to the idea of holding a carrot out for the two-ton beast.

Silas is about five feet behind us, so I take the opportunity to suggestively bend over while feigning interest in Phineas' thick, pointy upper lip. Ruby boldly takes charge, announcing, "Phineas, I have some carrots for you!"

I wave my ass at Silas before standing up to Ooooo and Ahhhhh, as the rhinoceros gently plucks the carrot from Ruby's small, trusting hand. If Phineas notices her sparkly, purple fingernail polish, he is unconcerned. He pulverizes the carrot between molars, rocking his robust jaw against the now pulpy carrot.

"That's fantastic. I'm getting great pictures. Really, they are superb." Silas says, and I know with complete certainty he is talking about the cheeky angle of my cutoffs when I'm bent forward, and not Phineas' thick-lipped, probing mouth.

My cutoffs are loose fitting and not all that short unless I hike them up before bending over, which of course, I purposely do just to taunt Silas. He is fun to tease, it's easy because he is so highly sexed that even innocent displays go through a filter before they get to his brain, turning everything sexual. So even something as innocuous as me loading the dishwasher will prompt some sexual innuendo from him, or at least a rub up against my ass.

When she runs out of carrots, the keeper stands, dusts her hands off on her smart, knee-length, khaki shorts and asks if Ruby has any questions.

Ruby, having waited for the green light, happily launches into the first of what's sure to be an onslaught of rapid-fire questions. "What is a Rhino horn made out of?" she inquires, with a glowing interest on her cherubic face.

As the keeper explains they're made out of Keratin just like hair and fingernails, I tug my wrenched up shorts back into place, ready to be respectable again.

It's going to be hard to beat feeding giraffes and a rhinoceros, but once Ruby finishes with her swarm of questions, we head off toward the other exhibits, with her skipping ahead and singing about having just fed a Rhino.

She is a cute little thing, she has Silas' deep blue eyes and light brown hair, though her hair is pin straight and halfway down her back.

He told me when he saw her for the first time, when she was just over a year old, that there was absolutely no denying she was his. So when I see the same facial expressions or mannerisms from both of them, it makes me giggle. Ruby is definitely his daughter, same looks, same traits.

In the back of my mind I wonder what would happen if Ruby's mother, Amber ever came back into her life. After all this time, after abandoning her in the first place, after however shitty of a mother she started out as, she is still Ruby's mother, and Ruby aches for one terribly. As wonderful as Silas and Analise are, they are not a mother for her, and Ruby sees this with crystal clear precision.

I don't know what Silas has told her about Amber, but I don't doubt that Ruby knows she has a mom out there somewhere. She probably has her on an enormous pedestal. Not knowing one's mother provides a six-year-old a plethora of unrealistic fantasies about how fabulous she *could* be, how glamorous, how perfect.

Silas breaks into my thoughts by draping his arm across my shoulders and asking, "What is that little smile about?"

"She is just so stinking cute, skipping along, singing about feeding a rhino. She doesn't have a care in the world. I hope she always has that light in her."

"You're great with her, you know," he says, squeezing me against him. I can smell his manly deodorant, and it gives me the urge to bury my face in his armpit and just breathe in the scent. Crazy? Yes, but the smell is somehow intoxicating and it reminds me of all the times I can smell that very scent when we are pressed together, naked and panting.

"Amber doesn't know what she's missing," I say this a little more wistfully than I would have liked. Then quickly add, "What was she like?" I've wanted to ask more about Amber but never felt it appropriate, however now seems like a good time.

"Besides being a complete narcissist? Well, she obviously wasn't good with commitments. Not much of a caregiver—"

"I don't mean like that. She had to have *some* redeeming qualities. Do you see any of her in Ruby?" I clarify, then lean my head against him.

"Yes, Amber was a free spirit, loved life to the fullest. She also was an artist, so Ruby definitely gets her creative flair from her. I would have said Amber was a people pleaser too before she abandoned her own child… Ruby definitely exhibits that trait. In fact, I sometimes wonder if Amber left Ruby just to please some man. You know, if a guy didn't want kids; or someone else's kid, I could see Amber choosing the man. She was like that, kind of molded herself into what she thought someone wanted," he says.

"She sounds insecure. I can't imagine choosing a man above my own flesh and blood child."

He takes my hand, "Yes, but you are a thousand times the woman she is." Touched by his words, I'm silent for a minute until he goes on.

"You know what I worry about sometimes?" He's plaintive and hesitant but sounds like he wants to share, so I look up into his eyes and wait for him to go on.

"Daddy, look at the flamingos! They look so silly on one leg! Like this, look at me, I'm a flamingo!" Ruby says as she teeters on one leg, then scampers ahead. She shouts over her shoulder, "Follow me to the Komodo Dragons!" Then she starts flapping her arms in camaraderie with the spindle-legged, pink birds.

"What do you worry about?" I ask, looking up into his contemplative face, reminding him where he left off before being interrupted by Ruby's exuberance.

"I worry Amber did it because some boyfriend was mistreating Ruby, and she was protecting her by getting Ruby away from him," he says quietly, as if giving voice to his thoughts will somehow make them true.

13

"Has there ever been any indication of that?" I ask, stunned but determined to know more. I can't imagine someone mistreating Ruby, but I guess I can't imagine anyone mistreating any child.

"I don't know. I was so new at being a father; I didn't even know you can't give a baby honey, or a kid Aspirin, or any of the million things you should know before becoming a parent. I was a deer in the headlights."

"Has she ever shown any lack of trust toward people? Or does she know more about bodies than she should? Was she withdrawn or plagued by nightmares?" Suddenly the concern is real, and I feel a visceral reaction, almost a seething need to invalidate his words or deny the possibility. What would I do if someone mistreated, or God forbid, sexually abused her?

"I don't think so. She seems developmentally on track, no unexplained past traumas to her body, no irrational suspicions of strangers. It's just knowing she was in someone else's care. Uncertain if she was loved and nurtured or was in the way, or an inconvenience, or worse."

"Daddy, Jessie! Guess which would win in a fight, a Komodo dragon or a King Cobra?"

"I'm not sure Rubes, a King Cobra strike is pretty quick. Would a King Cobra win?" Silas ventures through a proud grin.

"What do you think, Jessie?" she asks while hopping on one leg then the next, unable to still her excitement.

"I agree with your dad, a King Cobra."

"Wrong! They would both lose, you want to know why?"

"Why, Sugar?" Silas asks, indulging her glee.

"You're right, the King Cobra would strike right away, but the Komodo dragon's skin is really thick so not too much venom would penetrate its skin. It would still die but only after it bites the King Cobra too. The King Cobra would live for a few days, while the wound gets really nasty and infected because of all the bacteria in the dragon's mouth. Then it would eventually die from the infection."

"Ruby, did you just use the words *penetrate* and *bacteria* in the same explanation? You're six, are you sure you are supposed to be that smart? How do you know so much about Komodo dragons anyway?" I ask, grabbing her face and kissing her forehead.

"The Discovery Channel," she states, as a matter of fact. "Do you know the difference between venomous and poisonous?"

"Um," I pause, not sure if I should let her teach me, or demonstrate my own knowledge of the difference.

Silas scoops her up, placing her on his shoulders and says, "Poisonous is, if I eat you and I die. Venomous is, if you bite me and I die." Then to me, as if an explanation was necessary, "I watch the Discovery Channel with her."

***

After the Komodo dragon, alligator, turtle, snake, fish and frog building, we head to the next exhibit, the Polar Bears.

"Isn't it a little hot here for Polar bears?" I ask as we walk down the winding ramp to watch them swim from the lower level, behind a thick glass enclosure. The sun is scorching hot, and for animals that belong in the Arctic Circle, they must be absolutely miserable, melting into a puddle of thick white fur.

Without answering my rhetorical question, Ruby fires off another random animal fact, making Silas and I both laugh at her precociousness.

"Did you know Polar bears cover their black noses with their paw when they hunt? It's how they adapt to the all-white environment and don't spook their prey."

"Discovery Channel?" I ask.

"No, school," she says. "Daddy, can we have ice cream?"

"Let's go to the cafe and eat lunch first, then ice cream. Ok, my little scholar?" Silas says as he flips her down from his shoulders. "Lead the way."

***

After lunch and a menagerie of other animals, we are tired, our energy zapped from the beating sun. Ruby slogs ahead of us, face and hands sticky. She is wielding her empty cotton candy paper cone like a princess wand, granting mumbled wishes as she goes.

Silas releases my hand and tugs me close with his arm around my waist, and his lips pressed into my ear. "You are amazing. Such a natural with kids, I mean, re-applying her sunscreen... that was a powerhouse move."

"You are the powerhouse, Silas." I don't bother to explain what my fair skin would look like if I didn't learn a long time ago how to reapply sunscreen.

"Is it crazy that all I want to do is curl up with my girls and watch the Discovery Channel?" Silas asks.

I laugh and remind him that he is taking me home after the zoo.

"You are really adamant about this whole, take it slow thing, aren't you?" he states, not really asking a question at all.

"It's the right thing to do. She shared you all day, now it's her turn." I hold my ground, it will be better in the long run, I'm certain of it.

"Well, you and those shorts will have to meet me at the club tonight after she goes to bed then. You have been a naughty little cock tease all day, it's time I repay the indulgence."

His words prickle the back of my neck. After a whole day at the zoo with Ruby, silently but deliberately driving Silas crazy with my calculated taunts, my leaning over the exhibit rails and my deliberate brushes against his fly. I'm not sure what to expect at 1462. Payback for sure, but Silas has some pretty creative ideas when it comes to reparation, so I'd be lying if I said I wasn't a little nervous.

Chapter Three

Club

1462 is already crowded and electric with activity. The first and third Saturdays of the month are the orientation nights for all the new members, so the energy has a different feel. It's kind of like, accession meets yearning and out comes a sort of phosphorescence that clings to the walls.

I'm wearing a white burnout t-shirt that rests right on the edge of being see-through and the same cut-off jean shorts that taunted Silas all day. The shirt is kind of my power play, he *encourages* me not to wear panties, so I'll just be a good little toy and not wear a bra either. My dusty pink areolas show through the shirt, and my nipples are already hard against the flimsy fabric. It's funny how people brandish power in the world of kink. Sub or not, I have a certain amount of control to exert over Silas too.

I knock lightly on Silas' office door before pushing it open. I'm surprised to see a women leaning over Silas' shoulder pointing to something on his computer screen. She looks at me with fire in her eyes as she stands up, lifting her tits off my man.

On Silas' part, he acts as if nothing is unusual. "Hi, Sexy," he says as his eyes drift over my outfit, a thirsty smile curling his lips. "Jessie, this is Parker. Parker, Jessie."

Parker squints her eyes at me with the tip of her tongue paused on the corner of her lip in the most condescending look she can muster on short notice.

"Ah, Jess-ie, so nice to meet you," she gushes, overly sweet. Since Silas can't see her bitchy face, she actually sounds polite.

"Right, you too Parker," I say with my jaw squared a little more than normal.

"Silas, you sly little fox. She is nothing like what I expected from you, really, a complete departure." Parker sneers while she speaks, but she sounds playful, so Silas doesn't notice the game she is playing with me.

Silas pulls a key from the pocket of his jeans and holds it out to me. "Go on up, I just need five more minutes to finish this," he says, as he waggles his eyebrows at me.

Parker stands up straighter and crosses her arms across her full chest, the look in her eyes telling me to go back outside and fuck myself. Her hair is sleek and blonde, her eyes vivid blue, and her stance is one of total authority—she radiates the supremacy she no doubt feels. Her immediate dislike of me, tells me all I need to know about how she feels about Silas. Great, a catfight, and it's already in motion thanks to her snarling jealousy.

I already hate her. I stand where I am for a few seconds longer, scrambling for something clever to say when she snorts and says with a laugh, "Jessie, Silas and I have a few things to take care of, so you should listen to your Sir, *and go*." Just like that, she might as well have said, *You are dismissed, now piss off.*

***

I'm pacing the room, too flustered to notice the bondage equipment all around me when Silas enters. I had planned on waiting for him as I should, you know the good little sub, but I'm too pissed.

When he comes in, no less than twenty minutes later, I fire one across the bow. "What the fuck was that?" I demand, not at all submissive.

Silas cocks an eyebrow, "Uh. What are you talking about? What is this?" He gestures to my fuming agitation, still totally clueless.

"Her," I spit out.

"Jessie no, that's Parker. She owns 30% of 1462. She's my business partner, that's all. There was nothing shady going on."

I realize too late that Parker has already won this round. She came off perfectly lovely as far as Silas is concerned, and now I'm acting like a pitiful, jealous girlfriend. I have to shift gears and fast.

I slowly walk up to Silas, acting contrite. "Sorry, I think I'm just nervous. All this scary equipment. What's a girl to do, all alone, and afraid?" I avert my eyes, but arch my back and press my breasts more prominently forward.

He places his hands on them, dragging his thumbs across the thin fabric, teasing my nipples and immediately forgetting my outburst.

Placing a hand behind my neck, he pulls me in for a kiss, but stops just short of making contact. "Shouldn't you be on your knees?" he asks, but it sounds more like a command.

"Ooooo, I must have forgotten. I'm a bad sub. Maybe you should teach me how to be better," I say. Then turn around and lean forward, presenting my ass like I had done at the zoo countless times.

I had hiked my cutoffs up and folded down the waist before arriving at the club. So now, leaning forward my ass cheeks are presented to him in a raunchy, teasing way, even more salaciously than at the zoo.

"Pipes, do you need to be reminded of who's in control here?" he asks. "There is an art to submission, and clearly you haven't learned it yet." He breaks character for a flash with an amused smile. "Now, take off your clothes. Slowly, and I want you bent over when you pull down those infernal shorts."

I straighten up to face him but keep my eyes down as I slowly raise the hem of my shirt. I expose my breasts, or rather, further expose my breasts, as I tug the practically transparent t-shirt over my head. I grant him a long minute to stare at my exposed skin, my nipples hard as marbles. Then I bend over and pull off my brown leather cowgirl boots.

After tossing aside the boots, I slowly yank loose the buttons of my jean shorts. Then turn around, lean forward and unhurriedly slide the denim down my legs. I'm still bending forward waiting, as he takes in my explicit stance.

"Open your legs," he instructs and then groans when I do. "Slide two fingers inside." It's a command, but I know he is weak for me. He is giving the orders, but I know who has the power.

Feeling his weakness, I toy with myself before sliding my fingers in slowly then back out, then dipping in again. The exhibition of the act is very hot, and I softly moan. My fingers are mere pawns in my arousal, doing nothing to turn me on sexually beyond driving Silas crazy.

I arch my back further to adjust his view, as I slide deliberately slow, in and out.

After a few moments, he steps closer and says, "Now stand up and put your fingers in my mouth while you kiss me."

I straighten up, as he closes his arms around my waist. I kiss him, it's tender and languid and so passionate, but he breaks the kiss to say, "Your fingers, Jessie."

I close in for another sweet kiss, carefully sliding my fingers in his mouth at the same time. Our kissing mouths are crowded by the addition of my fingers. It kind of feels like three people are trying to kiss at the same time, but one is being treated as an outsider, three being a crowd.

He groans as he begins to suck on my fingers. I want him undressed too, to feel him against my skin. I'm frustrated by the unbalance of nudity, but I feel like his plaything, and it's surprisingly sensual.

He breaks our kiss, then in a whispered growl says, "Go get on the bondage horse." Feeling lightheaded and feverish, I look around for the first time, taking in some of the intricacies of the room.

It's similar to the predicament bondage room I had been in with Silas and Carson. Back before our lives diverged in an explosion of misunderstanding and regret. The floors are a marbled dark brown, stained concrete and the walls are mostly exposed brick with patches of plaster. There is a St. Andrew's cross and a spanking bench, both of which I'm familiar with. There's also a fairly basic looking massage table, save for the clips and rings that run the perimeter of the padded leather.

The other two objects are new to me. One looks like a narrow weight bench, with four stirrups hanging from it. The back two stirrups are lower than the front two, so I assume they are for knees and elbows. I roll the dice and start to walk toward this one. I know he is watching my bare ass as I go, and it makes me smile to myself. I do way too many lunges and squats at the gym to not appreciate his kind regard.

"No, that is a fuck bench. That," he says, gesturing toward the other piece. "Is a bondage horse," he smiles at my naiveté.

The contraption that is the bondage horse kind of looks like a sawhorse a carpenter might use. It's in the shape of an elongated "A" with ledges along either side, and of course, is covered in black padded leather.

"Climb up toward the front like you are riding a horse. Now bend your knees and rest your shins along the ledge here and here," he explains, as he guides my knees and shins into place.

"Beautiful," he says, as he takes in my spread legged, kneeling pose on the raised bondage horse. My core is already warming to the soft leather beneath me.

"Now lie back," he says, as he helps me recline awkwardly back, so I'm lying down, legs bent back at the knees.

I feel nervous, perched precariously on what seems like the top of a very narrow, peaked doghouse. With the bottom of my legs bent back, they offer little in the way of stability.

"Raise your arms above your head," Silas directs. I do as he says, the new position causing a deeper arch to my back as my lower back lifts from the leather and strains my breasts toward the ceiling.

Silas moves to my head and quickly binds each wrist snugly in sheepskin wrist restraints encased by stiff Velcro. He latches my wrist bindings to the top of the device with a clang from the metal clips.

My elbows spread wide to the sides while my wrists remain near my head, but hang off the end of the bondage horse. I feel a deep stretch in my quads as Silas tosses a leather strap across my body, just below my breasts and another one over my hips. He then moves to the other side and swiftly clips them before tightening the straps down.

Despite feeling a little like a human butterfly, I finally feel secure enough that I will not simply roll off, to one side or the other.

Silas slips a silky blindfold over my eyes, and just like that, my world goes dark.

"Is this too much?" he asks, his voice measured.

I pause, not sure what exactly he is asking.

"The stretch in your thighs?" he adds.

"No," I answer, already feeling the stretch loosening as I relax into the awkward pose.

"Remember, *'yellow'* means I'm approaching your limit, *'Red'* means I've crossed the line. I will stop immediately if you say *'Red'* or *'Rumpelstiltskin.'* Do you understand?"

I nod my head, feeling supremely naked as a shiver tickles the back of my neck. An amused smile plays across my lips that I hope goes unnoticed.

Just as I'm feeling a little cocky, I feel Silas fasten another strap. This one goes over the top of my right thigh, then around my ankle. He then tightens the strap, effectively pulling the heel of my foot against the base of my ass.

"Ahhh," I exhale as I again feel the stretch. I have to remind myself to calm down and breathe slowly and deeply.

He gives the same treatment to the left side then says, "Damn, you're so fucking hot. I can't wait to show you how completely you are mine."

As always, the fact that I'm displaying my body for him in such an erotic pose is an exhibitionistic thrill for me. I can already feel the delirium building from deep within my core.

The blindfold achieves a crazy synergy with the rest of my bindings, leaving me feeling hyper in-tune with my body. I'm chilly out in the open like this and already apprehensive. I know he will push what

I can handle, but it's so delicious when he does. He plays my body expertly, knowing it better than I do.

First, I feel his kiss. Then I feel an insane tickle/scratch in a thousand places down the inside of my arm, from elbow to armpit. The need to squirm right off the table is so intense that I'm only able to be still, and hold my pose because of the tight bindings.

"OhGod!" I pant, as I writhe in forced stillness. Then the sensation moves up the inside of my thigh. It tugs at my skin like a slow cat scratch with a hundred claws.

I'm alternately panting and holding my breath, unable to decide if the sensation hurts, or tickles. Actually, it does both if that's even possible. I can barely stand the intensity of it, and then it stops. There is a long pause, each millisecond worse than the one before, the building anticipation nearly unbearable. The absolute need to squirm is maniacal, but my restrained body is unable to move. My exterior remains still, while on the inside I contort like a thrashing animal caught in a trap.

Silas flicks one nipple with his tongue then exhales against it before taking the other between his teeth and gently tugging. The skill in which he uses his mouth never ceases to amaze me. He alternates between breasts, slowly fluttering his tongue against each straining tip.

The sensation in itself starts to pull me under, my excitement already starting to build. Then the crazy scratch, from armpit to hip as his tongue continues to strum against my wet nipples.

"Oh fuck, Silas," I groan. I'm straining my head back and trying to yank against the straps, enough to relieve the torment, or at least so the straps can rub against me and offer a trifling bit of relief.

The scratches continue across my hip then down my thigh, stopping at my knee. There is a squeeze of biting pain as the scratching stops then digs in a moment before letting up. My skin grips the pricks before surrendering and eventually releasing them.

I am held on the brink of insanity in those moments when I don't feel the scratch, but I know it's coming. It's almost better when I can feel it, and endure it, rather than wonder when it will bite in and snag my skin with its ruthless tickle.

Silas licks then kisses my sternum between my breasts, slowly making his way lower with soft, delicate kisses. The torturous snag of my skin follows the path of his warm mouth until stopping on my pelvis while his mouth delves lower. He licks and teases me while the threat of a thousand pokes hovers just above, taunting.

My legs are spread helplessly open to him, and the fear of the claws replacing his tongue is pervasive and relentless. His tongue flutters against my clit alternating pressure and pushing me closer and closer to the precipice.

I'm straining my chin as far back as it will go, my chest heaving against the straps when Silas says, "Let go, Jessie, come for me." The relief I feel, that the scratch is no longer imminent, mingled with the pleasure of his exquisite tongue is all I need to give in to the raging sensation.

The crashing orgasm against my tightly bound body is rapturous, as relief floods over me and release sets me free. When it's over, I lie folded up still bound to the table. My body, reduced to a dollop of liquid Mercury flickering on top of the bondage horse.

I feel the thigh strap loosen, and my foot drops back to the ledge as the stretch in my thigh is relieved. Silas loosens the opposite strap, and my other foot drops like a bag of quarters, just like the first one. I'm still arched back with my wrists and body bound when I feel the light touch of his lips against my inner thigh and feel his warm breath caress my skin.

He lavishes me with soft kisses and caresses every part of my body touched by the scratching device before I feel his smooth, latexed tip press into me.

I groan with gratitude as he begins to slowly bury himself deep inside me. When he starts rocking in and out, I shiver, and goosebumps pepper my skin. With each stroke, he takes a second to grind into my pelvis, pressing against my tender clit. His devotion to my body is so emotional and sweet, I feel like he is giving himself to me.

I moan with desire, desire for less sweetness, less tenderness. "Fuck me, Silas," I pant, hazy with need. He pinches my nipples hard, and I realize my mistake as electricity shoots through me.

"Fuck me, Sir. I need you," I groan. He has been inconsistent with the whole *Sir* thing, but I suppose in the heat of fucking me, *in his own club*, he wants to hear me say it.

He grabs my hips and begins thrusting with a new intensity, my breasts jouncing with each slam against me. Letting go of one hip, he moves his hand and yanks off my blindfold. "I want to see your eyes when you come this time."

I squint against the sudden light, before resting my eyes intently on him. His chest is glistening and tiny rivulets of sweat streak his temples. He drops his hand and begins pressing on my clitoris and rubbing small circles with his thumb.

"Do you like when I tie you up and fuck you hard?" he asks, while raking his other hand through sweat-dampened hair, leaving sexy rows behind.

"Yes," I pant, and then add, "Sir," quickly before my crescendo hits. Then I strain against my bindings, taken by another forceful orgasm. My spasming vaginal muscles bring Silas to his own peak as he clenches his teeth and grinds deeper into me, his body going rigid as a plank.

***

After unhooking all my restraints, Silas pulls me forward into him, gently like I'm a child. I'm quivering though not at all cold. He holds me and kisses me sweetly while cupping my face in his hand.

After helping me to my feet, he gives me a minute to steady my shaky legs, then walks me to the massage table. "Hop up here for me and lie down," he instructs. Suddenly I'm nervous for another round, but I'm wrung out and still very deep in subspace, so I comply without protest.

Silas walks naked to his jeans and steps into them, leaving the buttons undone, and then opens a cabinet. As for myself, I roll onto my side and curl up to watch him.

He pulls a fleece blanket out of the cabinet and gingerly covers me up. It feels like it just came out of the dryer, and engulfs me in comfortable heat.

"It's warm," is all I can say, as a smile creeps to my lips.

"Yes, I took it out of the warmer," he says with a wink, then drops a kiss on my forehead. He grabs a container of Cavicide wipes from another cabinet then casually walks toward the bondage horse.

"I'm just going to clean up real quick. Then I will see to you," he says, as he tugs three wipes quickly from the plastic cylindrical container.

I take this opportunity to lazily inspect my skin for scratches. I'm surprised when the most I see are red streaks, no broken skin whatsoever.

"What did you do to me?" I ask, almost puzzled by the lack of bloody scrapes.

He turns and smiles, "I did all kinds of things to you, Pipes."

I flush with the lewd memory of being bound, completely open and available to him. "You know what I mean," I say with a shy smile.

He finishes wiping down the bondage horse then walks toward me as he tosses the used anti-microbial wipes in the trash. "You mean the vampire glove?"

"That sounds about right." I sit up on my elbow. "Let me see it."

He shrugs then retrieves it from his bag. Handing it to me he says, "People use it for sensation play."

I snort, "No, really?"

My sarcasm is too much for him. He brings both arms behind his back, clamping his fingers around the glove. "You forget yourself."

"Whoops, sorry," I say, quickly pinching my lips together, so I don't smile.

He raises his eyebrows, pauses, then takes a step closer, handing me the glove. It's made of worn leather—soft and supple save for the aggressive little teeth lining the palm of the glove and the fingers. I hand it back, happy I hadn't seen it before we started.

"Lie on your stomach," he commands.

After I flip over, he adjusts the blanket over my legs and butt, leaving my top half uncovered. I close my eyes thinking, Ooooo, aftercare, I'm going to like this.

He pumps something into his hands, and then whisks them together for a few seconds before lowering his palms to my back and gently kneading my skin. He starts with some long strokes, encompassing my whole back, before focusing first on my neck, then my shoulders. He moves swiftly over my arms and low back and then adjusts the blanket to cover my top half, leaving the base of my ass and legs uncovered.

He presses his thumbs into my hamstring muscles and slowly moves down my legs. I let out a groan, not realizing how tight and sore my body had become, all trussed up for that amount of time. He works his way up, from the balls my feet to my thighs, working deftly until he reaches my ass.

"Spread your legs," he says, his voice sounding husky. When I do, he slows his pace and lavishes his touch on my upper thighs. I suck in air as he grazes the lips of my vagina, as though on accident—the inappropriate massage therapist taking liberties with his client.

Again and again, he *accidentally* skims my tender skin. I start to heat up, hoping he takes it further. The anticipation is already building again.

"On your back," he says.

I roll over, almost pouting. He adjusts the blanket over my lower half then begins to work on my upper body. "These marks will be gone within the hour," he says, as he grazes the pink streaks down my torso. I smile and nod, silently pining for him to caress my exposed breasts.

When he does, it's quick and perfunctory. All business, though my nipples strain for his touch. He surprises me by leaning down and timidly kissing each taut bud, then my lips before adjusting the blanket again.

He works longer on my thighs, kneading the sore quadricep muscles until they melt into his hands. This time, his stolen brushes against my sex are more invasive. He swipes his thumb solidly between my intimate lips, then leans in and follows his thumb with the point of his tongue.

My body is energized by his fondling and lit by his tongue, so I raise my knees to grant him better access.

He laughs into my flesh and says, "This is a wind-down, not a ramp up."

"Then stop ramping me up. No wait, on second thought, don't stop." His shoulders rumble as he takes another swipe with his tongue then blows on my wetness.

I shiver then sigh, as he straightens up and covers me with the blanket. Its warmth has dissipated, but mine has not, I feel like I will never be chilled again.

Chapter Four

Realization

Monday morning I emerge from my room tousled and groggy. I drop onto the couch, then slump over face first into the soft suede. It has the faint smell of Devin's cologne, mixed with pungent animal hide.

"Coffee?" Devin asks, glancing at me from the adjacent chair. He is quite used to my penchant for over dramatization and not really one to react much to it.

"Yes please," comes my muffled voice from within the couch.

He gets up and heads into the kitchen to pour me a mug. When he returns, I'm in the same position mostly, except I've turned my face to enable breathing. The wisps of hair across my face puff out with my exhalations and then settle back against my cheek. It's too much effort to swipe them away with my hand, so I don't bother.

"How was your night?" he asks, as though he's not quite sure he really wants to know. He furrows his brow as if he's expecting something reckless or mind-blowing.

"It was fucking amazing," I mumble.

"So why all the theatrics?" he asks, his face still covered in beard stubble and his hair all rangy from sleep.

"What about cream?" I ask, looking down at my mug of black coffee.

"We're out, you little ingrate. Now tell me about last night," Devin says, jerking his head to flick the hair out of his eyes.

"Silas taught me all about sensation play," I say, finally sitting up and moving my own hair out of my face with a swipe of my palm.

"Amateur," Devin quips. He is not a fan of Silas in the least. "What, like feathers and ice and shit?" he asks, already bored.

"Uh no, he is no amateur, trust me. Have you ever heard of a vampire glove?"

"No, but I've had a Wattenberg wheel all over my cock. Similar, yes?"

"I doubt it, I'm not sure a dick could take a vampire glove."

"Don't be so sure, some guys are into cock and ball torture. Not me...well, maybe a little," he smiles with ill-timed nostalgia. Then, as if snapped awake he adds, "Anyway, get to your issue."

"It's just that he is so experienced. He's completely knowledgeable about everything. I feel like there is nothing new I can bring to the table, so to speak."

"Earth to Jessie, he doesn't want you to bring anything to the table. He wants you to be his dirty little slut. He wants to do things *to* you, not the other way around." Then he stands and adds, "I'm late for work, call me if you develop a real problem."

I sigh, take a gulp of nasty black coffee and then head to the shower with the words *His Dirty Little Slut* ringing in my ears.

***

At work, Salinger and I have scheduling charts spread all over my desk. We need to get our report to our cost analyst before the end of the day. This is my least favorite part of the job. I like the face to face interactions with landowners and the negotiating, not the tedious, behind the scenes part.

Salinger is singing, what I can only describe as a slave song, in an attempt to break the monotony—or draw a comparison, however disgusting and unsuitable, to our work. *"Swing loooow… sweet char-I-oooot, commin' for—"*

"Salinger, can I ask you a question about something totally inappropriate?" I interrupt him while facing the carnage on top of my desk. I'm a little shy to make eye contact, though relieved to shut him up.

He drops into my chair, "JB, I would be kind of disappointed if you didn't."

Salinger and I do not have a typical working relationship, we spend hundreds of hours together traveling just the two of us for work, so we have become much more than co-workers. We are great friends…who have crossed the line on a few occasions, but have settled into a very functional working relationship.

When his marriage was falling apart, I logged endless hours as his personal therapist. I didn't care about work or the long trips, I just wanted to help him pick himself up and dust himself off. It had been my personal mission to help him see how great he was.

I could not do this job, and spend this much time with any other person. I can't even imagine how boring it would be with some stuffy guy or chatty girl. Really, anyone but him and the deal is off. I'm pretty sure I would hate my job.

"I know you have been going to 1462 and there are all sorts of kinky things to do there, but what could a woman do that would totally surprise you?"

"Jessie, every single thing that someone has done to me there is a total surprise. I mean, I've had my balls stretched with weights, my rectum filled, strangers have rimmed me, and I've had my dick in a locked cage for three days." His chin is down, but his eyes pierce through mine as he talks.

I get the feeling, Salinger is adventurous sexually, but would really prefer something... a little more sweet, more wholesome maybe.

"Why would someone even do that? Make you wear a cage...that's not even sexy." My focus on the cock cage overrides everything else he said. I've never heard of such a thing, I mean, really?

"So I couldn't empty my clip until I was with her." He widens his eyes until I get his meaning.

I finally get it, then in quick succession, I realize he must have spent at least one of those days at work with it on; the weekend is but two days. The thought is distracting, but I push on anyway.

"Ugh, I don't want to do any of those things. Plus, they are way too dominant," I say. I slouch down into the extra chair in my office, feeling defeated. It's hard to date someone like Silas; I want to be different from what he expects, not like everyone else.

"Oh, I get it. You want to do something for your dude that he hasn't experienced before, right?"

I push my sleeves up past my elbows and the gesture reminds me of Salinger's full arm tattoos. He is so measured and straight-laced at work, current conversation notwithstanding. Women adore him, the nerdy glasses, neatly combed hair. They would be shocked by his tattoos, his huge scar courtesy of the USMC, and the fact that he has been frequenting a BDSM club...and wearing a cock cage.

"I've got it! Get a Furry costume." His eyes twinkle behind his thick-rimmed glasses and his lips spread into a huge grin.

"You're fired." I laugh at the thought of me in a man-sized rabbit costume. "Ugh, never mind."

He is happy to drop it, so we dive back into work for about an hour before he sits back, inspiration having struck. "Do a sexy photo shoot," he says, finally feeling helpful.

"That might work," I say, letting my mind wander.

"Yep, it's the gift that just keeps on giving, page after page."

"I like it. I'll have to modify the typical shoot though."

"Let me know if you need any help with that. I have all sorts of ideas. Plenty of sexy images of you in my head to draw from," he winks.

"Stop sexually harassing me and get back to work."

We both laugh and turn back to the mountains of work at hand, but to be honest; I think he is on to something.

Chapter Five

Shopping

Devin, Corey and I are sitting at a yellow Formica table in our favorite little Greek restaurant. It always smells strongly of roasted chicken and feta cheese and is lively and boisterous at any time of day. Devin wipes his mouth and gives me a cold, hard stare. The bite of Gyro seems burdensome in his mouth before he begins a methodical chewing motion, his jaw tight and unmalleable.

Corey just smiles his delight at being asked to help. His military haircut has grown out in shaggy abandon. It's his latest futile attempt to resist the call of the Corps, with their sizable re-up bonuses. As a prior service Marine, and more so, as an Explosive Ordnance Disposal Technician, he would be eligible for over $50,000 in re-enlistment bonuses. Although he wavers in his decision, the tug of Semper Fi is strong.

"I just need a little help shopping for some naughty, BDSM-y outfits, that's all," I say this knowing they are my two best options for help. My girlfriends are all settled, most with kids and they would think I'm crazy for dabbling in kink. Plus, Devin and Corey would tell me, in a brutally honest way if something looks good or, say for example, that my ass looks big enough to sink the Titanic. Devin has actually said those words to me before, verbatim.

"You know I would love to help, Devin here is another story," Corey says. He gives a nod toward Devin, who sits smugly as though I've just asked him to tongue kiss a homeless woman.

"You know how I feel about Silas. So why would I willingly help you?" he asks. Then he takes a gulp of his water and swishes it around in his mouth like he is trying to get rid of the taste of burnt hair.

"How you feel about Silas is irrelevant because Devin, you care about *me*," I say. I know even he can't argue with that logic.

Corey pops an olive into his mouth then reaches out to lay his hand on top of Devin's in a consoling manner. "Saddle up partner," he says playfully, knowing I have just won the battle of the wills.

***

Devin begins very unhelpfully with some zip up masks and a full head and body, white spandex suit. "How about these?" he asks with a straight face, though it's laced with apathy.

"Oh sure, but it will take us a few extra hours if I need to try on all your disgruntled choices too," I say with a smile, and then reach out for the ridiculous white suit. I'll play his game, and we will be here for hours, I'll see to it.

"What I can't figure out, is when that's ever appropriate. Who needs a fully covered little gnome creature, who can't even open its mouth?" Corey asks over his shoulder, as he sifts through racks of leather corsets.

"It would be surprisingly handy. I can already think of a few uses for it," Devin remarks, as his listless eyes stare through me. He is so dramatic, it's like he needs to remind us that he doesn't want to be here. The funny thing is, he would be pissed if we went without him.

"Jessie, you can't go wrong with corsets and hot body harnesses," Corey says, as he dumps an armful of his choices into the arms of the eager sales associate. The sales lady spins around to deposit them helpfully in the dressing room. Then he adds, "Stockings and garters are a must...and crotchless panties I would imagine." His voice drifts off as he begins combing through shelves of silk and lace. His strong hands are the size of cake pans and look ironic against all the delicate fabrics, but at least he is being helpful.

Devin, on the other hand, drops onto an ornate chaise lounge, looking cumbersome and out of place. The chaise looks like it belongs in a brothel, not a high-end boudoir boutique. It is hand carved and covered in thick gold brocade, tassels, and a crushed velvet bolster cushion. His sulky expression and muscular frame dwarf the Louis style chaise. It's humorous how conflicting he and the chaise look. It mirrors his apparent disgust of being here, yet doesn't want to *not* be here.

"I'll just sit here while you two little squirrels scurry around. When you finally get around to trying stuff on, I'll give you one blink for no and two blinks for yes," he says, leaning back into the tufted brocade and relaxing as if for a nap.

"You do that, and I'll give you a lap dance in each and every thing I try on," I threaten. Corey and I make eye contact, and both burst out laughing. I would do it too, and they both know it, so it's that much more hilarious to see the tart look on Devin's face.

***

The dressing room is huge, and much too lit up by the black lacquer pendant light dangling above my head. I'm a little surprised when the saleswomen slips in with me, rolling up her sleeves as if headed into the trenches for battle.

"Where shall we start?" she wonders. Her eyes are sparkling at the thought of a hefty commission as she looks around excitedly. Every caliber of lingerie hangs politely from puffy satin hangers. And the hangers dangle from evenly spaced crystal knobs that surround us like peeping voyeurs.

The room is large for a dressing room, but much too small for all the sales lady's perfume. She smells like hot cinnamon, and it catches in my throat and singes the cilia in my nose.

"First, I think a proper measuring. Have you ever been fitted for a brassiere?" she asks. Her temples crinkle up like crepe paper when she expresses herself, this time in the form of a broad smile. She has lipstick on her teeth, and I can't help but focus on it, pondering if I should tell her, or hope it wipes off on the inside of her lip.

"Uh no, never been properly measured," I admit. I wonder if this is something most women do or if it's a marketing ploy to justify charging sixty-five dollars for a simple lace bra. I'm pretty sure I can tell if a bra fits by this stage of the game, but I'll play ball and see if I'm surprised by what she determines to be my *proper* size.

***

Once she finishes prodding, lifting, scrunching, turning, groping, and measuring me, she swings her measuring tape behind her neck and uses her cherry red, acrylic nails to tap a few more notes into her tablet. She is evidently satisfied with her deduction, 34 B, just like every other bra in my possession. The good news though, is that I can skip my next self-breast exam.

This whole song and dance feels completely unnecessary. It's kind of like bathroom attendants, who insist on pumping your hand soap and handing you a paper towel after you've rinsed off your hands. It makes for way too many cooks in the kitchen. How would you even explain this practice to someone in a disadvantaged country? *It's simply too much to turn on the faucet **and** reach for the soap.* I mean, can't I just dress myself and adjust my own buoyancy in the satin cups? I reaffirm my belief that it's just a marketing scam. A personal assistant is simply more justification for the inflated prices. Proper measuring? Check. Personal assistant? Check. She might as well have a tip jar out.

Hot Cinnamon reaches for a padded hanger and says, "I believe we will start right here," as she holds up a sexy, heavily boned, black satin corset. Then she stands back with her arms crossed, ready to spring into action should I require an assist in the removal of my t-shirt.

***

After deciding to mostly cooperate with the process, and only falling off the chaise once, (while laughing at a black, circle cutout, sheer body stocking that Corey had picked out, *for variety*). Devin chooses a leather cupless corset with matching G-string, a chainmail looking mesh dress and a very short, leather pleated mini-skirt with a cropped, front zipping vest. Apparently, he is casting me in a porno as a pillaging Viking.

I haven't failed to notice that Devin's tastes are of the harder, dirtier variety, while Corey's are sweet and almost demure. This is unsurprising and standard issue for their personalities, hard and soft, bitter and sweet.

On the softer side, Corey has chosen a deeply plunging, cream-colored lace teddy with cream thigh high stockings, and fuchsia pink, ruffled lace, booty shorts with a sheer black bandeau top. He seems to be envisioning more of the girl-next-door look.

After unanimous vetoes of a short baby-doll nightie, various boring camisoles, and frilly corsets, *I* finally choose a smoky gray, metallic-looking corset with matching panties. This middle-of-the-road number is much more my speed, more realistic to flaunt in front of a random photographer. However, there is a place for both Devin and Corey's choices too.

When I finally step out of the dressing room for good, I'm sweating, and my hair is frazzled and full of static like I just went five rounds in an octagon.

"Now I will just need a second job, and we are all set," I say, resigned at the mounting cost. I have readied myself, mostly, for the hit to my bank account. I reason that I will get a ton of use out of the items, Silas being who he is and all. However, when my very attentive saleswoman says, with an egregious smile, "Miss Hayes, that will be $864.17, will that be debit or credit?" all the blood runs out of my face like gravel from the back of an upturned dump truck.

"Uh, credit please."

Chapter Six

Work

I sit at my desk, ignoring the mountains of work calling to me. I'm blatantly refusing to stem the flow of my hemorrhaging bank account, as I add yet another item to my online *discrete* shopping cart.

I want to do this photoshoot for Silas, but it has to be amazing, really, really amazing. It also has to be authentic to his taste in kink, so I add a wide, tawny-colored leather waist cuff with dangling O-rings to the virtual shopping cart.

The cart currently contains some thigh-to-wrist cuffs, a ball gag, an over the door wrist and ankle restraint contraption, and a slinky leather harness. Actually, harness is a strong word for the strappy, body crisscrossing device that I had added, all the while wondering if I would have the nerve to wear the thing in front of a photographer. The harness is kind of like what a naked person would look like after Zorro rode past them, still naked, but now with lines across their body.

I'm deep in thought when Salinger barges in, only knocking after he already stands inside my office. This behavior is his typical M.O. when he needs to talk to me.

"Hey, can you re-send me the contract addendums for Morrison?" he asks, still looking down at the stack of title work in his hand. His neatly combed hair, now very short on the sides, with the longer top portion swept back in an old vintage style. Adding to his new look is a few days of beard stubble.

"Salinger, I like the Rockabilly look, you look mysterious and sexy. Are you sure that's fair to all the ladies in the office?" I tease, but actually, I'm taken aback. I can't see the tattoos under his neatly buttoned dress shirt and suspenders but knowing they are there, coupled with his new barbershop look, makes my heart beat a little stronger, and I'm reasonably sure my mouth is still hanging open.

"You like it? I want to look a little tougher these days," he says, still leafing through the pages and not even glancing up at me. He seems so oblivious about his attractiveness and the sizeable wake of squirming women behind him.

"Why tougher? You tired of having your asshole stretched?" I ask. Then I start laughing as he slowly moves his gaze to my eyes. His look is plaintive, but I can tell he is fighting a smile.

"It's my fault, right? Because I share that stuff with you, now you are going to fuck with me?" he asks through the wide grin that has split his stubbly face.

"Yes. But seriously, why the new look?" I ask. I'm curious, and not just a little impressed.

"It's called switch, right? When a submissive flips to a Dominant or switches back and forth between the two," he asks, standing there all perfect.

"I don't know. Something like that, I think," I say, not sure when I became the expert. I only know what Silas has taught me, so I'm hardly the one to ask about specifics.

"I just want to experiment a bit, that's all. But you like the haircut?" he asks, trying to redirect the conversation. I think he is a little uncomfortable being the office sex symbol. He is too humble, and real for that title.

"Yes, a lot." I minimize my screen of bondage gear before the conversation really takes a turn.

"Good," he says just as my phone rings. Then he backs out of my office while mouthing, "Ad-den-dums," in order to remind me why he came in in the first place.

"Hi there," I say to Silas, dissolving into my office chair and forgetting about the image of Salinger, standing there like he was on the cover of GQ.

"Hi yourself, are you busy tonight?" I can hear him typing in the background. Poor Silas, so many balls in the air, I don't know how he does it.

"Nope," I say, competing with his pressing real estate demands as he continues to type.

"I'd like to take you somewhere nice. Can I pick you up at 7?" He asks and then stops his typing long enough to wait for an answer.

"Sounds good, are you sure you have the time?" I ask, referring to his incessant typing.

"Sorry, I have a closing in ten minutes, and the net sheet is off. But I wanted to catch you now before I get caught up with the title company."

"See you at seven then. Leave the distractions at work, or I'll have to get creative in order to redirect your attention."

He laughs, and I can picture his easy smile, "Don't tempt me, Pipes."

Chapter Seven

Dinner

The restaurant sits perched on a rocky cliff with an overlook of the foothills. The impressive view captures the metro area in its entirety, with the city lights twinkling their silent applause in the background. Our table is private and nestled amongst the expansive windows, while the likes of Frank Sinatra and Tony Bennett croon their emotional serenades from unseen speakers. There is a savory aroma permeating the air, it smells of rosemary and dapper sophistication.

"This is beautiful, Silas." I smile, taking in the swanky restaurant with open astonishment and an all but gaping mouth. Refinement has never been my strong suit, so I hope I don't use the wrong fork or put my elbows on the table.

"I've always wanted to come here," he says, "Now seems like a good time." He winks, picking up a crystal goblet of water and taking a sip, never breaking eye contact.

"How does the five-course meal and wine pairing sound?" He is so casual; you would never guess what a frantic life he leads. He must thrive in chaos because he never seems overwhelmed or worried about all his responsibilities. I have a hard time picking up my dry cleaning and grocery shopping in the same week, and I *wish* I was kidding.

"It sounds fantastic. I've never done a wine pairing before," I say, sitting back and dropping my hands into my lap, not sure what else to do with them.

Our waiter approaches, "Welcome. If I may, I would like to go over your menu for this evening. I understand you would like to dine quietly and undisturbed."

I widen my eyes at Silas, but he seems completely unaffected. Of course, he would arrange for the wait staff to make themselves scarce, I should have expected as much. I do wonder, however, how one would eat a five-course meal with a wine pairing without being disturbed.

My answer comes when our highly starched waiter launches into the course descriptions. He continues for nearly three solid minutes, while Silas sits back easily in his chair, looking at me with a wolfish grin on his face.

"For your Amuse-gueule, we are featuring Foie Gras Torchon on Brioche with Summer Fruit Compote, paired impeccably with Chateau d'Yquem Sauternes, followed by your first course, Butternut Squash and Herb Oil Seared Sea Scallop, paired delightfully with Babich Avignon Blanc Marlborough. Followed by your second course, Warm Baby Spinach Salad, Manchego, Red Wine Onions, Candied Walnuts and Brown Butter Balsamic Vinaigrette, Paired beautifully with Domaines Schlumberger Riesling Les Princes Abbes. Followed by your entree this evening, Grilled Beef Tenderloin with Potato and Caramelized Fennel Gratin, Sautéed Lacinato Kale and Wild Mushroom Ragout, paired delectably with Frescobaldi Remole Sangiovese Cabernet. For dessert, a Molten Chocolate Soufflé, paired exceptionally with Manzanilla Sherry." When finished, the waiter tucks his head into his chest and backs up without another word, disappearing like an apparition.

"Now *that*, was a mouthful," I say lightheartedly. "Don't they need the space of a five-course meal to practice saying the names of the wines?" I ask. That was a lot to go over all at once. Although, it would have been distracting to have him describe the dish and wine pairing each time he advanced on the table. So this strange modification works for me, plus I would not have understood everything anyway, even if he broke it down and delivered it throughout our meal.

Silas just smiles.

"Seriously, I have no idea what we are eating tonight, but I'm pretty sure there is a sea scallop in the mix," I say, not totally joking.

"I don't care what we eat or what it's paired with, I'm just glad I have you to myself tonight." He takes another sip of his water, his eyes burning into mine with something rugged and unchecked.

As I sit across from Silas, so handsome and self-possessed, his model good looks and his undeniable success in life, makes me swallow back a little insecurity. Sometimes I wonder how I got here, but the crazy thing is, he thinks *he's* the lucky one.

Our *Amuse-gueule* is laid before us, and our napkins snapped violently before being placed in our laps. Our waiter stealthily places two crystal wine glasses before us then dissolves from sight.

"Ugh, it's Foie Gras," Silas says, disgusted by the tiny plate laid before him. "I was paying too much attention to your sexy lips while he was blathering on. I didn't hear him mention it."

"What is Foie Gras?" I ask, with no refined polish to my voice whatsoever.

"It's the fattened liver of a force-fed duck or goose." He has a repulsed twist to his mouth, and I'm happy for his own lack of polish, now I don't feel so out of my league.

I look to the spongy textured medallion before me. It's sitting haughtily on a swirl of fruit paste and garnished with some sort of micro-greens and small gelatinous cubes of something unidentifiable.

"So, you are morally opposed to eating it, or you don't like the taste?" I ask, amused by the disgruntled curve of his lip.

"I've never tasted it, but I assume it would taste like the metal pipe they jam down their throats… and baby tears." He snickers at his description and then smiles for real.

I appreciate his noble stance in defense of the ducks and geese, so in solidarity, we both slide the dainty plates to the side of the stiff, white tablecloth. Oddly, to see him act like this amuses me about his moral high ground. I do understand his sentiment, but he must not realize how all food raised animals are treated, because, with those convictions, he would surely be a vegan.

"Let's just hope veal is not our next course," I say sardonically as I fiddle with the stiff, completely un-absorbent napkin on my lap.

Shifting gears Silas says, "We haven't had the chance to talk about the new club. What are your thoughts?"

It surprises me when he brings it up. One of the few times we have discussed it, he said he intends for me to go with him, and I have a very settled life here. I have been avoiding the topic altogether if you want to know the truth, kind of hoping he forgets about it.

After a tentative sip of wine, I say, "What about my career?"

"Take a leave of absence. Or quit," he answers too quickly, having already thought about the stumbling block of my job, and knowing full well it will be one of my objections.

"Silas, I worked very hard to get to where I am. I can't just throw all that away." I furrow my brow, and then continue, "Is your plan to move there until the club opens? What about 1462? Would Parker just take over running it? And Ruby's school? You can't just pull her out of school and drag her around the country. Plus, what would Analise do? And your loft, what about that?" The questions come pouring out and would keep coming if Silas didn't start chuckling and holding up his hands in surrender.

"Jessie, don't panic. I'm not going to throw you over my shoulder and haul you off to New York. I can do a lot from right here, but there will be a decent amount of back and forth travel, and I would like you to come with me now and then." He finds my agitation amusing, and that alone lessens the strain.

I won't have to leave my family, friends, and job after all. I don't see my family or my girlfriends very often, but I still wouldn't want to leave them. And Devin, Corey, and Salinger? No way.

"Well, I do have a healthy amount of vacation days banked up." I wink at him and realize the instant relief I feel, not having to drop everything here to move. I had been repressing the thought of the new club, not wanting to choose between Silas and everything else, but his relaxed approach surprisingly makes me warm to the idea.

"Why BDSM clubs anyway? I'm not judging, just curious."

"I mentioned before that my introduction was to a more typical BDSM club. You know, the stereotypical dungeon where true sadists and true masochists come together."

"What do you mean true sadists and true masochists?" I ask.

"To give you an idea, I knew a man whose kink was blood splatter…and there was no shortage of women for him to play with."

"Noooo!" My shock registers plainly. "That's one sick kink."

"There was the element of power exchange but no real affection between the players, no kindness between the lashes, no meaningful aftercare, and certainly no aspect of protection or seeing to needs—sexual or otherwise. In fact, the acts weren't particularly sexual; it was more about dominating or being dominated."

"Why would people do that? I can't understand the mindset." My hands have stilled, but my imagination is accelerating.

"It's an emotional release, or escape for people. I've heard it said that a good scene doesn't end in orgasm, it ends in catharsis," he says.

"But hurting someone for sexual pleasure, or being hurt for this *catharsis* seems pathological to me."

"Some of it can be, but it's also a massive surge of endorphins, they block the pain and create a type of euphoria."

"So your introduction was more, what? Seedy?"

"Yes and no. It was very organic to the BDSM scene, but that particular club catered to more of the underbelly of society. Back then, clubs were trying to increase membership by being really laid back and welcoming. The result was that people stopped trying, they stopped dressing to impress, stopped taking pride in themselves and their craft. Now, the world of kink has evolved, there is a sexiness to it these days. In fact, it's more popular in upper-middle-class communities than the ramshackle, dungeon districts of the past."

"You told me once that you knew you could do it better, is that what you meant?"

"Yes, my vision back then was to create a club that catered to kink in a fun, sexy way and also restricted membership. I wanted to be in control of what types of people were allowed in."

"Isn't that considered discrimination?"

"Private clubs can discriminate. The First Amendment Freedom of Assembly allows private groups to pick their members. You will find every race, religion, creed, and lifestyle in my club and it is accessible to those with disabilities, but I *do* discriminate based on a person's psychology regarding kink...and sometimes, how attractive they are." He has the elitist attitude of someone admitting they only allow beautiful people in their club.

"I don't grant memberships to depraved or damaged individuals, and I revoke memberships if people can't follow basic courtesies."

"What are these basic kinky courtesies?" I'm being playful, but I do want to know.

"Communication, respect, and trust. Communication is so important when negotiating consent. As long as all parties are consenting adults, I'm happy. Respect is huge too. I don't personally believe someone can keep a sub caged for days, feeding them dog food, forcing them to shit in a bucket AND respect them. Also, trust is paramount, you have to be able to let go and know your partner will take care of you, as well as push your limits, and know you can use a safeword if they go too far."

"You're right, without those it could seem like perversion between social misfits."

"It certainly can be. It can also be straight-up abuse disguised as BDSM."

I watch the waiter approach and replace our plates with another. This time it's a proud sea scallop in an orange paste, with a sprig of tarragon all but saluting us. Our waiter stays dutifully quiet, as he places two new wine glasses in front of us. He tips the wine bottle with a sweeping flourish and pours a modest amount into each glass before he again disappears.

"When you open the new club, what do you plan to do about commercial real estate?" I ask.

"You know, it's funny. I used to think real estate would be flexible; I could work as little or as much as I wanted, have all the holidays off, and short work weeks. Perfect right? Well, as you well know, that's not the case. My real estate career has run away with my time. I won't be overly upset to ease away from it entirely."

"Really? Be done altogether?" I ask surprised, as I watch him over the rim of crystal before taking another sip of my wine, it tastes like chilled nirvana. It would be fantastic for him to lighten his load, especially as Ruby gets older and more involved with activities and sports…or girl scouts and whatever it is that little girls do nowadays.

"Yes, done. I would also like to be more hands off at the club too." He watches my eyes widen in further surprise.

"And just what will you do with all your free time?" I ask.

"I will raise my daughter and travel around the country opening clubs with my beautiful companion." He smiles and cuts into his scallop never really breaking eye contact.

"Sounds like a pretty amazing companion," I smile and bite into my own scallop. It's delicate, lightly crusted with herbs and it melts in my mouth.

"Yes, she is, and beautiful too."

I smile at this as the wine warms my veins. Jet setting with Silas, traveling the country and opening clubs, I think I could get used to that.

***

We are midway through our second course when Silas causes me to choke on my *delectably paired* wine.

"So, Pipes, why don't you tell me about your hard limits," he says, and then chuckles at my response. "You've been around the club enough now to have formed some definite opinions."

I lean in and whisper, though no one is around us, "Did you just ask me about my hard limits in this five-star restaurant?" I ask playfully, with a stern look on my face.

"Yes," he grins, and it's a feral one. Redirecting our conversation toward a sexually charged topic, mingled with the look on his face, makes me want to order an inordinate amount of scallops to go, and skip the rest.

I wipe my mouth and sit up tall, clearing my throat. "I don't want you to draw blood, hit me in the face, spit on me, choke me, suspend me by my feet, use electro-shock, of course, nothing degrading like cages, leashes, or dog food...and lastly, the basics... scat, urine, children or animals. I think that's about it," I answer. "Did I cover everything?"

"Any soft limits?" he asks, his voice is low as he brings his fork to his mouth.

"Anal, because as you know, I'm not a huge fan, but I'm slightly open to it."

"Got it," he grins and tips his crystal wine glass to his lips.

***

After dinner the waiter clears the dishes and scrapes the crumbs off the table with a stainless steel wand. Silas, while holding my hands, tugs me forward over the small table into his kiss. I have to rise up from my seat to make contact with his mouth. The position feels almost aggressive and demanding of me.

"I have something for you," he murmurs into my mouth.

"Is that so?" I whisper back, pressing forward and deepening our kiss, not even opening my eyes.

"Why don't you come around the table and sit on my lap," he says, as he sits back looking pleased with himself. It's a shocking suggestion, but my mood is warm and light from the decadent wine. Feeling playful, I deposit my cloth napkin on the table and stand, feeling emboldened and wicked.

My dress plunges deeply in the front, so access to my breasts is hardly hindered, and as Silas well knows, I'm not wearing panties under my above the knee, free-flowing dress.

I feel heady and scandalous as I lower myself to Silas' lap. My arm is draped behind his neck as I draw him into my parted lips.

With his arms folded loosely around my hip, I press into his relaxed body, cupping his jaw with my hand and holding him tightly against me. To my knowledge we are alone. Silas had set the expectations early for the staff, so I find myself strangely comfortable in this situation.

After a while, I break the kiss and murmur, "Touch me, Silas." He groans, and I feel him squirm beneath me. After a moment of contemplation, I feel him run a palm very slowly up my thigh, disappearing beneath my dress to tickle the inside of my leg.

"Spread your legs," he demands, but his composure is beginning to slip.

I spread my legs apart, granting him unchecked access, as I take his earlobe between my teeth and softly exhale into his ear, "*Yes, Sir.*"

He squeezes my inner thigh, hard, so I spread my legs further and arch my back in invitation.

As if in control again, he releases my thigh. Then he reaches up and partially exposes my breast with one swipe against the plunging fabric.

I roll my head back, shockingly unconcerned with the unseen wait staff, as I press my breast eagerly into his palm.

He swipes my nipple harshly back and forth while he delves into my neck, nipping at my strained flesh.

I can hear the other restaurant patrons, the soft music, muffled conversations, and clinking crystal. We are obscured, but hardly alone and it feels risky and wanton.

Our small round table nestles amongst spotless windows, sheer valences, and the shimmering lights of the city below. I have the distinct impression, on a typical night, there would be five or six other tables in our isolated room, or perhaps even a private party.

I'm a little surprised by my lack of concern with our wait staff. Although they keep their distance and haven't spoken to us since the earlier recitation of our meal and wine pairings, they still are attentive, and present among the shadows.

Silas drops his hand back to my leg, and I trill with beastly anticipation as his fingers crawl higher up my thigh.

He finds me eager, nearly desperate as he wiggles his fingers back and forth across the very tips of my lips. The motion is delicious and cruel simultaneously. His touch, salacious but purposely avoiding my need.

I rock on his lap, rubbing his steel against me as I covet more and more of his touch.

"All I can think about is burying my cock inside you," he groans.

"Then do it," I say as a shy smile lifts my cheeks. It occurs to me that I may have consumed more wine than I originally thought because all my inhibitions are out the window.

"Turn around," he says, low, almost a growl.

I slowly pivot on his lap and lean forward. I'm perched on his knees as he unzips his dress pants, my ass a breath away from his erection. I rise enough to slide my dress up, the fleeting motion enough for Silas to grab my hips and lower me down, entering me in one smooth motion.

The fullness is exquisite and complete. My channel feels taut around his girth as I begin to rock slowly on his lap.

"I don't have a rubber, I can pull out if you want, or we can stop," he whispers into my ear.

"No," I pant, "Don't stop."

He slides an arm around me, the flat of his hand disappearing into the plunging neck of my dress to squeeze my nipple between two extended fingers.

I rock gently, hardly moving but squeezing and milking him. The incremental movements of my hips are goading him, riding him— tormenting him.

Silas tugs both shoulder straps of my dress to either side, widening my neckline and displaying both breasts before cupping them in his hands. He twists and tugs both nipples until I'm gasping and rocking even deeper into his lap, the tingling pressure building masterfully deep within.

He releases one breast and drops his hand to make its way under my dress. His fingers deftly find my clit, pressing and rubbing against the slow, deep, undulating waves my body is making.

I can never last long once he employs his gifted clitoral stimulation, so in short order, I'm coming in muffled grunts and lip pinched moans.

He follows me with two deep plunges then stiffens with his own release, tightening his arms and crushing me so tightly against him, I can hardly draw breath.

In an exhausted motion, I rectify the top of my dress and then lie back against him. My back is resting on his chest, and I'm still clamping his penis within me, not wanting to release him just yet.

He holds me against him, content to stay just as we are for a long moment before he lowers something in front of my face, settling it on my neck. "Sit forward, hon, I need to clasp this."

My hand shoots to my throat, touching the necklace that's now resting cold against my heated skin. I sit forward and hear a tiny *snick* as the necklace clasps shut. I let out a burst of laughter because now I realize, this is what he meant when he said he had something for me. He meant a gift, a necklace.

I rise, letting my dress fall back into place, as Silas tucks his penis back into his pants and zips up.

Tenderly I sit back down on his lap, both arms around his neck and lean in for a steamy kiss.

Silas surprises me when he tucks his napkin between my thighs, ever the thoughtful lover and clearly mindful of my sullied state. He takes care of this detail without even a pause of his mouth against mine

"Thank you for the necklace, Silas," I purr.

"It's not just a necklace, Jessie. It's your collar. I'm marking you as mine. You are under my protection from this point forward." Silas follows his statement with a long, languid kiss.

"It seems like such an innocent little necklace," I say, excited by the progression in our relationship.

"Jessie," he says with some amusement, "It's symbolic. It doesn't have to be a leather dog collar."

"Well, I love it. Even though I can't see it, I love that you gave it to me," I whisper as I snuggle against him. To the touch, the necklace feels like a wide, herringbone chain, not at all overt or showy.

"Silas, I just thought of another hard limit," I say, as I rest my palm against my new collar. "I don't want to share you with other women. Ok? I mean, this collar marks me as yours, but what makes you, mine?"

"This does," he says, pointing to his heart, "But like any good Sir, I always honor my sub's limits." He says this with a smile while pulling my chin forward for our lips to meet.

He breaks the kiss but just barely, "Trust me, Pipes, you are all the woman I can handle."

Chapter Eight

Parker

"I hate that snotty bitch!" I exclaim as I hit end on my phone.

Devin comes out in boxer briefs, towel drying his hair. He drops the towel on the barstool next to the kitchen island before walking toward me.

"Now *there* is some venom, what's up?" he asks. His damp hair obscures his vision before he runs his fingers through it then drops onto the couch. A waft of his masculine body wash follows behind him.

"Fucking, Parker," I spit out. I can't even try to pretend she doesn't hate me. She is so relentless and overly vicious when it comes to me.

"This is Silas' business partner?" he asks, his tan skin bringing out his shimmering hazel eyes. I'm glad he has been paying attention to my, at least bi-weekly, ranting and is able to follow my clipped responses.

"Yeah, and what the hell is she doing answering his phone?"

"Uh—"

"And why does she always act like I'm imposing on *her* time with Silas?"

"Well—"

"I'm so sick of her head games. She is so calculating that Silas doesn't even realize she is fucking with me."

"Are you sure she is?" Devin asks pointedly. I'm a little surprised at his attempt to defuse me, that's usually more of Corey's approach. Devin usually jumps in with both feet, ready for a revolution.

"Trust me, she wants him, and she is manipulating the situation every chance she gets by planting little seeds in his head, *'Are you sure Jessie is cut out for the club?' 'She can wait; she should wait—that is, if she is a good little pet.'* Or, *'Jessie, why don't you fetch Silas and I a Starbucks—he will be so happy to have his submissive finally acting appropriately.'* It's so blatant; she doesn't even try to mask it. She even told me, if I ever need any tips pleasing Silas, to come find her!"

"Dirty whore," Devin mumbles, but he is smiling.

"Devin! She even said, *'Run along Jessie, you shouldn't even be coming to the office.'* RUN ALONG, like I'm some pesky kid! She is *maybe* a couple years older than me, yet she is so condescending—"

Pause

Pause

"Devin, why the fuck are you smiling?"

"Do you still have that naughty little chainmail dress, or did you puss out and return it?" he asks. His eyes are twinkling, and I know he is plotting something. Devin may not like Silas, but he doesn't tolerate people messing with his friends. The beguiling look on his face, tells me all I need to know about whatever crafty notion he has come up with.

"I have it, it's for the photo shoot," I say.

"Oh! That reminds me, you got your delivery of spreader bars and shit, I put them in your closet. Anyway, when are you supposed to see Silas again?" he asks, as his wheels continue to turn.

"Today. He said he would be finished up by 5:30. Analise and Ruby are making a big batch of pumpkin bread tonight to take to the homeless shelter tomorrow. So it's a good night for the club." I waggle my eyebrows and wait for him to go on about his master plan.

"And he works in the office with Parker?"

"Not usually, she just always finds a way to be in there when she knows I'm coming. It's part of her game."

"Well Jessie, I *too* know how to play games. Now go put on your chainmail dress."

***

At Devin's urging, I arrive twenty minutes before Silas expects me. As usual, Parker is in the office with him. I can hear her laughing, and I picture her putting her hand on his bicep, in an *innocent* gesture that Silas completely misses. Or bending over across from him, as if she doesn't know her tits are rolling out of her signature rhinestone tank top, while strategically at his eye level.

I walk over to the bar and ask for a bottle of Champagne, then text Silas.

Me: *I was wondering if you could indulge the aggressor in me just once before I relinquish her forever.*

His reply is immediate: *Sounds fun, should we discuss my hard limits?*

I smile, knowing he is kidding, grab the Champagne and leave a tip on the bar. Now, I head determinedly to his office.

The chilled bottle has a sticker on it, marking it with Silas' member number. This is how the club gets around the legalities of not being allowed to sell liquor. Members and guests simply bring in their own alcohol, some monthly, some with each visit. The 1462 bartenders are paid well to simply provide the members with their own alcohol and any mixers they may require.

I can't even begin to think how all the libations are cataloged and so readily available to the patrons. But I have seen the cavernous walk-in where they are stored, and it rivals the Library of Congress in its enormity. Silas' personal stash could practically supply Bourbon Street during Mardi Gras, less one bottle of Champagne.

Silas' office was a storage room a few weeks ago. He was adamant about not having a dedicated office at the club, but Parker thought it was a great idea, of course. So now accounting is done from the storage room office instead of from the *real* office at the front of the club, where Mrs. Delacroix sits primly behind the *real* desk.

***

I knock two quick raps then push the door open, swiftly closing it behind me and leaning against it. I mean to trap Parker in here; she will need to see this.

Silas smiles, then leans back in his chair with a mischievous look on his face.

Parker is sitting on a low filing cabinet, peering just over Silas' shoulder. Her skirt is hiked up to a ridiculous level, and she's wearing her predictable, rhinestone studded, biker tank top. It's torn at the neck, into a skanky, tit-baring atrocity. As expected, she makes no move to leave. A girl has to take a stand, I suppose.

I'm still leaning against the door, Champagne bottle in hand, eyes locked on Silas, when Parker says, "What can *we* do for you Jessie?" as she cocks her blonde head to the side and stubbornly stands her ground.

"Well, actually, there is quite a lot you can do for me," I say, keeping my eyes trained on Silas'. I deposit the bottle on the desk and untie my knee-length jacket, letting it drop succinctly to the floor.

I'm standing with one hip cocked, as two sets of eyes take in the chainmail dress. Silas stares with heart-pounding lust—Parker, with rueful disgust.

The dress isn't *chainmail* per se; it's more like a heavy metallic mesh, with cutouts about the size of dimes. It hugs my nakedness and leaves nothing to the imagination. It feels cold and heavy as it brushes and moves against my breasts with each inhale.

"Why don't you come over here? I can be very helpful when the situation calls for it," Silas says with amusement, as he slyly sits back in his chair and adjusts his pants.

I walk around the desk, eyeballing Parker and willing myself with everything I have, not to wink at her.

She steadfastly holds her ground, because leaving would be too easily seen as defeat, just as Devin had predicted. In fact, she is reacting *exactly* how Devin said she would, and it emboldens me to a wicked degree.

Silas scoots his chair back, making room for me, as I edge onto the desk in front of him, legs spread slightly. He is completely unconcerned with Parker, as he revels in my short dress and partially spread legs.

"Well, for starters, I can't seem to get my shoe unbuckled," I say, as I raise my ankle strapped stiletto to his lap and press down on his erection.

Silas holds his breath for a beat with the light pressure. Then his eyes trail up my leg to my pantyless core, now visible with the rise of my leg.

He holds my foot, pressing it harder against his shaft. Then he raises my ankle, placing it on his shoulder while kissing the inside of my calf.

Parker coughs, "Silas, shouldn't we wrap this up?" Her statement is a last ditch effort to maintain his attention.

"Nope," Silas says, as he makes his way up my leg, kissing the inside of my knee.

I lean back on my forearms, pushing my stiffend nipples against the metallic mesh and moan when Silas makes his way to my unguarded sex.

I'm watching Parker's sour face as she hops off the filing cabinet, glaring at me.

My eyes follow her glare as I lick my lips and moan, "Oh God, Silas. You're so good to me." And then she is gone, out the door with a slam. Leaving behind nothing but her hatred of me and a waft of her too fruity perfume.

***

With my release, comes the feeling of the chainmail trying to bury itself deep in the flesh of my ass and shoulder blades. Even so, the satisfaction I feel is enthralling, and it has nothing to do with my orgasm.

"Is there anything else I can do for you?" Silas inquires, through glistening lips and a huge smile.

"Actually, yes, I think my dress may have a broken zipper," I say this, as I climb up onto the desk on my hands and knees. I also know full well the dress doesn't cover my ass while I'm bent over.

"Hmmmm, this is very distressing. There doesn't seem to be a zipper on your dress," he says, not at all distressed. "Perhaps if you spread your legs a little more, I will be able to find it."

I spread them more, as Silas begins caressing my inner thigh with one hand and unzipping his pants with the other.

He opens a desk drawer and retrieves a condom. In less than thirty seconds he has both hands on my ass, clutching my cheeks and parting me before him.

"Still no zipper. Perhaps a button?" he says devilishly, as he reaches around to press on my clit.

I jerk with the pressure to my sensitive, post orgasm nub, but he doesn't let up.

Instead, he presses inside me, pulsing with need and burying himself deeply with a groan of pleasure. He pumps three slow, deep, rocking thrusts before he asks, "Why the Champagne?"

"Because we are celebrating," *Parker's downfall...* "My beautiful collar," I say. I crane my head back, changing the angle of his thrusts with the deep arch of my back. His slick head pressing past my G-spot over and over.

"In that case," he says, shoving my dress up to the small of my back and pulling out. "Turn back over."

When I turn, he pulls the dress over my head, leaving me naked and panting on his desk. I wrap my legs around him, while he tugs his own shirt off and flings it to the floor. Then he reaches for the bottle and enters me again, quick and hungrily, pumping while he pops the cork.

He holds his thumb over the opening for a few extra seconds while the pressure inside the bottle builds, then begins to gush out, all over my naked body. The fizziness of the chilled champagne sparkles against my bare flesh, it feels like I have rolled in snapping, pop-rocks candy.

He makes a minimal effort to avoid the computer next to my hip but is completely unconcerned with anything else that may get doused in the celebratory process.

Pulling me off the desk into his lap, he sits back in the executive chair. He lets the Champagne flow over my breasts as he licks and sucks it off. The Champagne is fizzy against my skin, and his mouth is hot as he nuzzles my neck, licking the liquid sensually and making me squirm.

I position my knees then begin rocking against him, sticky breasts poised for his nipping teeth.

He pours the last little bit of sweet bubbles into my mouth then drops the bottle to the floor. Gripping my ass, he adjusts my rocking into more of a hopping motion, making my breasts bounce before him.

"Fuck me harder, Pipes," Silas snarls. He is needy, like he can't get far enough inside me to mold us together. I increase my pace, squeezing him harder with my deep kegel muscles.

He clutches me against him as he stands and hurriedly deposits me back on his desk. He presses me down, working my legs over his shoulders and pumping hard and fast. The sweat is beading on his forehead as he rails against me, over and over. He pins my arms above my head and clasps my hands possessively. I'm bent almost in half, powerless against his deep thrusts and engorging advance as he conquers my body.

I'm writhing beneath him as the vigorous sex pushes me to the limit and I scream, maybe a little louder than is absolutely necessary, "Oh, Yes! Silas, Yes!"

He bucks and captures my mouth, folding me even more as he grunts, jerking with his own intense orgasm.

I lower my stilettos from his shoulders, to wrap my legs firmly around his waist. Minutes go by as he lies on top of me, our chests heaving and hands still clasped together, before I say, "Silas, take me to the bathhouse."

Chapter Nine

Referral

Devin, Corey and I are having dinner at our dining room table while Devin fills Corey in about my club revenge. He is proud to be the mastermind behind the whole thing. I think Devin has unchecked emotions inside that goad his evil genius and stoke the fire within.

"So, not only did she get fucked across the office desk, but the Champagne got all over everything! Now, if that doesn't mark her territory, I'll go straight."

"Easy on the straight talk," Corey says, with a sly grin. "And remind me never to piss you off." Then he adds, "Wait, I thought you hated Silas?"

"I do, he was just a pawn in my evil plan…and besides, I hate Parker more," he smiles but avoids looking at me.

"One of these days you will realize that hanging on to hate like that, only hurts you. Silas has turned out alright hasn't he?" Corey asks.

"He hasn't redeemed himself yet," Devin says dismissively. He scoots his chair out from the table and folds his arms across his chest, all but daring one of us to push the issue.

Diplomatically, Corey retreats, "At least every time Parker is in the office, she will have to walk across the sticky floor, and picture you all splayed out, getting nailed by Silas." He smiles, "Did you really wear that cage dress?"

"Absolutely!" I gush, "He was hard before I even rounded the desk."

"It's classic," Devin says, perking back up. "I knew Parker wouldn't leave right away and that played so well into my plan. Even if she would have left, there was still the champagne. When that shit pops, it gets everywhere," he laughs at his cleverness, and all but pats himself on the back.

"The only thing better would have been a trip wire and a poison dart for Parker on her way out," I say, through a mouthful of salad as the dressing drips down my chin.

We all laugh, but Corey adds, "Jessie, that's just not right," while his shoulders rumble with his stifled laughter.

***

After putting food away and loading the dishwasher, Corey turns to me and asks, "Are you still looking for a photographer?"

"Yes, do you know one?" I ask, excitedly. "It can't just be any old photographer though—you know family portraits and senior pictures."

"Right, wedding announcements and split beaver shots don't really call for the same type of shutterbug do they now?" Devin says through a snort as he re-wipes the granite countertops.

Corey rolls his eyes at Devin, "I do know someone. He would be great…but he's not gay." He says this apologetically, as if only someone attracted to men would not behave like a lecher during the shoot.

"Aw, so Jessie, you will just have to settle for a photographer sporting a huge boner," Devin says, sarcastically disappointed.

"He specializes in Boudoir Photography, so he is a professional. I'm sure he has seen it all," Corey says.

"How do you know him?" I ask curiously.

"We went to college together. I haven't seen him in a while, but we keep in touch." Corey shrugs. "I know he will be respectful and that's important with this kind of shoot."

"Yeah, you don't want some horny, sketch ball guy getting a little *too* close for your close-ups. Or someone who would rub one out between sets," Devin puts in needlessly, not even trying to be helpful.

"Thanks for that Devin," I say blandly, while nervously wringing my hands together. I'm nervous to do something like this. It's a little like getting naked for the random guy at the deli counter—and then whipping out a ball gag and spreader bar.

"Anyway, his card is at home, so I'll text you his number tomorrow," Corey says on his way out of the kitchen.

I look at Devin, "Can I borrow your camera for this?"

"You don't think the professional photographer has one?" he asks. His eyebrows rise, and he sounds a little disappointed in me.

"If you think he is keeping any trace of our shoot, you don't know me at all," I say.

"That's my smart girl, my smart, paranoid girl." Devin loops an arm around my shoulder and gives me a squeeze.

Chapter Ten

Studio

It turns out Corey's photographer friend is a professional in his field and completely legit. I enter his loft space and look around, noticing I am alone in his vast studio. It's impressive, with all kinds of lighting, giant filters, lighting mounts, and umbrellas. There are several different areas, all set up and staged for different scenes.

There is a corner full of furniture, all mostly vintage or Hollywood Regency in style. One piece that catches my eye is a battered old claw foot tub with a rain shower fixture above. Its usefulness demonstrated by the rusty drain below the chipping porcelain tub. Hot, but not for this shoot.

I have brought my gym bag full of bondage devices, a garment bag of risqué outfits, and Devin's camera case. I stand, weighted down with provisions in the studio. My damp hair, piled up at the back of my head with a wide clip. I'm wearing sweatpants, a t-shirt, and flip-flops and feel rather silly, as I look around for Matthew my photographer— who is still nowhere to be seen.

I'm alone in the open loft space, but the quiet is broken by my own heartbeat, it sounds like, 'WhatTheFuckAreYouDoing?' 'WhatTheFuckAreYouDoing?'

Breaking my solitude, a man emerges from the freight elevator. He's pushing an empty, rolling clothes rack and nods curtly in my direction. He is a lot younger than I thought, and I groan inwardly, trying to do the math about Corey having gone to college with him. Perhaps when Corey was a senior, Matthew was… a child prodigy I think sourly to myself, discomfort settling in my knees and making them feel stiff and achy.

"Are you Matthew?" I ask.

"No, I'm Craig, that's Seth." He points to another youngish guy carrying a bunch of equipment into the room. "We are Matthew's assistants." He speaks with pride and a little puff of his chest.

I close my eyes and exhale a long breath. So there are three of them? Now I'm not just naked for the deli counter guy, but two meat and cheese reps too.

I was told that Matthew has his own hairdresser and makeup artist, so when I hear a trilling voice call to me from the back, I assume it's her. I cautiously make my way toward the beaconing call of the unseen Macaw.

***

Sitting in the hair and makeup chair while a gum-snapping, apple-cheeked, teenager winds my hair around the thick barrel of a curling iron, I watch Craig and Seth setting up equipment and adjusting the lights and filters.

Craig is tall and lanky, the body of a long-distance runner and the haughty attitude of a Nobel Prize recipient. He has pale blonde hair and arctic blue eyes—the same eyes that will ogle my body, with the same steady focus he currently has directed on the lighting.

Seth is very much the opposite of Craig—doughy and thick-necked, with his shaggy brown hair rising in anarchy around his square face. Seth's roomy jeans cling to the extra twenty pounds around his midsection, with plaid boxers bunched up above the denim. His demeanor is more relaxed, or maybe kind of blunted, as if he was stoned or coming off a bender.

Both guys are tending to the equipment, paying me no heed. I try to convince myself they are consummate professionals, not raffle ticket winning, seedy voyeurs along for the ride.

"Trust me, you are going to look hot," the girl says, breaking into my thoughts. "Matthew's pictures always turn out amazing, you know? (gum snap) He will get discovered someday, and his pictures will be on all the magazine covers. (gum snap) He is good with direction too, in fact, I have learned a lot from him about angles and posing."

"Yeah?" I ask, curious if she is doing some sort of photography apprenticeship with Matthew.

"Totally. I have my own webcam business, knowing my good angles is essential." She says this as if she were touting her position as an astrophysicist. She shows no concern for her future beyond the age-centric world of sexual exploitation. As if having her own webcam business serves as a master's degree or something wildly influential or worthy of a diplomat's designation.

"How old are you?" I ask, surprised and a little disappointed by her webcam announcement. If I had done something like that as a teenager, my parents would have slapped a jagged, rusty chastity belt on me and thrown away the key before pouring copious amounts of Drano into my computers' hard drive.

"Twenty. (gum snap) I know I look young. (gum snap) Lots of pervs out there like the young ones though. You know, you gotta give em what they want, even if their predilections are gross. You know, I can help you if you want, I know what guys like." Again she overvalues herself as more than just a piece of meat guys hunger for.

"Ok. Thanks," I stutter. I'm thinking, this poor girl only sees her value as a sexual object. It's a shame because she must be at least moderately smart to start her own business, and she must have *some* computer savviness and intelligence, right? I'm staring slack-jawed at her in the mirror, with no further response jumping to mind regarding her offer to help me. I'd like to think I could teach *her* a thing or two.

"Craig and Seth will help a lot too, they *really* know what guys like," she says with a giggle that announces a certain familiarity with the two. It all makes me uncomfortable to get almost naked in front of them. Her little giggle and statement about them really knowing what guys like, makes me feel like they are jeering, amateur porn directors, instead of professional photographers' assistants.

I suppress the instinct to tell her to stop talking, but the more she keeps blathering on, the less comfortable I feel. So far, it seems I'm in the hands of a peppy, showboating egotist and two ogling gawkers.

I need to change my perspective, and fast. Maybe instead of focusing on my discomfort with these three, I should embrace them. It might be good to receive direction from them… awkward, but maybe better in the long run. In any case, I have no choice, I better make the best of it.

"Oh look, there is Matthew now," Webcam states, directing my eyes toward a man sifting through my outfits, now hung on the rolling clothes rack.

He is wearing a suit, which seems overly formal but fine, I guess. He is talking with his assistants, and after some pointing and basic direction, Craig and Seth move to comply, attending to their individual tasks.

Webcam is finishing up and blowing on my eyelids to dry the eyelash adhesive when Matthew finally approaches to introduce himself. My eyes are closed while she blows. I'm also holding my breath against the gale of old cigarette smoke and stale Parmesan cheese, so I don't immediately notice his presence.

"Jessie! So nice to meet you, Corey has told me a lot about you," he says eagerly, with a slight British accent. "How is that handsome gaffer anyway?" When I open my eyes, I look into his narrow face and strawberry blonde hair. He speaks warmly, though his face is almost stern. It looks like it's been etched with hard lines and a difficult life.

"He's great," I say, unsure what gaffer even means, but too nervous and preoccupied to speculate.

Matthew seems very professional and replaces the stiff, rookie air with an experienced, cultured atmosphere. He has the look of a British aristocrat, with long sideburns and an upturned starched collar. I half expect to see flowing lace coming from his narrowly cut jacket sleeves.

"Brilliant! Shall we begin?" he asks, taking off his suit jacket and handing it to Webcam. "Let's have a look at your adornments and discuss the direction you would like this photo shoot to take," he says, taking my hand and pulling me from my chair, leading me off toward the garment rack.

I clear my throat, "Well, I want to do something for my boyfriend that will totally surprise him," I say, and it sounds trite and cliché as I gulp down my insecurity.

"Sure, sure," Matthew says while nodding earnestly. His pale blue eyes are encouraging me through wisps of strawberry blonde hair, overgrown yet still tamed and stylish. He has the grace not to mention that a sexy photo shoot isn't all that new and exciting; at least not to someone who sees it every day.

"The problem is that he doesn't surprise easily," I say weakly. I'm trying to impress upon him Silas' capacity for having seen it all. It's hard to explain that my boyfriend is steeped in the sexy and enigmatic world of BDSM without announcing myself as a little kinkster, or whatever other imagery his blown mind may come up with.

He is nodding, so I continue, "Well, you know how people describe someone who is very prude or boring as *vanilla*?"

"Yes, yes, of course." He is squeezing and releasing his chin, in deep thought or consternation, I can't tell which.

"Well, Silas is the opposite of that," I finish and Matthew looks relieved. It's like he had been thinking he would have to scrap all his props and preparation and start over with a more wholesome shoot. As if anything hanging from the rack in front of him is appropriate for a vanilla photo shoot.

His relief takes on another look, it's almost like he is accepting the challenge to shock Silas. Now I'm really hesitant. There are many levels to kink. I know this because only the top two floors of 1462 are private playrooms, the rest are very, very public. The variety of things that go on there range from public missionary sex to stuff that would shock a Las Vegas call girl.

"These your toys?" Craig interrupts, holding up my gym bag. His cockiness surprises me, and his smirk is a little patronizing.

The direct mention of *my toys* catches me off guard. I try to swallow the lump of dryness deeper into my throat. "Yes," I reply, timidly. What if they are familiar with lingerie shoots, but not ones with restraints? What are they going to think now? Please don't let him snicker at the contents of the bag...*please, please.*

"Awesome, let's see what we've got to work with," he says, kneeling down and unzipping my bag. He pulls out the crisscrossing body harness. "Let's start with this!" he says, and all at once the atmosphere of leering men returns.

"Um, yeah, I think I'll need to warm up to that one. That, and the cupless corset," I say dryly, and I'm pretty sure I roll my eyes at his eagerness.

I wish Matthew's crew was more professional. You know, less like two eager frat boys and a stripper with facial contouring expertise, and more like polished, high-level advisors.

At least the pictures will be sexy. I'm guessing each one of them will see to that in their own unique way.

Chapter Eleven

Photoshoot

After a great deal of preparation, we start with the smoky gray metallic looking corset with matching panties. Because of course, my choice in outfits is the tamest. I already feel like I'm about to give a speech at a conference about horned owls or something else I know nothing about…naked and lit up with a spotlight.

When I emerge from behind the smoked glass folding partition used for changing, I see the four of them gathered around an insanely garish, full-length, standing mirror.

They collectively turn, and Matthew throws his hands up, clasping them together in the air and says, "Brilliant."

"Get it girrrl," Webcam says, eying my black thigh highs and towering heels.

"I've chosen a sort of Moulin Rouge, French Rococo design for your set. I love the idea of lavish, extravagant furnishings paired with naughty cabaret poses and vicious props," Matthew announces, blessedly familiar with this type of shoot.

I take my first breath of quiet relief. He said *naughty cabaret poses* and *vicious props,* with a totally straight face and the others didn't giggle into their hands. Maybe this kind of shoot isn't all that unusual. I shake off my delicate sensibilities and remind myself that I have served sushi off my naked body. It's time to stop being such a tender little prude.

"There's just one thing. I, uh, would like you to use my camera. I'm sort of uncomfortable with someone, ahhh, retaining possession of the camera cards and digital images. It's just a bit—"

"Compromising?" Matthew interjects, not looking up from his sleeve rolling. I get the impression I have requested something completely unheard of, and Matthew is weighing how much of a diva I might be, against his level of allotted patience.

"Yes. Is that ok?" I hedge. Now I feel stupid, like I'm trying to keep the paparazzi from selling my images to the tabloids.

"May I see the camera?" he asks, skeptically, as though I would hand him an Instamatic camera with the removable flash cartridge plugged into the top.

Oddly, his air of camera superiority makes me feel better about the whole thing. A certain snobby confidence is always an attribute in delicate situations where nudity and the permanence of a photo are combined.

"It's right here," Seth says, stepping forward with Devin's case. "It's an Olympus E-M1 OM-D System Camera with both 7-14mm and 12-40mm lenses. Not too shabby."

"But my cameras are calibrated for the lighting and for this setting," Matthew says, as he studies the heft of Devin's camera and raises it to his un-squinting eye.

After a few moments of deliberation, Matthew announces, "I need to use mine. However because you are a friend of Corey's, I suppose you could buy the memory cards if that would make you feel better. But, you should know, it will cost quite a bit more to retain all of my work. You also need to understand that part of my expertise is my photographic eye. You may not recognize a potentially brilliant image."

"Um, thank you." I feel weird saying it, and it comes out like a question, making me feel even more awkward.

"Let's begin shall we?" Matthew calls out while making some quick adjustments to his camera. Then he begins barking orders. "Jessie, step in front of the mirror, both hands on the glass and arch your butt toward me. Missy, I need her hair off that side of her face so she can look back toward the camera.

As if the starting pistol at a track and field event has suddenly fired a loud shot, everyone jumps to comply.

As I step cautiously into place, I feel gratuitous, standing with my legs planted in towering stilettos while arching my butt toward four sets of eager eyes. It's as if the swatch of smoky gray between my legs holds the answer to the worlds' complexities. The way they all tune in is unrestrained and a bit overindulgent if you ask me.

Webcam, or Missy rather, bubbles with excitement, rising to her toes in gleeful little hops as she takes one tendril at a time away from obscuring my face and places it methodically behind my shoulder.

I do as Matthew directs, place my palms against the mirror, and then look back at the camera. My panties mostly cover my ass, but they have a little stitch up the middle, making them pucker and accentuate my cheeks.

Without being told, Craig steps up to adjust the panties, revealing the top of my ass crack and making my cheeks look like two melons in a slingshot.

He says into my ear, "Press your tits more toward the mirror and arch your back even deeper." When I do, Matthew says, "Yes! Just like that, now open your legs some more so we can have a little peek."

***

The next set-up goes much the same, Matthew giving directions and his three assistants snapping to attention, to move furniture, touch up my lip gloss, or adjust giant gray light diffusers. Matthew speaks in code to the guys about exposure values, strobes, and softboxes and they seem to hardly take notice of my bright pink booty shorts and sheer black bandeau top, which conceals my areolas and peaked nipples not at all.

"Missy, get the silicone mist. I want extra dewiness on her collarbones, shoulders, and tops of her breasts. I'm also going to need more highlight above her cheekbones."

Missy hops to attention, spraying me with an oily mist, and then swiping a highlighter brush across the tops of my cheeks before blowing in my face to remove the excess shimmer.

The new set has a furry rug and what Matthew describes as a Louis Philippe settee, with white leather upholstery and shiny black lacquer trim.

The posing here starts with me on the settee, on my knees with my arms over the back of the chair.

"Arch your back, yes now spread your legs a little more. Brilliant, now drop your arms some so we can see your breasts, yes, turn more to me, now drop your head back. Missy, arrange her hair down her back." He speaks with a constant stream of directions. "Craig, get the wrist to thigh cuffs, Missy help Jessie with her top."

As the command to remove my top settles in, Seth approaches with a shot glass. "It's Jagermeister," he says, as he hands over the chilled shot glass. His shaggy hair obscures the fact that he doesn't look me in the eyes.

"Very timely, thanks." I toss it back, grateful for it and wish there were more. Missy approaches ready to help me remove the sheer top.

Up until now the focus has been more on my upraised booty and spread legs. You would think a treasure chest remained between my thighs. You know, where X marks the spot. The pose itself is surprisingly uncomfortable, and they kept reminding me to arch my back. It felt like the camera was looking for a perpendicular shot, up my vagina. Maybe it was, but now my low back is on fire, and this is only my second outfit.

When it comes to helping me remove my top, Missy takes extra caution not to disturb my finely tuned hair. All the while, she gives absolutely no thought to not stretching the bandeau top halfway to kingdom come. She does, however, manage to scrape the sheer material roughly across my nipples. It makes my breasts strain against the fabric, and then jounce free, in what feels like a purposeful calculation on her part. Perhaps she does it for the benefit of the attentive assistants or perhaps for her own indulgence. Either way my raw, freshly scraped nipples are now on display, out and proud; my hair, unruffled.

Once topless, I stand as Craig Velcro's the straps around my thighs, then my wrists. My newly chafed, naked breasts are inches from his eyes, as his attention darts from the cuffs to my tits and back. His stolen glances feel invasive due to his proximity, and he takes a clumsy amount of time simply fastening the Velcro.

I wonder if I would have the same impression of the three helpers if Missy had kept her trap shut. Maybe if my only impression of them was professional like Matthew, I wouldn't feel like I was providing them with a private lap dance without the benefit of tips.

The Louis Philippe settee is removed at Matthew's direction, leaving just the furry white rug. Once Craig fastens the cuffs, he helps me to kneel. Then with no direction to do so, or warning for that matter, he tugs up the booty shorts to further expose my ass cheeks and give me more of a wedgie. The ruffled lace looks decidedly less demure with the hasty adjustment.

Seth approaches with two soda cans, and before I can register what he is doing, he presses them against my breasts. The iciness of the cans causes me to inhale sharply and my cold nipples to throb, while Seth attempts to hide his boyish grin. I'm surprised and affronted by the jolt of glacial aluminum, but before I can protest, Matthew is belting orders again.

"Turn toward me Jessie, point your torso at the camera and bring your finger to your mouth, yes, now look down, nice and coy yes, perfect. Craig, what is the reflective light meter reading off her chest?"

Craig holds a handheld meter an inch from my bare collarbone while his knuckles brush against the inside of my breast. He calls out, "18%."

"Grand, now let's get the ball gag," Matthew says, as he moves around snapping shot after shot. "Chin down, yes. Missy, I want some tendrils of hair on her breasts, not too much, we still need to see her nipples." He moves around me to the front. "Spread your legs. Craig, I need her shorts lower on her waist, can you roll them down some?"

When Craig steps up to comply, again, he is more interested in my partial nudity than Matthew's running commentary.

Seth approaches with the ball gag, but Missy snatches it from his meaty hands. "Let me, I don't want her hair messed up," she says, as if she knows him to be clumsy with her work.

Having a ball gag in my mouth is something new for me, and it's awkward to swallow with my lips stretched taut around it.

With my wrists bound to my thighs, I feel vulnerable and meek. Now I understand the need for trust between people regarding kink. The feeling I have when Silas binds me is vulnerable yet taken care of, here I just feel ogled and defenseless.

"Someone grab something for her to lean over," Matthew orders. I swallow awkwardly against the ball gag. A large white, frilly pillow arrives immediately. Someone helps me bend forward on my knees, with my ruffly pink ass in the air, and my wrists cuffed tightly to my thighs.

He snaps a few more pictures with my booty up, and again with my legs spread and head wrenched back, then Matthew yells, "Change scene."

Craig helps me stand, then unfastens the thigh to wrist cuffs and finally, unhooks the ball gag. As he eases the ball out of my mouth, I have to slurp the saliva that has pooled in my mouth to keep it from running down my chin.

Matthew hands me the leather pleated micro-mini and the tight, zip-up leather vest. "We are going to skip the lace teddy for today, it's far too demure," he says.

I think of Corey's *demure* choice. Poor guy, I guess in this case nice guys do finish last.

***

Skipping the lace teddy leaves this outfit as the last somewhat respectable one before the cupless corset and the Zorro body harness.

When I walk out from behind the partition, clad in all leather, I see two things. One, the set has changed and two, there is a pile of bondage equipment I didn't bring.

"Lie down on the Palace bed on your back, feet toward the headboard," Matthew directs. I notice he has unbuttoned a couple buttons of his shirt revealing golden tufts of chest hair. Hopefully, this was due to the heat and not something skeevy. I certainly don't want him getting so comfortable that he sheds one of the few professional aspects of the shoot, one being himself.

The bed is, of course, ornate with a high, ostentatiously carved headboard and rich merlot colored satin sheets. Matthew stands at the foot of the bed, camera ready while Craig slips thick, leather cuffs over my wrists, and then binds them together.

"Bend your knees and tip them slightly to your right, arch your back, bring your wrists up toward your face. Yes. Craig, that zipper isn't working, unzip it halfway."

I move my wrists so Craig can unzip the tight leather vest, then he unapologetically adjusts my breasts, so they sit high and proud against the opening but are still, strictly speaking, held within in the top.

"Crane your neck up and back against the bed, now look into the camera, yes, thrust your breasts up, fantastic. Craig, help her slide off the edge of the bed some, just to her shoulders. Now, Jessie, can you hold the zipper with your hands cuffed? Yes, gorgeous. Craig, now undo the top completely and tuck it against her sides. Seth, get the cans, we need her nipples prominent for these next shots."

Even though I see them coming, the cold is as much of a surprise as it was the last time. The frigid chill takes my breath away. Seth rolls the cans back and forth across my nipples, pressing with more force than is absolutely necessary. I know my wrists are bound together, but perhaps I could have managed the cans with a bit more finesse myself.

"Beautiful! Now arch your back and pop your ass. Yes. Drop your arms back behind your head, off the end of the bed. Seth, the blindfold."

Matthew never stops clicking the camera, constantly giving orders and directions. "Lose the top completely and switch out the cuffs for the neck to wrist ones."

They help me to my feet at the base of the bed. Craig takes off the cuffs and slides the leather vest down my arms, again eyeing my breasts closely. There is a look of perverse memorization on his face while Missy dusts powder on my cheeks and forehead.

I should feel flattered by Craig's frank appraisal of my puckered nipples, but the idea of residing indefinitely in his masturbation realm is somehow too invasive.

Seth brings a thick, neck collar with a chain and two cuffs connected. He fastens it to my neck allowing the cold chain to drape down the middle of my back. It bumps freely against my skin with cold little jolts before he connects the cuffs to my wrists. This device effectively pins my wrists to the sides of my waist. Besides the bindings, the very short leather skirt is the only scrap of clothing I have on, and it hardly covers my ass.

Matthew fires off directions immediately, "Now stand tall, press your breasts forward, spread your legs, yes, chin up, more, yes. Now pop your butt out toward me...more, so we get a glimpse of what's underneath. Craig, tuck one of the skirt pleats under her wrist cuff."

Craig adjusts the skirt so that my ass is more exposed, and Matthew lies down on the floor to get a better view up my skirt and between my legs. It's like he's a peeper with mirrors on his shoes, except I have essentially given him license, a green light access to whatever glimpse of flesh he would like.

"Wrench your head back, like you are more tightly bound. Now turn toward me and look like you've been naughty. Yes! Perfect, your boyfriend is a lucky man, Jessie," Matthew states between clicks.

As I am bending and contorting to Matthew's every whim, all thoughts of surprising Silas evaporate. These are intensely dirty pictures, and Silas won't be expecting me to have performed in this way, for anyone else.

"Craig, get the zip ties. Missy, I want part of her hair up. Seth, remove those bindings and grab the wire-backed chair." Matthew barks his orders, and once again, everyone snaps to attention.

Once everything is as Matthew desires, he directs me to sit backward in the chair with my knees spread, high heels flat on the floor and zip tied wrists resting on the back of the dainty chair. "Beautiful, now bite your lip. Brilliant! Arch your back and raise your breasts higher so we can see them over the back of the chair, beautiful. Craig, another zip tie on her forearms."

To think I was worried about shocking Matthew is absurd now. I have heard him refer to all my most intimate parts as if he were talking about the weather. His references to my nipples are so commonplace now; I hardly register them as uncomfortable.

"Jessie, these have been a warm-up and very tame. Are you ready to shock your man?" Matthew states, as if everything thus far has been on the Girl Scout level. The fact that I have become tolerant of the manhandling and the elicit poses has clearly emboldened them.

***

The next outfit is the cupless black leather corset and matching G-string. I have to take a few deep breaths before rounding the corner of the folding partition; with trepidation leading the way. Although I have been mostly naked for the whole photo shoot, I have not had to walk out from behind the partition this exposed.

The walk to the set is particularly nerve-wracking because Missy has me so tightly cinched in the leather waist corset. I feel like my breasts are overfilled water balloons ready to burst. Displayed like this, they precede me onto the set. My discomfort is honed intensely by Craig and Seth's open stares and frozen smiles.

The set is arranged around a makeshift door, with a four-point restraint system. Two wide restraints hang limply from the top of the door and the other two pool on the floor.

"Come, ladies, this set will be quick; there is not much we can do with a four-point harness. Jessie, I need your back against the door. Craig, the restraints. Seth, I want you setting up the next scene. Change the sheets on the bed to those black vinyl ones."

After maybe ten minutes, first with my back to the door, and then with me facing it, Matthew yells, "Change scene." Everyone scurries into action, first unhooking, then directing me to the bed.

"On your knees, Jessie, look back toward me, yes, now elbows down, I want you to crawl away from me very slowly, yes just like that. Now, kneel up and reach back to grab your ankles, just above your heels, um-hm, now loll your head back, shoulders out, breasts up. Perfect."

I feel less nervous as time ticks by, but I do feel like the assistants should be putting money in my G-string, especially when Craig and Seth start piping in with their ideas.

"On your back, knees up and drop your hands between your legs," Craig says. He positions himself to better view my open legs, yet stays just out of the shot. "Maybe just one hand between your legs, like you are playing with yourself, fling the other one back behind your head for now."

"You should do that same pose with the blindfold," Seth adds, and soon, said blindfold is lowered over my eyes.

I know without seeing them, they are leering at my spread legs. There is hardly a thread of fabric concealing my core, and I can feel the heat of their stares. The intensity of their focus is almost as strong as a physical caress. I am grateful for the G-string, but its coverage is laughable, with its vain attempt to cover anything.

For his part, Matthew doesn't seem to find anything particularly voyeuristic about his assistants, but he is busy with the clicking and shifting of the camera. Every few minutes, he blows his strawberry blonde hair out of his vision, in a practiced, automatic response to its rogue strands.

"Someone get the Astroglide," Matthew says, after indulging his assistant's input, but now ready to regain control.

All of a sudden I'm worried about Matthew's intentions. If he thinks I'm getting dirty with sex toys for the shoot, he is dead wrong. Even *I* know Silas would find that too dominant of me. Not to mention, I'm just not going to masturbate for these people, period.

Just then, a cold squirt of lube to my chest startles me and my eyes fling open beneath the satin blindfold.

"Keep that one hand between your legs Jessie and play with your nipple with the other." I know it's Craig who says this though I'm still blindfolded. I hesitantly follow his directions, working the lube into my chest then finding my rigid nipple.

"Head back, really arch, and shift your knees a bit toward us. Now lick your lips—Missy we need gloss," Craig demands, as he takes charge of the set. His voice is quick and eager, I can picture his hand in his pocket, boldly fondling his hardness, though I sincerely hope this is not the case.

Missy tends to my lips, as someone loosens the corset and slides it damply from around my body. Now I have nothing on but a skimpy G-string, a blindfold and the beads of sweat left from beneath the corset. I'm cold from the spray of lube and the plastic sheets, and I self-consciously hope goosebumps don't show in the photos.

"Jessie, real quick I need a shot of the blindfold strap between your teeth as you tug it away, yes. Now a sly smile while tugging, great," Matthew says, "Got it."

While the blindfold is off, I look around at the wet, slippery sheets. My body has grown clammy in the puddles of lube.

"I need her in the ankle to wrist spreader bar and go ahead with the ball gag again," Matthew instructs, retaking control. "Missy, I want her hair damp for these."

Missy approaches with a spray bottle and a wide-toothed comb, as Seth squirts another round of lube directly on my breasts, then on my thighs. It drips thickly over my skin, accumulating on the sheet in wet channels and irregular pools.

I'm shivering now, as Missy combs gel through my hair. Craig attaches the spreader bar between my ankles then wrenches my legs widely apart.

With my legs splayed open and Craig closely between them, I feel vulnerable and pornographic. With nothing but a tiny string to cover my girl parts, I am struck again by his cockiness.

I think it's his sense of entitlement that bothers me. It is as though he relishes doing these things to me while suffering no repercussions. Almost delighting in pushing my consent and testing my limits. In this context, it's weird and anxiety provoking, not fun and sexy like a power exchange with Silas.

For me, the exchange is uneven and debasing. It doesn't feel like my typical power exchange. He is taking from me with impunity, and I wish Matthew would notice and put an end to it. You'd think he would be able to attach the spreader bar without being so close to my crotch. Front and center, rockstar parking if you will.

Craig should be able to assist the photographer without drinking me in as if I were his own personal refreshment. He could still do his job without the intense focus on my body and the liberal handling of it.

Craig says, "I know you are cold, we are almost done. Reach down here so I can bind your wrists." He sounds kind instead of lecherous, *finally*.

I smirk at his timing because we are almost finished. Perhaps if he ends on a professional note, that is all Matthew will notice, and his illustrious career can continue unabated.

With my knees bent, he binds my wrists to the inside of my ankles, drawing my torso forward. "Now the ball gag," he says, with indifference.

After various obscene and slippery position changes, I begin to clamp down on the ball gag and openly shiver. I am wet, naked and tensing up from being cold when blessedly, Matthew shouts, "That's a wrap."

Missy holds a robe out for me, as Craig hurries to unbind my ankles and wrists. I'm drooling through the gag before they finally unhook it, and my jaw is sore from the intrusion.

"Come with me, I'll show you where the shower is," Missy says, kindly. In the back of my head, I can hear Silas, *Aftercare is an important part of coming out of subspace; we can't just high five you and send you home, Jessie.* I smile at the thought of him, but mostly I'm just happy to not be naked and bent over, or stretched out in front of these people anymore.

It is pure relief when I realize the Zorro harness is still hanging boldly from the clothes rack. At least I've saved that for Silas. I prefer his power exchanges anyway, and that little harness, that is going to be fun.

Chapter Twelve

Ruby

I realized pretty quickly that although I had purchased the memory cards from my photo shoot, I still needed Matthew to work his photographer magic on the images. So, after perhaps too much input from Devin, I contacted Matthew to let him know which images I decided on. It had been surprisingly hard to narrow them down. Some made me blush, and a bunch made me cringe, but for the most part, they were amazing.

As I page through the finished portfolio now, I marvel at the photos. They are all incredibly sexy, dirty centerfold pictures and in each one, I am heavily bound and appropriately submissive.

As awkward as the whole shoot had been, the pictures turned out insanely good—thanks, in part, to Photoshop. You can't tell how uncomfortable I was, or how contrived the whole scene had been.

While flipping through the book my phone rings. It's Silas, and I'm suddenly embarrassed, as if he caught me masturbating on a city bus or something.

"Hi, Sexy," I say, attempting a composed sensibility.

"Hi yourself," he says, and I can tell he is smiling. "Analise is leaving town for a few days, and Ruby and I would like to spend some time with you."

"That sounds great."

"I asked her to pick something fun to do tonight, so we are at the mercy of a six-year-old. I hope you are comfortable with that."

"Of course, how bad could it be?" Then I picture her obsession with Barbie fashion shows and ask, "Is she there?"

"Ruby? Yes, she's here." After a bit of jostling comes a small voice, "Hello?"

"Hi sweetheart," I say. "Do you have any ideas about what we should do tonight?"

"What about a spa night?" She asks, her voice timid and unsure.

"You want to go to a spa?" I ask in disbelief.

"No Silly, I want to *play* spa," she says, while managing to sound a little disappointed in me for not knowing better.

"Oh! Right. Yes, of course." I say, and it sounds lame, even to me.

"We can do our nails, and curl our hair…and put makeup on." Then, as an alternative, she adds, "I also want to get a hedgehog." She delivers this information with a puff of confidence and a genuine belief in the possibility.

"A hedgehog?"

"Well, I really want a dog, but daddy said he would have to have both feet in a crazy house to have a dog with no yard."

I laugh, "How about the two of us cook dinner for your dad tonight, and then do manis and pedis?"

She giggles, "Sure, what should we cook?"

"We will think of something. Ask him if it's ok for me to pick you up in thirty minutes."

I hear Silas in the background, and then Ruby speaks into the phone again. "Eewwww! Daddy says he wants hedgehog stew for dinner."

***

After what feels like an eternity in the grocery store, idly perusing each and every aisle, some, multiple times, Ruby has decided on hot dogs, macaroni and cheese, corn on the cob and smores for dinner.

"This will be great, too bad we're not camping," I say, letting go of her hand to retrieve my wallet. I had decided to let her choose the meal. Which is why; after many attempts to steer her in another direction, here we are, with glorified camping food and nothing else.

"Ooooo! Could we? Please?" Ruby lights up like a Christmas tree, hopping up and down and clapping her hands.

"Uh," I insert my card as the cashier looks apologetically at me, like I've just stepped in something and have no way to scrape it off.

"Please, Jessie? Please?" Ruby begs, and in her eyes, I see she has already made up her mind as to the direction of the evening. The fact that she has the same bewitching blue eyes as Silas plays strenuously against me and my resolve.

One of the *very* last things I want to do tonight is go camping. I have a choice though, be *fun Jessie* and pay no heed to the tremendous hassle camping would bring, further enamoring Silas' daughter. Or, say no, break her spirit, and have a quiet ride home while she glares at me in the mirror and reminds me that I am not her mom.

I hedge, "Ummm. It's kind of late to get started tonight, hon," I say while glancing at my watch, it's 5:11.

"It's early, Jessie! Please? I've always wanted to go camping!" She pleads, and my resistance wavers.

"Ok, BUT we won't be able to go far, like *at all*. Ok?" I say. My wheels are spinning as I wonder how a six-year-old has managed to completely take control. She is definitely her father's daughter.

I text Devin: *Can you grab your tent and sleeping bags out of the storage closet for me? Please, Please, Please?* I secretly hope Ruby's technique works as well for me.

Devin need only go to our parking garage to retrieve the stuff, but he is awfully bristly when it comes to Silas. He still holds a grudge about how Silas abandoned me after our first scene together and the resulting sub-drop. He doesn't even process my words when I explain that it was all just a big misunderstanding. He prefers to remain bitter instead…on my behalf, as well as his own.

***

After a quick stop at home to grab camping gear and an overnight bag, we are on our way back to surprise the hell out of Silas with this evening's turn of events.

When we arrive, Silas openly gapes at me. His eyes are wide as he looks me up and down. My arms are laden with sleeping bags, and I have a tent strap slung across my body.

I drop the sleeping bags at our feet as he gently slides the tent strap over my head. He looks at Ruby, who is holding two grocery bags and, as you might have guessed, is beaming like a prom queen on stage.

Silas clearly recognizes which one of us is the orchestrator behind this latest calamity. "Are we going camping, Ruby?" he asks, as she nods fervently, mirroring his excitement. He sees the look of resignation on my face but must read it as playful cynicism the way he laughs and pulls me into him.

"We have smores, daddy!"

"Well then, you better go get the marshmallow roasting sticks." He says this mostly to her back because she's already dropped the grocery bags at our feet and is sprinting to the kitchen.

He draws me tighter into his arms and nuzzles my neck. "This is a brilliant plan. She goes to bed at 7:30, and we can't very well go camping without you spending the night."

***

It turns out that Silas is quite adept at setting up a tent, even though it *is* on his terrace, next to the gas fire pit *and* in the midst of bustling downtown streets and high-rises.

Ruby insists on the legitimacy of the camping trip. Her only begrudging modifications are that we tell jokes instead of scary stories— then, in a conciliatory and subsequently hilarious tone, she also requires our use of the indoor facilities.

Silas heartily agrees with his daughter, all the while wearing an ironic smile on his face. He is probably wondering when she became such a delegator. My guess is, from birth.

Once we set up the tent, Ruby sets to making it comfortable, complete with about fifteen of her most treasured stuffed animals. Finally, after fevered preparations, countless pillows, and three armfuls of extra blankets, she ties the tent flap back and announces its readiness.

Her proclamation demands all the fanfare of a mayoral ribbon-cutting event, so Silas and I clap and cheer with reckless abandon—though it's a bit contrived and completely excessive.

We squat down and peer into the tent. Silas declares it worthy of a Turkish Sultan, which makes me laugh because it *does* look more like a harem bed than it does sleeping bags inside a tent. However, anything that cushions the terrace floor is good with me because I am not exactly excited to sleep on the ground.

After a thorough appraisal of our sleeping arrangements, I spear a hot dog and hand it to Ruby, though she can hardly sit still at the fire pit long enough to take the rawness off of it. She demonstrates her excitement at the idea of making smores and sleeping in a tent in the form of constant, buzzing movement and a vocal chattering that never stops, only slows.

For his part, Silas wraps the corn on the cob in foil then sets them on the threshold of the glimmering fire pit crystals. He then takes his own skewer and settles back into thick cushions to roast his hotdog. He is relaxed, and he balances Ruby's exuberance with his own wistful contentment.

As Ruby flutters around the terrace, now and then thrusting her hot dog into the glow of the crystals, she asks, "Jessie, if April showers bring May flowers, what do May flowers bring?"

"Uh...bees? Or butterflies, maybe?" I glance over at Silas. He is slowly shaking his head, in disappointment I think, though he is smiling.

"No, Silly. They bring Pilgrims," she says, as she climbs into Silas' lap, handing him her skewer and mostly cold hot dog. "Right, Daddy?"

Silas nods while taking a huge bite of his hot dog, then tries to guide Ruby's flailing skewer back to the heat. I love how he teaches and encourages her without stifling her own quest for autonomy. She is precocious and independent, but I can see his parenting at work. It's subtle, but he definitely is molding and shaping her.

"Ok, Ruby. I've got one for you. What do you call a fish with no eye?" I ask, watching Silas ponder a clever answer but come up empty.

"I know, blind!" she says in triumph, and the cocky look on her face is *all* Silas.

"Nope. Fff-Ssshhh," I say as I sound out all the letters except the i.

Silas chuckles at the obvious answer and pops the cap off a beer with his key chain, then hands it to me. We settle in for a bit before Ruby surprises us by asking Silas to tell her about her mom.

Silas stammers for a while and then looks to me for help.

"I heard she was very creative, just like you," I say.

"Did she hate me?" Ruby asks, and it's a shot to Silas' heart. I think me being around has re-ignited her interest in her mother, but I still don't think Silas is prepared for her inquiries.

He scoops her up. "No, Honey, she didn't hate you."

"Then why did she leave?" When she asks this, I am struck by how young she looks, how vulnerable she is.

"She left *because* she loved you. She knew she couldn't be a good mother to you. Your mom knew how special you are and knew she wasn't good enough. She wanted you to have more than she was capable of giving." His answer is heartfelt, but I think Silas still wants to convey more.

"And Rubes, in her heart, I think she knew how desperately I wanted you. How much I need you to breathe," Silas says, and I know he is reeling.

Ruby thinks about this for a minute, evidently satisfied with the answer. Then, in the way only a child can, promptly changes the subject.

"I'm going to name my hedgehog Stewart, just like Jessie's dad." I cough out a laugh because she has incorporated one of a billion questions she's asked me over the last few weeks. The fact she remembers my dad's name lets me know she is paying attention to every single thing I do and say.

Relief visibly washes over Silas as he realizes he's off the hook for now about Amber. He has dodged a bullet he didn't even see coming but has feared for years. It's this very deliverance that finally has him agreeing to a hedgehog named Stewart.

By the time we finish our campfire dinner, we have made a mess of the limestone floor tiles with streaks of melted marshmallow webs and charred balls of discarded attempts. Ruby is falling asleep in my lap with her angelic face still smeared with melted chocolate.

"Honey, is it time for bed?" Silas asks, though it plainly is.

"Uh-huh, we should go to sleep," she says, without even opening her eyes.

"Come with me so we can do jammies and teeth while your dad puts this food away. We don't want to attract bears," I say, with a wink toward Silas. I guess the benefit of all the excitement is that she is wiped out, and the night is still young.

***

The tent is roomier than I expected, as Ruby nestles in her little spot in the corner, only halfway in her sleeping bag. Silas tucks her in and kisses her forehead sweetly, then sits back on his heels.

"What now, Pipes?" he asks, with his hands on his hips.

"Let's finish our beers, then *obviously*, we should take advantage of these five-star accommodations. Plus, I'd hate to ruin a good camping trip by not getting enough sleep," I say with a wry smile.

We settle back in around the glowing crystals, and I ask, "How long will Analise be gone?"

"Just until Wednesday, she is visiting her family in Vermont."

"Then Wednesday, I want to see you at the club. I have something for you," I say while leaning into his shoulder.

He slides his warm hand up my thigh. "You got it, Pipes. I certainly wouldn't want to disappoint my girl. Especially if she comes bearing gifts," he says, while giving a light squeeze to my very unsexy, oversized sweatpants.

"I want to thank you," he says, suddenly shifting from playful to serious.

"For what?" I ask, looking up into his penetrating eyes.

"For always being so great with Ruby, and for understanding the delicacy of my situation." He leans in and traces the neckline of my tank top with one finger.

His mischievous caress invades my consciousness. "Awwww," I respond to his appreciative words, but all I can think about is his touch.

"I mean it. You said the perfect thing when she asked about Amber. I completely froze. I couldn't even think, let alone produce an audible response. It's like you instinctively know what to say. You gave her something tangible about her mother, something she needed, even if it was just that she had something in common with her. You're a natural."

"Stop, I just needed to give you a second to think. You are the one who set her mind at ease and let her know Amber loved her. Be ready though, it probably took her a long time to work herself up to asking that.

I bet she has a ton of questions, and now that she is giving them a voice, they are going to start tumbling out."

"I better have my game face on, you mean? I can't just stand there and stammer like an idiot?" Again, tracing the neckline of my shirt. He sounds contrite, but he is not acting that way at all. In fact, he is taunting me, and he looks ready to pounce.

"I'm just saying her questions are going to come easier for her next time."

"I'll be fine, as long as you jump in and wave your arms around or start singing, to distract her while I think of something intelligent to say," he teases, but he isn't finished with my praise because he adds, "You truly are amazing with her. It was your idea to ease in and not overwhelm her right away. I think that was a good call, because now she's not jealous of our time, and she gets to know you for herself." Now, he drops his finger inside the neck of my tank, tickling the skin along my neckline as he follows the stitching just above my breasts.

"I know if she sees me as competition for her daddy's time, this won't work. She will end up hating me or resenting me, or both. I know that well enough, that's just basic human psychology." I say as I lean closer, inviting his touch.

"She asked me if you could be her mom," he says after a long pause, and while moving his arm over my shoulders as if I was about to bolt.

"What did you tell her?" I ask, reeling from the candid delivery of such heavy information.

"I told her I would like that too. Does that scare you?" His face is lit by the fire pit, and there is sincerity in his twinkling eyes.

"Not at all," I say, nervous but surprisingly comfortable at the thought of being her mother. Mostly, I'm completely struck by the fact that Silas doesn't seem scared by it either. This is the guy who never wanted to be tied down to one woman, never wanted a family.

"Good, now get those insufferable sweatpants off and get in the tent."

***

I creep into the tent with Silas following right behind, grabbing my ass as I go. It's dim inside, and I can hear Ruby's soft, raspy breaths, rhythmic in her sleep.

Silas piles up a buffer of stuffed animals and blankets between her sleeping quarters and ours and then flops down on our erratic stack of blankets, sleeping bags, and the down comforter from his room.

Ruby had neatly arranged the beds reminiscent of the Princess and the Pea, heaped with pillows and blankets of all sizes. It's an eight-person tent, which is good because at least five of those people are blankets.

Silas pulls off his shirt, shucks his jeans, and holds open the comforter with a provocative look. I sit back on my heels, looking back and forth between him and Ruby's tiny sleeping frame. "You can't be serious," I state. I'm unnerved by the idea of his daughter in the same tent as his look of ravenous intent.

"Oh, but I am."

"No," I shake my head.

"Just come over here, I only want to cuddle," he says, grin broadening.

I leave my sweatpants at the edge of our makeshift bed within easy reach should the need arise, and crawl toward Silas.

He engulfs me in his arms and kisses me gently, then, not so gently. I can feel his erection against my leg and reach down to pinch its tip. "Stop it, Ruby is right there," I whisper, still skeptical of his insistence. Sex in the same tent as a sleeping child has to be some sort of child abuse, right?

"That's not how you get me to stop. Pinch me again, Jessie," he says into my ear, his voice low and rumbling. "I told you, I just want to cuddle." He says this with persistence, as he flips me over with my back to his chest. Then he sucks my earlobe into his mouth and nips it with his teeth.

Shivers run down my body, and he feels my acquiescence as I melt against him. He drags my tank top down, unveiling my breasts above the stretched neckline, and then tickles and plays with my nipples.

I press my ass into his shaft, rubbing against him and making his breaths come heavier into my ear.

We are facing away from Ruby when he reaches around my hip and, from the front, eases my panties to the side. He raises my top leg and bores in with a slow, deliberate press. The walls of my vagina seem to marble with the stretch of his bold advance. The absolute fullness feels glutinous, the pressure, engorging.

Knowing he is inside me, claiming me is intensely erotic. I grind my teeth together to keep from making a sound as he uses my panties to give an erotic wedgie that presses against my clit as he tugs them up toward my belly.

His slide is slow and rhythmic as he pushes in and drags out, all the while exerting constant pressure on my tiny bundle of nerves with my bunched together panties.

I bend more at the waist to press against him harder. I'm aching for him deeper and faster, though this pace is more appropriate with a sleeping child six feet away.

He keeps up his deliberately slow, grinding motion for an eternity. His movements almost timid, which is the only indication he's as fearful of waking Ruby as I am. One of his arms cradles my body while his other hand tugs my panties. His hips rock and strain against me, but his ministrations are hardly noticeable above the blanket.

"I'm going to pull out, but first I want you to come for me," he whispers ticklishly into my ear. He knows I'm getting close.

"I crane my head back while still clenching my teeth together, as the fullness builds. A minute later my body quietly spasms, constricting and releasing in rapid-fire succession, squeezing and tugging against his dick.

He takes two quick inhales then pulls out, his cum drenching the inside of my thighs in thick squirts that are warm against my skin. Pulling me tightly against him, his penis still anchoring us together, he whispers, "I love you, Jessie."

With my throat dry, and my voice hoarse, I utter, "I love you too, but you better wipe up that cum before it gets on Devin's sleeping bag."

Silas buries his chuckle in my neck and suffocates it with a wet kiss. I turn to face him, no longer concerned with Devin's sleeping bag, and melt into his profession of love.

Chapter Thirteen

Inquiry

After work, I go straight to the gym and flail through a ridiculously hard boot camp. There is no doubt in my mind it's taught by a sadist, looking to inflict as much suffering as humanly possible. The intensity of the workout itself makes my legs shake, and nearly buckle under me as I walk down the stairs, headed to the locker room.

***

Once home, I find I can hardly lower myself onto the toilet seat because my quads hurt so bad. Groaning, I hobble to my bedroom and pull an oversized t-shirt over my head. Then I walk tenderly to the couch, where I tip back into it like a pregnant woman, instead of bending my legs.

"What's up with you?" Devin asks, as his face contorts with misunderstanding. "Did Mr. Big Swinging Dick finally get the best of you?"

"No. Boot camp," I exhale.

"Oh, is that all? Good. Can we talk?" He says, shifting gears faster than Dale Earnhardt Jr.

I slowly turn my head toward him, "I thought we were."

"I want to ask Corey to marry me," he says casually.

I light up, "Really?" Suddenly, my sore quadriceps are all but forgotten.

"Yes, and we have been talking about having a family too," he blurts out, without meeting my eyes.

"Devin!" I squeal, "That's amazing. I mean, I'm not totally sure about the logistics of having a family, but I'm happy for you!"

"The logistics are easy…Now, don't say no right away… suck on it…let it marinate for a few days." He is stammering, and he completely lacks his signature haughty confidence.

"You want me to have your baby," I say, crestfallen. The joy I feel for their approaching nuptials is squashed entirely by the implication of me carrying their baby.

"Will you just think about it? It would be turkey baster, you wouldn't have to have sex with us," he says, as if the sex part were the big deal.

"Fuck, Devin," is all I can say, as he leans over and kisses my temple.

"Just think about it."

My spent leg muscles are forgotten, as I sit on the couch with my mouth hanging open, but nothing to say.

Chapter Fourteen

Work

Now that Wednesday is finally here, and Analise will be back, I can't wait for tonight to give Silas the naughty photo book. I want to watch his face as he turns each page, growing harder and more crazed with each sexy photo. However, even with all the building excitement, I'm still consumed by Devin's casual dropping of his nuclear question.

Salinger knocks on my office door while pushing it open, not even looking for permission to come in. "You ok? You seemed very distracted in the meeting." His trendy new, vintage haircut looks distractingly sexy, and he has the office ladies squirming even more than usual these days.

"Do you think I would look good pregnant?" I ask, not even bothering to evade what's on my mind.

He sinks into the chair facing my desk. "Are you pregnant, Jessie?" he asks, his question tinged with disappointment.

"No," I say flatly.

"Oh, good. So you're saying there's a chance?" he asks while smiling that hundred-watt grin he has perfectly mastered.

I roll my eyes, "Stop," then decide to fess up, "Devin wants a baby."

"Oh, wow. That's a little sticky isn't it?" he asks, finally relaxing back into the chair.

"Yeah," I scoff, and then change the subject. "How is the club going?"

He scrunches up his face with the sudden change of subject, but answers anyway.

"It's good, I met someone," he offers shyly.

"Oh shit, please tell me her name isn't Parker," I say with alarm.

"No, it's Bradley. Do you know her?"

"I don't think so. You like her?" I'm still uncomfortable with him frequenting the club, so the idea that he has met someone is good— maybe they will stay at home more.

"Yeah, for now. Jessie?"

"Hmmmm?"

"You would make a beautiful pregnant woman." He doesn't look away, and for some reason that feels really supportive, like he will always be there for me, no matter what hair-brained idea I come up with.

"Do you really think so?"

"Yeah, I really do."

***

Just as the door closes behind Salinger my cell phone rings, it's Silas.

I answer the phone, "Hi."

"Baby, I have bad news. Analise isn't coming back until Friday. She wants to stay with her family a couple more days. So, unfortunately, tonight is out for the club. I still need to see you though, I gotta get my fix. Want to come over instead?"

"Um, sure," I say, and I can't hide the disappointment in my voice. I wanted to give him the photo book so bad. With Analise gone, that means dinner, bath, and bedtime stories instead of a hot photo book and dizzying sex.

"Alright, Hon, see you after work."

Our phone calls are always so brief because of his work schedule. It makes me that much more desperate to see him. I have never *craved* a man before Silas. I've always been kind of disappointed in men in general and in sex specifically. I never felt like I *had* to fuck someone, but great sex is like a drug, and the withdrawal is real. I seriously need to be with him, and tonight would have been perfect.

After he hangs up, I have a better idea, so I call Devin.

Chapter Fifteen

Gift

"Can you at least pretend to be nice to him?" I ask Devin while he fidgets in the elevator.

"I'm not making any promises," he quips, adjusting the trendy messenger bag that he has slung across his chest.

Once we get to Silas' door, I give Devin one last pleading look then raise my hand to knock on the door. After a moment, and an indifferent shrug from Devin indicating that he may, or may not be nice, Silas swings the door wide open.

Devin marches inside exclaiming, "Where is Ruby? I have a design emergency. Ruby, where are you?" He is so animated in his storming of Silas' loft that both Silas and I step back a little stunned, and to make room for Devin's huge personality.

Silas' face lights up when he sees the wrapped box under my arm. "What have we here? You brought me a present *and* a sitter?"

Ruby runs into the room upon hearing Devin's distress call, curious about his stated design emergency.

"Ruby, I'm Devin. I need your help," he says, as he slips his messenger bag over his head and extends his hand proudly for her to shake.

"Hi, Devin," she says, with a huge smile creeping to her sweet face. It's as if she can sense the fun and uninhibited nature of Devin right off the bat.

As I said before, people love him. They flock to him just to be part of his world. For his part, though, he lets few in, damaged by his past as he is. His expectations of people are high, but the return of his love is an unmatched gift he doesn't even realize he is bestowing.

There is a similarity between Ruby and Devin. It's unspoken, but it's there, and they both feel it—like a sixth sense. Perhaps the souls of the abandoned sing to each other.

She beams, and just like that, they are a part of each other's worlds. Devin begins emptying the contents of his messenger bag as they both sit in the middle of the floor, perched on their knees.

She really is an accepting little girl, but I also see her carefully measure people up, probably afraid to grow attached. Silas has kept her away from the steady stream of women in his past, perhaps knowing the frequency of the pendulum to swing, and wanting to shelter her from it. She has accepted me with no reservations, I think, due to her eagerness for a mother. Her immediate acceptance of *Devin* is more in the way of the circus having just come to town.

Analise is a nanny, grandmother, playmate, and mother to her, but Ruby still craves something deeper, with the rawness of a child who has known profound loss and sudden abandonment.

Devin starts pulling a fuchsia pink feather boa from his bag, and Ruby's mouth drops open. She cannot believe her good fortune. Fashion emergencies and feather boas are right up her alley, and Devin knows this with the certainty of a prophet. When he pulls out a makeup kit, he has her full attention.

***

Silas and I slip into the club and make a beeline towards the elevator. We are anxious to avoid any club business, but halfway to the elevator doors, I hear Parker and my hackles go up. Even her voice is like liquid nitrogen, freezing everything in place moments before it shatters into a million shards of pure loathing.

"Jessie, could I steal Silas for a minute? I promise he won't keep you waiting too long, and I'll return him *almost* as good as new." She winks at me as if knowing I can't very well say no.

"Actually, we are in—" I try, but I'm cut short.

"Jessie, don't be silly, this is club business that *Silas and I* really need to see to. This is *our* club you know," she says, with a treacherous glint in her eyes. As if I need to be reminded of the fact they are banded together in the same alliance, appalling as it may be for me.

Silas looks at me and then back to Parker, "Five minutes," he tells her sternly. Then he holds out a room key to me, who, by the way, am growing tired of this new routine of heading on up and waiting for him.

"Of course," she says, as she drapes an arm around him and leads him away. As they are walking, she actually raises the hand not clinging to him, up next to her shoulder, and gives me the finger. My anger flares just as she's adding a little pretentiousness to the swing of her hips.

How can Silas miss all her bitchy overtures? He finds her genuine and insists she likes everyone, just sometimes needs to warm up a little. Well screw her, even warmed up she is still frigid, and I don't play well with nasty, conniving women. Never have.

***

I walk into the room, a new one for me. It's on the smallish side and contains a medical chair complete with stirrups, and a hospital gown draped across it. Above is a bright surgical light. Next to the exam table are a stainless steel medical cabinet and a strange device sitting on the floor.

The thing on the floor looks like a giant mailbox, but I can see a long submarine-like attachment running down the middle of it. The device looks odd against the vibrant Oriental rug on the floor. It seems to be smirking at me, taunting me to approach before it lets out a maniacal laugh. As I stare at it, it looks almost sinister in its simplicity, just sitting there, goading me, waiting for me to make a move.

I put Silas' gift down on the stainless steel cabinet and hop up on the exam table, swinging my legs while I wait for that scheming bitch to finish with my man.

I ponder if I should strip down and put on the hospital gown, but quickly decide I like my short black shorts and off the shoulder top better than a frumpy hospital gown. Not to mention, I want to give Silas the photo book right away, and not dressed as the infirmed.

As I sit and wait, I can't stop eying the mailbox. It mirrors my mood, dark and brooding. Parker knows she can get to Silas just by appealing to his business side, and he is too nice of a guy not to accommodate her. The whole Parker thing is maddening, and I'm constantly amazed he doesn't see it. Maybe he does, but he can't acknowledge it because we are two women that won't be going away.

What he needs to realize, though, is that he can't be neutral. I'm not saying he needs to take sides, but he needs to establish certain boundaries for her. The fact that she treats me the way she does, and talks to me the way she does is easily attributed to him not wanting to make waves.

When what he needs to do is stand up for me, not leave me hanging like low-lying fruit for her to pick off. If he stood up for me just once, that's all it would take. Boundaries. I'm not saying he needs to tell her off, but a simple, "That's enough, Parker," or, "You can't talk to her like that," is all it would take to squash it. The fact is, she does it because she *can*.

As I sit here analyzing Silas' role in the whole pissing match between Parker and me, I'm getting angrier. I'm supposed to be under his protection. Isn't that what he said when he put his collar/necklace on me? How can he sit back while it goes on right under his nose? I shouldn't even have to tell him, *he* should know women better.

Now, if I can only get him to stand up for me without screaming, stomping my feet, and demanding he do so, unintentionally making *me* the psycho one, I'll be all set.

***

By the time Silas comes in, it's been a good half hour, and I'm lying down with my forearm shielding my eyes from the ridiculous surgical light that hangs above me. My high heels are in the stirrups and as exasperated as I am, I make no motion to move or get up.

"What did that little saboteur need?" I ask, muffled into my arm.

"I'm sorry, Jessie, it was our accounting software. You look fucking hot like that though," he says, deflecting my comment like a pro.

Approaching me, he takes one of my hands and helps me to sit up. "I'm really sorry it took so long," he says, and his voice is soft, his eyes contrite.

"I expected nothing less from Parker," I say.

"I'm surprised you are not on the Sybian," he says, through a huge grin. "It would serve me right, leaving you here waiting for me."

"Sybian, is that what that contemptuous little thing is?" I ask, raising my chin to the mailbox contraption. "What does it do?"

"Shall I show you?" Silas asks playfully, as he pulls a funny little dick attachment out of the medical cabinet, walks toward it, and begins securing the silicone phallus to the submarine part of the Sybian.

"No, not yet. I want you to open your present," I say, hopping down from the exam table and leaning forward provocatively to retrieve the photo book. I refuse to let Parker's games affect our time together. I need to put my anger toward her, and my resentment toward him in a little box and set it aside for now. Not forever, mind you, because this needs to be addressed, but it's not going to happen while I'm burning this much for him, and we are finally alone together.

Silas takes the present, gives me a skewed smile, and pulls out the rolling stool. He sits down, rips off the paper, and gapes at the cover of the book. On the cover is a 12X12 black and white photo of me on the satin bed. The angle of the picture first shows my face; sexy look to the camera, then my cleavage, and finally my cuffed wrists. My lower body is out of focus but in a really beautiful, artistic way.

Silas pales and looks up at me with a questioning look on his face. He very cautiously opens the cover, as if a cobra might strike, then slowly pages through a few bawdy photos before he says, "Jessie, is this a joke?" I'm thrumming with excitement, but with that single comment, it's snuffed out like a candle in the rain.

"What? Don't you like it?" I ask, completely stunned. I had been anticipating a far different response. His dismay doesn't compute right away.

He turns a few more pages with thick fingers, swallows heavily then tosses the book onto the exam table. "No, I hate it," he says, his face ashen.

"Whoa, that's a little strong, isn't it?" I'm angry now, so when tears well up in my eyes, I swipe them away hotly.

"No, it's not strong enough. In fact, I *fucking HATE* those pictures," he says, standing so fast the stool falls over. For a few seconds, the casters on the legs of the stool sway back and forth before coming to a rigid stop.

"Who did that to you? Was it someone here, at the club? AT MY CLUB?" He is talking fast and loudly now as his anger gears up.

"Is that all you can think of? Who did that to me! Well, screw you, Silas!" I yell. "I'm sure you would rather I give you a leash for my collar. Right? Well, excuse me for trying to surprise you with something hot!"

He is looking at the ground, shaking his head. I can tell he is trying to rein himself in and compose himself as much as possible.

"You are the only man alive that would hate those pictures!" I spit out. "What's wrong? Not sexy enough for you? Huh! Not bound tightly enough? Maybe I wasn't naked enough?"

"You shouldn't have done that, Jessie," he grinds out slowly, almost quietly. He still hasn't looked up, has yet to face my fury.

The effect of him not meeting my eyes is a sudden and profound insecurity. Does he not like how I look? What's wrong with me in the pictures? My mind is snatching at all the insecure possibilities, but inside I am crumbling with his rejection. The pictures are of me at my most raw, most trusting…most vulnerable, and he hates them.

"I did it for you! I was a dirty little slut in those pictures because I thought that is what you wanted!"

"Jessie! You are **my** dirty little slut! Do you get that? Huh? Can you at least understand why I am so angry?" he is shouting now, face twisted in blistering anger. He is looking at me, his eyes boring through me with his question hovering like an executioner's blade above my neck.

"What the hell did you just say?" My words soften as they spill out, and his meaning becomes more apparent.

"You are **my** *dirty little slut.* You wear **my** collar. You are under **my** protection. You submit to **me**. No one binds you but **me**," he annunciates each word, fire blazing in his dark blue eyes, though he is no longer shouting.

"Is that why you hate the pictures? Because someone else did that to me?" I ask, feeling nothing short of flabbergasted.

"Isn't that obvious?" he asks, cocking his head to the side in a questioning manner. I notice his pupils are mere pinpricks.

"No," I say methodically, "I thought…you thought I…looked ridiculous…or unattractive."

He is exasperated now. "No, *Jessie.* It's that you looked **that** sexy for *someone else.* You let another man bind and dominate you."

I don't have the heart to tell him that three men did that to me, so I say, "Oh. That didn't even occur to me." I'm lost for other words, but my outraged demeanor takes a spiraling nosedive.

"Tell me, would you take wedding pictures with another man and then give them to your husband as a gift?"

"Well, no…" I feel foolish now, "Of course not. Not unless we were into the whole cuckold fantasy," I say, cracking a smile and trying to break the tension, with perhaps, ill-timed humor.

"*Fuck*, Jessie," he scoffs. "Come here," he says, more gently now.

I walk cautiously into his arms, and he squeezes me tight. "*Fuck, Jessie,*" he mumbles again. His anger has dissolved into disappointment, a far more hurtful emotion for me to absorb, especially coming from him.

After standing enveloped in his arms for a few minutes, I'm feeling better about his unexpected reaction to the images. He did like them, just hated the idea that someone else took the photos. Ok, so his reaction was possessive, I guess I can understand that. Though I don't exactly relish the idea of being possessed by someone, I think his heart is in the right place.

"This seems like a good time to remind you how unsatisfying *anyone* or *anything* else is for you sexually. Because you *obviously* need to be reminded of a few things."

"Oh crap, is this where you spank me?" I ask, resigned but not totally surprised.

"No, I'm not into punitive spanking," he says lightly, maybe too lightly.

I pull back and look into his eyes questioningly. I remember how he had taught me a lesson when he thought I was flirting with Carson. Being familiar with his emotional responses and knowing how wildly they swing, this lesson will undoubtedly be one for the record books.

"Take your clothes off and get on the exam table. I need to go get a few more items, but when I get back, I want you naked and in the stirrups." He is not smiling anymore, and as he turns to leave the room, I wonder what the return of his sovereignty will cost me.

Chapter Sixteen

Club

Once naked and in the stirrups, I find that I am shaking. Not really *shaking*, but quivering, or maybe humming with nervous intuition. I've heard of medical fetishes, heard stories of speculums and urethral dilators, enemas, and douches, but none of these are sexy and playful to me, so I pray Silas doesn't think some sort of exam is in order.

The overhead surgical light is blinding and illuminates my naked body like a solar flare. Due to the bright light, I can't see Silas when he enters. I only hear him as he approaches.

He tips the light down my body so it's no longer blazing into my face. Shadowing my eyes with my hand, I see he is wearing a lab coat and is holding a clipboard. *Shit*. His hair is parted and combed in wet rows to the sides. His glasses are coke bottle thick and distort his face by making his eyes look too large for his head, like a fly, or something else un-sexy.

"Miss, I understand you are having trouble finding release through orgasms. Is this why you came to see me today?"

I roll my eyes and groan. He can't be serious, right? This kind of role play is not *at all* sexy for me, and if he thinks he is giving me a pelvic exam, I will use the club safeword in a hot second. Truth be told, I'm a little disappointed in him. This seems too cheesy for Silas.

"Uh—" is all I can get out, my mind is spinning.

"I see. Luckily, I can help you. I have many tools for correcting such sexual dysfunction at my disposal. Let's get started," he says. His words are short and clipped as he grabs one towering heel and begins wrapping a silk scarf around my ankle. Then he binds my strappy-shoe-clad foot into the unforgiving metal stirrup. I think I've been more at ease during an *actual* pap smear.

I am supremely uncomfortable with the turn of events, and the soles of my feet begin sweating while pressed against the metal footrests.

"I… Uh," I stammer, but can't put words to my thoughts. I would rather he spank me. I'm wrenched open, naked before him, and instead of feeling sexy, I feel ridiculous and annoyed.

After tying my other ankle, he sits on his stool, rolling it forward between my stiff legs and cold countenance. "Slide on down and let your knees fall to the side," he commands. Then lightly caresses my inner thighs as if sensing my discomfort. However, his touch feels like that of an awkward doctor copping a feel, not of a seductive lover.

When he begins toying with my lips, the awkward doctor mystique intensifies by tenfold, and I drape my arm across my eyes in mortification.

After a few fluttering touches and blundering fondles, nothing like Silas' skilled, confident touches, he announces, "Everything seems to be in order down here."

I hear the snap of latex gloves and groan with annoyance again. Suddenly, something very cold and smooth touches my clit. I gasp and try to pull away, pressing into the stirrups and attempting to back up in a quick, yet involuntary motion.

"Nothing more than a chilled spoon, just relax," he says. "Perhaps some lubrication will help." He withdraws the spoon for a moment before resting it wetly against my nub again. This time it's coated with KY jelly.

As he rubs it gently up and down across my clit, I settle in, finally relaxing a bit with the erotic sensation.

"Let your legs fall open, Miss. I can hardly help you if you restrict my view. I need to see your naked sexuality up close and personal," he says with his words still cropped short.

I drop my knees more, opening myself to his ministrations with the spoon and warming to the idea of his touch. The spoon slips up and down with a light pressure. My breaths begin to come faster. Up and down, up and down, over and over, gradually picking up speed and sliding easily over my clitoris. My orgasm is quickly building, and now I'm straining against the spoon.

"Oh, Doctor," I exhale as I near my peak. He slows his movements then gives a final slippery swipe down my vaginal lips. He rolls his stool back with a squeaky protest from the casters.

"That didn't seem to work, let's try some of this tingling gel. Then I have a very special tool, designed with you in mind." He swipes a dollop of cream across my bud, then continues dragging his gloved finger back through my vagina.

I immediately feel a cooling sensation, but after a few seconds, it warms, then turns into a prickle. It almost creates the sensation of all the nerves in my vagina having fallen asleep. It's a maddening tingle, and again I try to push away from the stirrups.

"The gel seems to be working, so now I will utilize this very specific, patent-pending medical device. It's called a *Pearl Necklace*, not to be confused with the one made of cum around your neck," he judiciously explains that which needs no explanation.

I flinch as he begins rubbing a strand of pearls up through my folds, bumping distressingly into my prickling clit, one pearl at a time. The bump of each pearl against my tingling bud causes a jolt of pain/pleasure that has me ferociously trying to close my legs. My knees are straining, trying madly to come together.

"Now, now, that simply won't do. I need unfettered access to your vagina if I'm to help you with your sexual dysfunction," he says, through his doctor facade. "It appears lubrication is not your issue," he chuckles, breaking character for a split second.

I'm twisting under the ankle restraints and panting with each bump, bump, bump of the pearls.

"Doctor! I need you to fuck me," I grind out through gritted teeth, orgasm descending like mist.

"Absolutely not, Miss! That wouldn't be proper. I am a board-certified physician. I couldn't possibly fuck this tight little pussy."

"Oh, yes, Ahhhhh," I moan, as I thrash my cheek to the side and press it into the exam table, about to let go.

He stops and again scoots back, squeaky casters screaming my torment, *again*. I can feel my pulse in each part of my vagina's anatomy. It feels like a deliriously tingling, beating heart. I'm sweating with need and beyond frustrated.

"Why?" I ask, and it sounds whiny and combative at the same time.

"Your treatment, Miss, it's called *edging*. What do you think so far?" he asks, clearly amused.

I'm speechless with realization. Edging is a nice little term for withholding orgasms, with the intent of building toward a monumental release. But he is punishing me for the photo book, so this may not lead to fireworks.

He doesn't care about my dreaded epiphany, as he holds up a funny little wheel. It looks like a handheld Ferris wheel with pink flaps protruding from each pod.

"This is a favorite of my patients, it simulates oral sex. It's really quite adept at treating the common female hysteria," he says, as he turns it on and it begins rotating.

I blanch as he holds it to my core. The color runs from my body and pools against the exam table like some sort of sexual lividity or dread, I'm not sure which.

The little tongues slap against my clit, nudging it down in sequential thumps. I can't say it feels like a tongue, but the constant, ceaseless clap against my swollen and highly sensitized tip has the desired effect. Soon I'm rocking my head from side to side, in resignation and rapture. Surrender and torment.

I know he won't let me come, my only hope of release is to trick him. If I can just calm myself and quiet the building climax, maybe I can fool him into waiting just a moment too long.

I quickly find that my plan has holes in it, namely the relentless little slapping tongues. The incessant attention is incredibly hard to overlook, and it's impossible to maintain my distance from the edge.

My back is arching, and sweat is saturating my hairline and temples, as I try to pull away from the stimulation. It's too much, my need to orgasm. I feel like if I don't let go, I will drown. As expected, Silas removes the device just as I graze against the edge of oblivion.

"It's too much, stop," I beg. "I'm sorry. I didn't know you wouldn't like the photos. Please," I'm crazed yet listless in my begging.

"Perhaps a firmer touch then?" he asks.

"Yes," I pant, praying my ordeal is over—my apology accepted.

"Ok, let's try this." He holds up what I think is a camel hair shaving brush.

"No," I whimper, mania oozing from every pore.

"Don't worry, it's soft, and I've never used it before," he says consolingly, as if that was my resistance to the thing.

I grind my teeth as he pushes the bristles against my flesh. He pokes and wiggles the brush as it grinds into me, stabbing against my delicate parts. The tamping is almost driving me off the table with crazed sensitivity.

"Fuck!" I yell, as the sharp little points stipple against tender flesh. Sweat glistens on my body, and for the first time, I feel an ache in my ankles from pulling against the restraints. Inside my shoes is now wet and slippery with my sweat.

My teeth are vibrating with the flood of endorphins. The need to orgasm is well out of control as he pokes, jabs, and scratches against my raw clit. I'm powerless against his daunting stimulation, and I'm flooded with the visceral need to summit the peak of my orgasm and then throw myself over the edge. The withholding is beyond merciless. It's cruel.

Blessedly, he stops his torment. "Well, it seems direct clitoral stimulation is not helping with your sexual dysfunction, Miss. I have one more medical apparatus to try, though."

He walks away, and I realize I am gripping the edge of the exam table so tightly that all the knuckles in my fingers are throbbing. The table is wet with perspiration, and I can't unclench my jaw because I'm so tightly wound. My chest is heaving, and my mind is spinning.

When Silas returns, he is pushing some sort of cannon-shaped device. It scrapes heavily against the stained concrete floor before he has to lift it onto the rug and position it between my legs.

I realize what it is when I see him attach a dildo to the end of it. My resolve plummets. It's a fucking machine, and he has every intention of using it on me. I have heard of these, but never actually seen one and certainly never been on the receiving end of one.

"To be thorough, I will need to examine your internal structures as well," he says, as he eases the spear end into my vagina.

I'm exhausted with the intensity of this game, and my mouth is as dry as a cinder block, but the purple dildo slips easily into my body, betraying my exhaustion.

Silas comes to my side holding a remote control box and saying, "Just relax, Miss." He has a dubious glint in his eyes, so I close mine, all too aware of the building dread.

With the sound of a small humming motor, the dildo begins to bob in and out. The suction sounds audible against the hum of the motor. The pumping increases in depth, but besides feeling repeatedly impaled by a silicone phallus, with no clitoral stimulation, I am in no danger of orgasming.

Silas watches my reaction, which beyond a fluttering beneath my eyelids, is minimal. He has controlled the depth of the plunging machine, so it doesn't hurt, only dips shallowly. However, the thrusting isn't stimulating—it's only, well, mechanical. Silas bores quickly and withdraws the device, only to attach a different mechanism to the arm of the machine.

This time he rests a heavy, bulbous tip against my clitoral hood. The top of the attachment feels spongy and is about the size of a tennis ball. When he turns on the vibrating massager, my eyes fling open in surprise, the direct assault way too intense.

"Too much, too much," I cry out, and when he does nothing, I simply breathe, "Yellow."

He immediately slows the massager, and I calm a mere fraction, though my body is still held stiffly in a type of live rigor mortis.

After a few minutes, he can tell by my hard set jaw and my hurried breathing that my orgasm is threatening. In reaction to that fact, he simply slows the hum of the machine to nothing more than a low insinuation. Climax averted.

I've long since tired of this game, and my body feels like it's on the edge of Blitzkrieg, when he moves the machine and silently slips between my legs.

"Give me your hand," he says.

When I do, he helps me into a sitting position.

"Slide down a little more," he says in a soft voice.

I do, and then adjust my arms behind me, supporting my sitting position as I lean on them. My hands feel otherworldly against the leather of the exam table, and my legs are still wrenched apart and held securely in the stirrups.

The pose is overtly sexual, as Silas drinks in first, my spread legs, then my breasts, and finally my eyes.

"You look so fucking sexy like that," he says as he tugs off his latex gloves and unbuttons his lab coat. He is bare-chested beneath the coat, and he quickly disengages his hard-on from his jeans. He steps forward, never breaking eye contact.

My feeling of being conquered and mentally broken shifts a bit when a smile flutters across his face. He cups my breasts, thumbing my erect nipples, and I realize it's the first human touch I've had since the gauntlet began.

He steps closer, his silky penis brushing my splayed core as he leans in. He places one hand on the back of my neck and pulls me into his firm kiss.

I almost dissolve into him with the realization that the ordeal is over. Tears unwittingly spring to my eyes, and I begin to cry against his mouth.

"Shhhhh," he coos, as he wraps his arms around me, caressing my back and holding me against him. Next, he tips my chin up with a finger and kisses me gently.

After wiping my tears with his thumbs, he begins to kiss my ear, breathing into it, "I love you, so much." Then he starts making his way down my neck.

Goosebumps speckle my body as he moves languidly down to my nipples, flicking and sucking each one in turn. When I flop my head back, he drags his tongue down my abdomen grazing it wetly against each hip before delving lower.

When he begins kissing my thigh, I can feel his hair brush against my sex, and the tickle is somehow magnified. He feathers kisses against each thigh then settles his warm tongue into my silkiness.

He works tenderly, as if knowing how heightened my sense of touch is. For the first time tonight, I find that I am trying to wrench my legs more forcefully apart, opening further for his wet probing tongue. I moan toward the ceiling, as he continues to savor my virtue, flicking and rubbing gingerly.

I'm arching into him as the tidal wave approaches, then recedes with fear he won't let it come to fruition. Each time the wave gets stronger and stronger, and I begin to moan in ecstasy, hardly able to control the fury building inside.

When I do let go, I fall back onto the table as Silas holds my thighs, pinned tightly between his forearms and biceps as he slows his ministrations but doesn't stop, his face still held tightly against my core.

The orgasm is incredibly strong. The intensity is suffocating as it crashes and splinters over and over again. Silas stops all but the gentlest pressure, slowing his tongue, as I shudder against his mouth, my vagina spasming violently.

My heart is pounding out of my chest, and I'm still not under control when another orgasm rips through me. "OhMyGod! Silas, Yes!" I'm disoriented now. I have never had multiple orgasms so close together and *never* of this magnitude. I feel feral as I grunt and writhe against the ferocity of my release.

Heart still hammering, I've only just recovered from the last crushing wave when another one hits. My body tenses with the first spasms, but this one is more of a stutter of the last two, nothing like the strength of the preceding ones.

Once my quaking stills, Silas stands up, his mouth glistening with my triumph, and pulls me into him again. He holds me against his body, knowing I am boneless and completely unable to stay upright on my own.

I feel him press and slide into me, hard and long. My body welcomes him like part of my own anatomy.

"Silas, I love you. OhGod! I love you so much," I lament as he begins to thrust. His ability with my body is staggering, and like nothing I have ever experienced before.

"I love you too, baby," he grinds out as he increases his slippery tempo.

Before long, I feel him clutch me tighter as the building tension between my legs breaks again, and we orgasm together. For me, it's a gentle storm. For Silas, a crushing squall as he plows into me a few more times, his neck veins nearly bursting with his strain.

***

After a few moments of my vision being speckled, Silas helps me lie back again so he can untie my ankles. I feel like not a single muscle in my body will respond when I need to move, so I'm relieved when he scoops me up and lowers me down to the Oriental rug. He cradles me against him because neither of us has the strength to move more than a few feet.

We lay there for a long time, feeling the closeness of our bodies, our exertion fusing us together. We are both exhausted and content to stay on the rug, naked and spent, forever.

I'm nodding off when he whispers, "Stay here, I'm going to clean up." As he peels away from me, I'm too tired to protest. I just make a noise that sounds like, "Humpf," before my eyes flutter closed and I fall asleep, mindless to the world around me.

***

When we arrive back at Silas' after leaving the club, we both grin at the sight that greets us.

Ruby and Devin are sprawled out on the couch. She is tucked into him. He has one leg draped over the back of the couch and is clutching her in one arm like an old favorite doll. His other arm is flung behind his head, over the armrest of the couch.

Devin has several bows in his hair, and his scarlet red lipstick is smeared across his cheek and on the back of his hand, as he open mouth breathes in his sleep. The aqua blue eyeshadow has been applied with a heavy hand and looks like two nesting birds on his eyelids.

Ruby, also open-mouthed, is snoring softly. She is cradled in Devin's arm between him and the back of the couch. She has an array of erratic braids and clips in her disheveled brown hair. Her makeup is softer, but her lips are bubble-gum pink.

A blanket is haphazardly strewn across their sleeping frames, but a vibrant purple tutu peaks from under the covers.

Silas chokes on a snort in an attempt at not laughing too loudly, but the sound, along with his subsequent stifled laughter, wakes Devin.

"Lord in Heaven, what took you two so long?" he says, while sliding out from under Ruby. There is a little drool spot on his t-shirt from where she was sleeping.

"Sorry, Dev."

"No matter. How do I look?" he asks with complete seriousness, though he is being facetious.

"You look stunning, and Ruby obviously had fun," Silas says, as he scoops Ruby into his arms then carries her to her bedroom.

Once Devin and I are alone, I whisper, "Thank you, Devin."

"You got it," he winks, and then straightens up, clearing his throat as Silas returns.

"Thank you, Devin," Silas says, as he extends his hand to him. Devin looks at the offered hand for a moment, before shaking it slowly.

"You're welcome, I guess. I didn't know we were so formal." He releases Silas' hand and then wipes his own on his jeans, not caring in the least that Silas sees him do it.

Devin yawns and stretches dramatically again, "Well, I better get this lil' firecracker to bed." He means me, his smudged lipstick giving comic relief to his statement, as well as adding a little sneer to his words.

"I'll pull up out front," he says, as he walks out the door unfazed by the bows in his spouting hair and freakish makeup—if you can even call it makeup.

Silas pulls me into him and mutters into my ear, "Are you sure you can't stay?"

"I'm sure. I still don't want to force too much on Ruby."

"Maybe we should have re-thought the whole Devin thing then," he says, with a hearty laugh.

Chapter Seventeen

Trip

Salinger and I are in a company car. We look like the secret service in the black Suburban with dark tinted windows, although one look inside would blow that whole image. Salinger is blasting SiriusXM. It's set to a rap station, and he is belting out every word of every song. His flailing hands and rapper moves make me have to squeeze my legs together, so I don't pee myself.

"Ok, ok, one more and then I'm done," he promises, as he dives into his next gangster rap montage. He's rapping to me like I am front row at his concert, his words spilling out with voracious speed and surprising accuracy.

I'm laughing so hard I finally have to tell him to pull over. He flashes some sort of gang sign in acknowledgment and then rolls to a stop on the deserted country road.

I drop out of the hulking vehicle and mouth, "No peeking," as my feet hit the gravel, rustling the dirt into a minimal protest.

Salinger pauses his verbal assault long enough to say, "As if," then launches right back into his lyrical grandstanding.

I squat by the rear tire and pee a long forceful stream, still giggling at Salinger's theatrics. Silas was not happy about this business trip, but the fact that it's not far enough away for my company to deem it worthy of an overnight expense made it easier for him to swallow. Although, he still had a sour look on his face when I told him I had to go.

When I get back into the car, Salinger calmly announces, "You splashed on your shoes."

I give him a squinty-eyed glare for peeking, then say, "Tell me about Bradley."

He looks stunned, lowers the volume and asks, "Why do you want to know about her?"

"Maybe, because we will be in the car for another three and a half hours," I press.

"Um ok, she has blonde hair, blue eyes, tattoo sleeves like me, she's hot as fuck, killer bod..." he trails off.

"Boring, tell me something good."

"She's a circus freak in bed. How's that?" he asks innocently, plying me with something he thinks I might consider *good*.

"That's a little better. What do you mean by *circus freak*? Are we talking contortionist stuff?" I ask, playing into my aroused curiosity.

"No, just freaky and adventurous... and completely insatiable. She's a total nympho, and I'm not even exaggerating," he says, and his eyes are wide as if he is still trying to get his head around it.

"You met her at the club, right?" I ask.

"Yeah, she was performing in the peep show room. Have you been to that part of the club?"

I slowly shake my head, no.

"There are all these little rooms where people can watch her strip and dance and eventually play with herself... or others." He raises his eyebrows, insinuating he has been one of her *others*. "She is a total exhibitionist, and I mean that fondly."

"Are you two exclusive?" I ask, with maybe the slightest twinge of unwarranted jealousy.

"I'd like to say yes, but there is no chance of tying that girl down. I'm not even sure I could handle her all by myself." He scoffs a bit and adjusts himself more comfortably in the seat of the Suburban. He seems a little shy to admit he can't handle her by himself, like he is admitting he is not man enough.

"What is her personality like?"

"That's just it. I can't get a solid read on her. She is really into my scar, and I think she likes the whole *damaged* aspect of me, but I kind of get the feeling that's so she can counterbalance her own issues. You know? Her own damage."

"Are you certain she even *is* damaged? I mean, that's kind of a leap isn't it?" I kick off my shoes and tuck my legs under my body in an attempt to get comfortable in the deep captain's chair. It has become somewhat of a second home for me in the company SUV.

"Oh yeah, she's damaged," he says, with unabashed certainty.

"You're sure?"

"Positive. I just don't know what damaged her. I know enough about the psychology behind emotional wreckage though, and I can spot it from a mile away. Trust me, she's suffering from something," he says, with total conviction.

"Tell me something about her that makes you so sure," I push. I'm resisting the idea that she is somehow emotionally wrecked just because she is a member of 1462.

"She pinches her nipples before asking someone for directions that she doesn't even need, just to see if they stare at her tits."

"Salinger! That just points to her being an attention seeker, not fucked up."

"All right then. She masturbates at red lights when she knows a trucker or bus driver can see her."

"Again, attention seeking," I say, exaggerating a yawn.

"Ok then, she works as a prostitute, and I'm not just talking high class, call girl stuff. She will do the whole *lot lizard* thing at truck stops too." He stares straight ahead, afraid to look over at me.

"Ok, you win," I say, stunned.

After a long awkward silence, I jump right back in. "And you have sex with this chic?"

"Jessie, she is under court order to test every three months. She is also very strict about condoms, even for trucker hand jobs. The truckers usually like to fuck her in the ass though."

"What the hell are you thinking? Court ordered? Truckers like to fuck her in the ass?" I'm astonished.

"And, if all that isn't enough, she is really into gangbangs, like...serious gangbangs. Her ultimate favorite though, is when a guy gags her to the point of throwing up from a forced blow-ie." He hazards a glance at me, and then quickly looks back to the open road.

I gawk at him, open-mouthed and stunned into silence.

"Don't even get me started about her record for how many men can come in her mouth at one time." His lips slowly curl into a smile before he bursts out laughing.

"You asshole! I thought you had gone crazy from syphilis or something," I say, then punch him in the arm.

"But, seriously…she does pinch her nipples before asking for directions," he says, unapologetically.

"So she really isn't damaged?" I ask.

"Oh no, she's completely wrecked," he says, committing wholeheartedly to his initial assessment.

"Does she really masturbate in the car for bus drivers?" I ask, still interested in this enigma of a woman.

"No, she slides her skirt up, and I do it for her." He looks over at me, and I'm pretty sure he can see the gulp of saliva squeeze down my throat.

"Although she *has* been known to spread her legs and knock one out on the subway if someone is looking. Jessie, I'm serious about her being a total exhibitionist. If someone is watching, she's performing."

"Don't exhibitionists just become strippers?"

"She used to be a stripper, but it wasn't enough. She *needs* people to watch her get rimmed, or double penetrated, or spread open with vag spreaders. I'm totally serious, there is actually such a thing as vag spreaders. I'm telling you, she's hardcore."

"I wonder why she is so desperate for attention," I say, as I puzzle it over in my head. Those kinds of displays are highly objectifying, and speak to an insecurity that I, thankfully will never understand.

Salinger adds, "Or why she only sees her *value* in those kinds of raunchy displays. Could be a lot of things, my hunch is—"

"Low self-esteem? Daddy issues?" I interrupt, while looking out the window at miles upon miles of farmland.

"Sexual abuse," he says flatly, eyes on the road. "In fact, I think her tattoos started out as a way to disfigure herself, to make her ugly or unappealing."

I can plainly see Salinger's arm tattoos, and the *last* thing they do is make him ugly or unappealing.

When he registers my silence and notices that I'm staring at his arms, he quickly changes the subject.

"So, is Devin serious about you having a baby for him?" he asks, smiling at my frank appraisal of his tattoos. He likes the idea of me knowing he is a little edgy. His new haircut and stubble, the grungy, hip way he dresses now when we are not working. Now that he gave up trying to hide that side of himself in the interest of professionalism, I feel closer to him. It's like he is opening up to me more, now that I know about his injury. He is no longer hiding a part of his darkness from me.

"Yes, he is completely serious," I say, as I sit heavily in the seat, almost pouting.

"What do you think about that?" Salinger asks.

"I don't want to do it, but how do I say no? I'm the only chance they have if they want kids."

"I don't know about that," he states, dismissively.

"They would be such great parents. I want them to have the opportunity, but I don't think I'm ready to get all, you know…pregnant. I get birth control shots for precisely that reason."

"I fucking *love* pregnant women," he groans, "Their bodies all supple and their full breasts. Oh my God."

"Are you getting a boner just thinking about pregnant women?" I tease.

"Not yet, but if I keep thinking about them, I might."

"Do you think I should do it for them?" I ask, changing from playful to serious.

"It's a big decision, JB, would the child be yours, or would you be inseminated?"

"I don't know. I haven't thought about it."

"It makes a big difference, don't you think? It would kill me to see my child raised by someone else," he says adamantly.

For some reason, that statement chokes me up. Not at the thought of Corey and Devin raising my kid, but because Salinger sounds like he wants to have kids. I've never really thought of him as a dad, but knowing he wants to be one, is somehow very poignant for me.

"I wouldn't care about that, they would give my kid an amazing life." *Would* it be harder for me if the child was genetically mine, versus me just being the vessel? I'm not sure, but I do need to start considering these very pertinent questions.

"What does Silas think?" Salinger asks, as he turns into a gas station and un-clicks his seatbelt.

"I haven't brought it up yet," I admit, and then start to get a little panicky.

He gives me a look that says, *You need to be discussing this with him*, as he gets out of the vehicle and saunters to the pump while shoving his rolled sleeve further up his arm. While Salinger is pumping gas, I send Silas a cryptic text.

Me: *No inappropriate touching...yet.*

Silas immediately fires back: *Watch yourself, he may be staging an ambush.*

I crinkle my nose at his humor, I'm happy he is adjusting to the fact that I work with Salinger. He may not like it, but at least he trusts me. As a matter of fact, he likes me working with Salinger about as much as I like him working with Parker.

Salinger gets back in the Suburban, checks himself in the rearview mirror, and then swipes his fingers through his rockabilly hair.

Since I'm thinking about Silas working with that conniving bitch, Parker, I ask, "Have you ever met a woman at the club named Parker?"

"Who is this chic? You asked me about her the other day." He turns to me before starting the vehicle, while listening sincerely.

"She owns part of the club. She is trying to sabotage my relationship with Silas."

"Oh, is that all?" he says dismissively, then turns the key and points us back toward the highway.

"What, you don't want to help me plot her downfall?" I say, appealing to his dark side, though that is really more Devin's department.

"Not really... wait, why? Is she hot?" He waivers suddenly, his decision to help plot her downfall apparently depends on how she looks.

"Yes, if you like slutty, egotistical, manipulative, catty women," I say, without any inflection in my voice.

"Well!" he guffaws, "Sounds like my kind of woman!" He smiles and enthusiastically nods his head, though he is being completely sarcastic.

"I'm serious, I hate her."

"Jessie, don't waste your energy hating her. Hate is just a wasted emotion that grows inside you like cancer, or a tapeworm. In the end, you are the only one that suffers, not her." He accelerates and slips his arm back over the steering wheel in a very relaxed, somehow satisfied manner. Is he happy someone is trying to sabotage my relationship?

Chapter Eighteen

Movie

It is becoming more and more apparent that Corey is going to accept the hefty re-up bonus from the USMC, which would mean another four years in the Corps. He hasn't said as much, but he seems to be tying up loose ends. He renewed his apartment lease on a month-to-month basis, he is selling his F-150, and he is getting his mother settled in an assisted living situation. His mom had a stroke a few years back, and if he deploys again, he wants to know she is being taken care of.

I suspect Devin figures as much, and his distress in the matter is driving his engagement plan. Not that they wouldn't get married eventually, it just seems like it's on the fast track to me.

Who knows where all this marriage thinking leaves me. Our condo is owned by Devin, not that he would put me out on the street, but I couldn't stay if they both lived here, the space is way too small for all that testosterone and me.

Anyway, tonight it is the three of us, copious amounts of wine and an endless supply of streaming horror movies. I love nights like this, they remind me of the days when things were simple. No gay marriage restrictions to think about, no babies to carry, no sick mothers needing assistance with their living.

My thoughts are interrupted by a piece of popcorn hitting me in the chin.

"What?" I ask.

"Just seeing if I could get it down your shirt," Devin says, as if I should have expected as much.

"What are you daydreaming about?" Corey asks. He is so wonderful and caring, all of a sudden my throat pinches together, and I feel like crying. He can't re-enlist, the constant worry and the very real danger of possibly losing him are too much. His job as an Explosive Ordnance Disposal Technician is incredibly dangerous. When he was overseas, every time Devin or I got a bad feeling about anything, we were just sure Corey had been killed at that exact moment. Every buzz from the intercom indicating a visitor was met with a wave of nausea, tunneled vision, and sweating palms.

It is agonizing to have someone you love in harm's way, yet at the same time, the pride you feel for them is overwhelming. The kind of person it takes to say, *I got this,* and then put all their dreams and expectations in life on hold. To go away from everyone they love and care about to fight a war is beyond heroic. It's like there is more honor in one enlisted person than can normally be found in ten. It seriously takes more courage to deploy than most people can ever hope to have.

I straighten up and clear my throat. "Uh, just about this woman Salinger is seeing from 1462," I lie. I can't open up a discussion about Corey leaving; it's all-consuming and far too crushing. Just talking about it would ruin our night.

"You are daydreaming about her? Shouldn't you be daydreaming about a dude? Or have Corey, and I opened your eyes to something wonderful?" Devin teases. He leans back against the base of the couch, stretching his legs out in front of him with one arm slung across Corey's lap.

"I wonder what she is like, you know? I can't very well ask Silas," I say.

"Why not?" Corey asks, puzzled why I wouldn't be totally open and completely honest with Silas.

"I'm not ready for him to know Salinger goes to the club, *his club*. I live in fear of the day Silas sees his name show up in his accounting software. He has a hard enough time with me working with him. Also, there is no way in hell I am ready for them to meet. If Silas knew Salinger was spending time in his club, he would march right up to him and knock him out. Don't you remember the whole video chat fiasco?"

"He would not," Corey says, dismissively. "The longer you wait to tell him, the deeper you get," he says, and it's in a premonitory way. Then he adds more soothingly, "Come sit, I'll brush your hair."

I stand up to go sit in front of him, on the floor next to Devin. Brushing my hair is our ritual while watching scary movies. Corey has a hard time just being still, so he loves to brush and play with my hair, it relaxes him.

As for me, I would rather have someone brush my hair than almost anything else. The tug of the brush against the strands, the Zen-like tickle—it almost puts me in a trance.

It also happens to be the only way I will participate in these horror movie nights because these boys like the psychological, emotionally disturbing, messed up movies. They don't bother with the campy slasher, creature, or zombie movies. They make me watch the ones that get under your skin, like a faction of black widow spiders. Their kinds of movies keep me up at night, all tense and disturbed. I have lost indeterminate amounts of sleep due to my lingering psychological fears and moral ambiguity following our movie marathons.

"What do you know about her already?" Devin asks, startling me back into our conversation about Bradley. His practicality regarding the matter trumps any concern he may, or may not have for Silas.

"Just that she is damaged, a total exhibitionist and a circus freak in bed," I say flatly, "Oh, and tattooed and beautiful," I add this regretfully, though I can't fully explain why I don't like that she is beautiful.

"Hello! If she is an exhibitionist, how hard would it be to watch her at the club?" Devin says, as though he were talking to morons.

"You're right. Salinger said he met her in the peep show room!" I blurt out. I'm excited by the idea of being able to check her out with complete anonymity.

"Well then, there you go. Can we start the movie now?" Devin asks as he raises the remote, dismissing Bradley as a non-issue.

Chapter Nineteen

Peep Show

From work, I am able to confirm that Silas will be with a client this evening. He is finally closing on a 200,000 square foot medical building he has had listed for ten months. Apparently, this closing requires a certain level of wining and dining, so he plans to take his wealthy client out to a testosterone-laden cigar lounge. Where the two will sip scotch and puff on sweet, woodsy tobacco until glassy-eyed and prostrate.

So tonight, it turns out, is a great night to check out Bradley. Silas finds my curiosity amusing, not about Bradley, mind you, but about the club. He even suggested I explore the Shibari room. Then, after a superfluous lesson in the difference between Shibari and Kinbaku rope bondage, he felt better about my explorations in his absence.

Now, if I were to psycho-analyze my ridiculous compulsion to stalk Bradley, I would say I was jealous of her, in a creepy way. But I rationalize that it's really more about my inquisitive nature, or maybe my concern for Salinger, that has me brandishing my key card at the fortress door of 1462.

I really care for Salinger, and besides, *he* is the one who said she's fucked up, right? I'm just doing my civic duty, my social responsibility as his friend. You know, kind of like fulfilling my fiduciary obligations on his behalf.

I can't have rumors starting, so I'm wearing the modest dress of someone *not* participating, a breezy romper, belted at the waist. The hem is a little above mid-thigh, and I'm wearing ankle wrapped wedges to still look sexy, just not available. As if a single person in here doesn't know Silas collared me weeks ago.

The cocktail area is full, yet from across the room, as if lit by a spotlight, I see Parker. She is surrounded by adoring minions and is eating up the attention, practically with a spoon. She always has to be the center of attention, it's so needy. How people don't see her as a clingy, sapless bitch, I will never understand.

When she sees me, her eyes squint into a haughty glare. She literally drops whatever conversation she is having and cleaves through the crowd toward me. I'm beginning to think my presence actually causes her physical pain the way she winces, and her face corrodes over when I'm around. I think her personality genuinely changes for me because everyone else thinks she is perfectly lovely. However, when I'm near, she acts like she has sharpened bamboo sticks shoved under her fingernails.

"What are you doing here?" she challenges. Her blonde hair falls around her shoulders in layers, and her icy blue eyes spill contempt. She has on more eye makeup than an Egyptian Pharaoh, and it distracts from what *could* be her natural beauty. Well, that and her venomous attitude.

"Well, Par-ker, as a valuable member of 1462, I am here to enjoy the many splendors Silas' club has to offer," I say, and it's perfectly condescending. I look almost frumpy, compared to her in her shimmery club dress and thigh-high boots, but I'll be damned if I let her see my insecurities.

"Well, you look like a stray dog," she quips. She crosses her arms across her ample chest in an authoritative manner, posturing like a warrior ready for battle. "You are *SO* beneath Silas. You *ARE* aware of that, aren't you? You're just a pathetic wannabe and should go back to the bush league where you belong."

"Oh Parker, you're just mad because I still have Silas' cum buried deep inside me," I say with a smile. "Right, Parker? But you should know, jealousy doesn't look good on you." I hold my ground, daring her to say something smart.

"Trust me, Jessie, I know all about Silas' cum. In fact, more than you will ever know." She winks and then turns away, walking calmly back through the crowd, while I stand here and choke on her petulance.

***

Parker's words leave a bitter taste in my mouth, almost like I have coffee grounds on my tongue. I'm not worried about Silas being interested in her now; it's more like revulsion that they may have had something at one time.

I don't *want* to know about all the women in his past, and I can hardly challenge him about them now. I would, however, like to think he wouldn't stoop to someone like Parker. That his taste in women would veer away from the straight-up hussies, and gravitate toward a classier girl, but who knows.

She is toxic for sure though, every time I encounter that woman she leaves my skin a little more chapped.

I'm still brewing about her as I slide into a little room, the promise of secrecy and isolation contained within. The room is the size of a small walk-in closet, empty except for a padded stool. It has a niche in the wall that holds a lotion dispensing pump, a tuft of tissue from a hidden receptacle, and a similar tuft of sanitizing wipes, smelling strongly of lavender.

What's surprising to me, are my various voyeuristic options. I can simply move a teardrop shaped piece of wood, toggled at the top of the tear, to the side, and view the show with one eye and total concealment. Or I can slide the whole front cover open, leaving myself visible behind nothing but a pane of glass. Yet another option for me, is to open the cover but slide a black mesh curtain over the window. This option allows the viewer to retain some semblance of obscurity, but not have to watch through a hole in the wall like a perverted school janitor.

I decide to open the cover and slide the mesh between myself and the glass. Bradley has no idea who I am, or *why* I would be watching her, so I take a deep breath, trying not to feel like a self-sacrificing lamb. I have no way of knowing if she will even be here. For that matter, I don't even know what she looks like besides blonde with tattoos…and beautiful.

Once I open the cover, close the mesh curtain, and sit back on my stool, I see a small round stage and not one woman, but three. Each one is kneeling down on a knee, with her back to the others. The stage is slowly rotating on a hydraulic lift.

The room itself is like a small gladiator arena, with rooms identical to mine circling the rotating stage. After a quick glance around the ring, I estimate at least twenty peeper rooms. The amount of them is shocking to me because I had ducked into the first one I saw with a lit green light by the knob, which by the way, was only the third door on my path.

I adjust my perch on the stool and again look at the performers. The women wear cropped football jerseys with their breasts peeking out from underneath, skimpy, laced-up shorts, striped tube socks, and cleats. They also all have thick black lines smudged under their eyes. Football players, they are not, but the look is sporty and undeniably sexy.

None of the three women are blonde. One has short, disheveled brown hair, one has long brown pigtails, and the third has bright copper hair, rumpled in waves to just above her shoulders.

They each hold their pose, perhaps waiting for rooms to fill up, or for a certain hour to strike, but for long minutes there is no movement besides the slowly turning stage.

Once finally given the cue to begin by some unknown source, they simultaneously stand and step forward to their respective spots on the edge of the rotating circle.

Their stance is firm, with cleats shoulder width apart and hands on their hips. They stand like this for maybe a quarter of a rotation before the music starts. In unison they turn, backs to the concealed audience, and lean forward, never bending their legs. They slowly lower their shorts until they expose their pink lips and cherry centers to the crowd of voyeurs.

After the girls have slipped out of their sporty shorts, they help each other remove their cropped jerseys. Following, perhaps the slowest shirt removals ever, they are left standing naked except for the tube socks and cleats.

With their backs to the darkened rooms, and while facing each other, the girls begin sliding in unison into the splits. Once their cores are nearly touching the stage, their legs spread widely apart, all three lean forward reaching for each other's hands. They lean all the way forward, pressing their breasts against the stage, while their legs remain open for the viewing pleasure of the observers.

The position makes me cringe, the unfettered views of their round asses and lady-bits, all displayed on the slowly turning stage. It's so incredibly bold and yet intensely vulnerable.

The music pulsates as the women slowly join hands, pulling themselves forward enough to break the splits' position and then slide their legs closed.

In unison, choreographed no doubt to the song, they roll to their backs. Then they each lift one leg, cleats pointing to the ceiling, then lower it slowly to the side, again providing views of their exhibitionistic, dewy centers.

At this point in the stage rotation, I am almost eye level with the short-haired brunette's open legs. I notice she has her clit pierced with a little hoop and ball. I'm imagining what must have been an absolutely searing, *white-hot* pain; having someone shove a needle through that tiny explosive fuse when she leans forward in a slow sit up. As she rises, I see she has both her nipples pierced as well. A shiver runs through me.

Suddenly, my cell vibrates loudly from inside my purse. I recoil with alarm and almost shriek out loud before I pinch my lips shut. So much for a stealth mission, you would think by my behavior and frazzled nerves, that I really was a peeping Tom; lurking in someone's bushes.

By the time I look back at the show, the three women are lying down with their heads hanging off the edge of the round stage. Their feet are clustered together in the middle of the platform when they begin toying with their breasts.

This is where the tempo of the music changes, and the synchronization ends. The two facing away from me pry the pierced girl's knees apart. From my vantage point, I'm looking down her body. So, closest to me is her head, then her fingers; still rolling her nipples, and then the other two—now holding her legs widely apart.

I can tell they are stroking and teasing her because her reaction is overdone for the observers; like a B-rated porn star.

By the time the stage rotates around to me, the pony-tailed brunette is on her knees and elbows with her face in short hair's lap. She is flicking at the clit ring with her tongue while keeping her legs spread open. The copper-haired one is straddling ponytails and playing with her own nipples. The whole scene is ridiculously excessive and dripping with the type of lust that caters to a male audience.

The rest of the show continues for another twenty minutes or so before a window cover slides down from the performer's side.

I'm wrapped in darkness for a moment until a dim light turns on down by my feet to counter the pitch. A low voice startles me from an unseen speaker, *"The next show will begin in t-e-n minutes."* The computerized voice sounds like it's announcing a self-destruct mode in 10...9...8...

I decide to wait for the next show. The first one wasn't bad, just predictable. Men like seeing women together, and I get it, but I personally found them far sexier when they were standing in their uniforms—and I use that term loosely, with their breasts showing from under their half-shirts. The precursor to the show was more titillating for me than their overt sexual acts, but this type of room is frequented chiefly by men. They undoubtedly prefer the raw, woman on woman sex acts to the timid displays.

I pick at my nail polish while I wait for the next show, deciding to leave right away if I don't see a blonde with tattoos. While picking the thick gray lacquer, I start to wonder if Silas would like to see me with another woman—or more importantly, if I could even be with a woman.

***

My ruminations are cut short as the cover slides open, revealing a darkened room lit with a bluish light. The mournful croon of a bagpipe begins playing as a hoop slowly lowers from the ceiling.

A woman sits in the circle like a swing, but it's too dark to see her hair color until she descends further into the light.

The bottom of the hoop stops about ten feet from the ground, then the women spreads her legs and falls backward, effectively stopping her free fall with her open legs. She is now in an upside down position that looks like a capital T. She is obviously flexible, obviously extremely talented, and also obviously blonde and heavily tattooed.

I watch her as she moves seamlessly through an incredibly impressive routine, from gymnast poses to gravity-defying feats, to horribly painful looking positions. She is a performer at heart and belongs in a Cirque du Soleil show, not a peeper's paradise.

After a completely absorbing demonstration, the ring starts to lower her down again. I can see a man standing on the ground below her. I have to lean in and squint my eyes before I see, to my horror, that it's Salinger, and he's shirtless.

I jump back and quickly close the window cover in a panic. I can't let him see me, not behind a window, not behind a black mesh curtain, not watching him at all.

I'm scurrying around, back and forth like a rat in a cage. It's a small room, but it holds a lot of chaos for the moment. While I wring my hands together, my thoughts are firing off like mortar rounds, yet they offer no discernible solution to my current dilemma. I know I should leave now— while Salinger is out there with her, and he can't see me slip out of my dark room, but I need just a peek of them together.

Once I calm myself enough to slide the teardrop to the side, I see that she is at his level now, still perched like a Fairy Godmother. He stands behind her as she sits primly on the hoop, both of them facing directly toward my concealed room.

He is kissing her neck as he slowly lifts his hand from her waist, grabs the shimmery bikini top between her breasts, and rips it off in the quick release fashion of stripper clothes, and then tosses it to the ground.

Her tits jostle with his show of force, while he continues to nibble at her neck. Then he reaches up to play with her nipples as she lolls her head back against his chest.

My heart is pounding, it feels like I shouldn't be watching, but I can't look away. The way he touches her is so experienced, so, um, gifted.

While still standing behind her, he spreads her legs as she adjusts the hoop more sturdily under her ass. It's like they are performing a private show just for me. There is no rotating stage, no view of their backs, just them—and me. I'm feeling anxious about being the nerve center for their performance, but I'm hoping it's because there is a similar red/green light system inside, so performers know which rooms have occupants.

Bradley is currently reaching her arms back, draping them around Salinger's neck as he pinches her nipple with one hand and slides the other under the waist of her skimpy, sequined thong.

I can see clearly, as he teases between her legs for a moment, his fingers working expertly against her clit. He withdraws his fingers long enough to unsnap the crotch of her shimmery costume.

When the middle of her thong falls away, the shimmery waist portion remains, and her explicit nudity is exposed to me, front and center.

His hand travels down, spreading her open with two fingers as he continues to kiss her neck and tweak her nipple. He starts twiddling her swollen clit with his thumb, while two of his fingers start to dip in and out of her.

I can't believe all this is happening right before my very eyes. This is crazy. It's such an intimate act, and the fact that it is broadcasting to *anyone* who might be watching is ludicrous but surprisingly hot.

My legs are crossed, and I'm squeezing them together against the building pressure. I feel like a dirty old pervert, but I can't stop watching. It's so erotic, nothing like the three women. Shit, am I ever going to be able to look Salinger in the eyes ever again?

He makes his way to the front of her as she holds the top of the ring and leans back, her legs still splayed widely apart. I'm sweating buckets, as he lowers his mouth between her legs. It's insane to see him sexually like this; it is completely out of context for me.

I will *never* be able to get this image out of my head, his muscular shoulders, full arm tattoos, and the horrendous scar; puckering his once smooth skin.

The scar is appalling the way it embraces him, below his shoulder blade and around his ribcage, like a hideous barnacle. The fact that there is no indication of the wound when he is covered belies the gruesomeness of the near-fatal injury. It clings to him like a demon, a constant reminder of a malignant military experience. I can't see the names of the fallen Marines on his opposite ribs, but I know they are there. Even unseen, the names are more chilling than his injury.

Bradley breaks my focus on Salinger's scar by orgasming wildly against his tongue. She is animated in her climax, shuddering against his mouth and crying out in exultation.

Once her outburst calms, he stands and drops his pants to reveal a massive, rock hard erection. He is so controlled, so casual as he handles his bulging extremity. As I openly gape, he stealthily rolls on a condom.

He told me *she* was an exhibitionist, but *his* comfort level with this whole process is unsettling for me. It seems perfectly natural for him. He doesn't even mind his scar being on display. He wears it like the badge of honor it is. Although, it *did* take him years of hiding that particular honor before he finally accepted it as part of his journey and opened up about it to me.

His penis is thick and impressive. It causes me to cross my legs harder and squeeze my thighs tighter, as well as unknowingly lick my lips. His nakedness is completely taboo for me, this is my co-worker and friend, and I'm watching with shameless focus and downright awe.

I find I am straining against the tiny hole in the wall, trying to see more clearly. One eye is hardly sufficient to take in the whole scene, but I wouldn't dare open the cover. Even with the mesh, it's way too risky.

Salinger holds the hoop on the lower sides of the metal circle to steady it as he pulls her into him, firmly and completely possessing her. He's fucking her as he eases the hoop forward and back, his biceps bulging with the effort.

She moans in ecstasy as he speeds up his tempo, plowing into her over and over. His strong, tattooed arms flex against each pull of the hoop. His hair is sweaty and hangs over one side of his face as she slaps against him over and over. Her own half-sleeve arm tattoos are on display as she holds tightly to the top of the hoop. Her long, silky, blonde hair swings back and forth behind her, jerking with each exquisite thrust.

She wraps her legs around his hips and releases the ring in order to dig her nails into his back. I flinch when she rakes across his massive scar, but he is lost in her.

He stands, easily taking her weight as he grinds into her. Their fucking is almost artistic in its raw magnetism. However, one thing that doesn't escape my notice is that they do not kiss, not even once.

I see his ass clench with his orgasm, and I know I have to get out of here before they completely finish, or I'll risk running into him. I'm flustered and breathing heavy, but I turn and bolt out of the room, desperate to forget what Salinger looks like naked.

Chapter Twenty

Mortified

I'm keeping my head down at work, trying not to make eye contact with anyone or otherwise invite conversation. I came in this morning, closed my door, and have not emerged since. The headache brewing in my skull is a testament to me not even bothering to get coffee from the staff lounge when I arrived.

I am praying technology will see me through the next few days. Emails, texts, and IM's are my saving grace because now and then, I actually need to have work contact with Salinger. I feel heavy with the certainty I will blow my cover if I see him. I simply will not be able to act normal this soon after seeing him fucking Bradley.

Right now, I am trying to calculate the best time to storm into the break room, grab a coffee, and then haul ass back to the safety of my office. It needs to be soon because my head is starting to split open like a Halloween pumpkin.

It's 10:17, too early to leave for lunch, but it's beyond time to make my move. I smooth my hair and stand up stiffly. I'm nervous as I head out of my office and through the catacombs of cubicles.

There is an artificial glare to the windowless space. The fluorescent lighting and lack of vitamin D affect the forty hour a week atmosphere in a subtle but impactful way. Accompanying the dismal office ambiance is the latent hum of computers and printers, as well as all the non-specific chatter of countless phone calls and office conversations. Together, the lighting and incessant commotion do horrendous things to my greedy migraine.

I keep my head down as I pass Adelaide, the receptionist. I'm moving at a fast clip for intra-office dealings, so she must think I'm headed to the bathroom to explode in one fashion or another. Honestly, I would rather her think that than know I am trying to avoid Salinger.

In the lounge, there are four interns gathered around the coffee machine. It's one of those ridiculous corporate coffee machines, where you push upwards of five buttons to make your selection and stand back as it creates your elaborate concoction. It takes much too long for a simple cup of coffee, but on the bright side, I get to make meaningless conversation with people who will never know my name, or me theirs.

"So, what's it like working with Salinger?" one of them asks. She is young with a cute pixie cut and way too much makeup. Ballsy question for an intern if you ask me, but office crushes on Salinger are far from uncommon.

I cringe inwardly before answering, "He is a good guy, very good at his job." *For the love of God, coffee machine!*

"I mean, how can you stand to be so near him all the time?" she presses, thinking I'm good for some girl talk.

"I know, right? I would play with myself under the desk all day." The one who says this is wearing a pantsuit, looking like she has never played with herself a day in her life, and flushing at the thought.

"Yes, he is very good looking," I admit, as I awkwardly back away from them thinking, *you should see him naked.*

"I know! I can't even concentrate if he is in the vicinity of my cube," Pixie cut says, chewing on her voluminous bottom lip.

"You girls should get to know him, he is much more than just a pretty face, uh…he might be seeing someone though." Following this random statement, I instantly turn beet red and heat washes over me like a lava spill. *He is seeing someone alright, at least the inside of her.*

I'm embarrassed by my reaction, and they will probably misread it entirely. I feel like I need to somehow let them know, despite my ridiculous response, that the person he is seeing is not me. So I carry on like an idiot, "Actually, he *is* seeing someone, and office romances are frowned upon anyway, you know…never get your honey where you get your money, right ladies? Well, have a nice day." I spin on my heel, coffee in hand, and bolt. I'm desperate to get back to my office before quite literally running into Salinger.

The interns must think I'm socially awkward or somehow touched, or dim-witted because my discomfort was *radiating* off me in blurry waves.

***

Safely back at my desk, I chug the coffee. It singes my mouth and esophagus, then pools in my gut like hot tar. I have to get ahead of this headache, or I'm going to put my face through the computer screen and then go home to collect workman's comp. After my categorical fail in the office lounge, it really wouldn't be a bad idea.

My door flies open, "JB…Wait, first of all, do you hate it when I call you JB at work? Should I just stick with Jessie Belle, or do you prefer plain Jessie?" Salinger asks, and he is amped up about something.

"What do you need, Salinger?" I try to keep calm, but I'm overcome with the irrational thought that he knows I was watching him last night. My hands are shaking, so I drop them in my lap, squeezing my skirt with both fists to dry the sweat and still the tremors.

"I just got a call from Paul Weinritch. He is ready to play ball." Thankfully, Salinger shows no indication of knowing anything about last night.

"Oh good, I'll get the contracts going." I turn my face away from him to fixate on the computer screen. My eyes are crossing with anxiety, and I'm praying he leaves.

"Ok then." He stands there for a minute, obviously expecting a bigger reaction from me. When I don't look up from the monitor, he finally closes the door and heads back to his own office.

I let out a huge exhale and notice my hands are still shaking. How did Salinger act so normal at work after he walked in on my racy video chat with Silas? A good looking co-worker is bad enough, but once you introduce nakedness into the equation, it feels impossible. Literally, all I could think about when he was discussing the Weinritch property was how his mouth looked on Bradley's skin and wondering if his dick brushes against his thighs when he walks.

***

As I'm collecting the survey information for the Weinritch property, my cell rings, it's Silas. "Hi there," I answer, smiling for the first time today.

"How is your day going, hon?" he asks, and I forget Salinger and my headache altogether.

"Rough start, but it's on its way up. What about you?"

"Intensely busy, but I need to ask you a favor." He cuts right to the chase. "Would you mind going by my place after work? Analise is taking

Ruby to Disney on Ice and won't be there for the cleaners. Would you mind letting them in?"

"Sure, what time?"

"They are coming at 5:30, and I will be with a client until about 6:45 or so. I figured we could grill something for dinner after I get home."

"I'll let them in, but it's going to cost you," I say playfully.

"Trust me; I have every intention of paying up." His words have an instant warming effect on me.

"I'll expect payment immediately, once services are rendered."

"You got it, Babe."

***

After a virtually endless day at the office, dodging Salinger and memories of his glistening mouth, I head to Silas' to let the cleaners in. While they clean, I'll just take care of a few errands. First stop, a lingerie store for a sexy maid outfit. After that, I'll stop somewhere for takeout because we won't be grilling tonight.

I figure the Disney on Ice show starts at seven o'clock, probably runs two hours, then another hour for Analise and Ruby to get home. That means we should have until about ten o'clock; and trust me when I say, I need every minute for Silas. It's been a few days since I have seen him, and my body is as tight as a fully drawn archer's bow.

Between his two jobs, my job with travel and Ruby, we don't see nearly enough of each other. Most of the time we end up doing mundane things like cooking dinner or taking Ruby for ice cream or to a movie. The problem is, even doing those everyday things, I'm still around Silas, and he has a way of making me burn for him.

He will cook shirtless, so the sway of his low back into his perfect ass drives me insane. It provokes the most sinful images to play in my mind. Or, he'll just lie on the couch, all rumpled and sexy, with Ruby snuggled against him. It's perplexing, the riot he starts deep in my pelvis without even trying. The way I respond to his proximity is like he has his own pheromones pumped into his loft, like oxygen in a Las Vegas casino.

I can always tell when it's been a few days since being intimate with him because now, my over-sexed, professionally stroked libido aches for sex when I used to be just fine without it. Now I think about things like Salinger's dick brushing against his thighs, or what the grocery store clerk's orgasm face looks like, or what my CEO masturbates to. Everything gets viewed through the erotic, rosy glasses of a lustful, sexually charged woman—I can't help it. I see *everything* more sexually now, and it's hugely distracting.

In fact, I never would have guessed I would be the one eyeballing the guy pushing the mail cart through our building. It's just that he has these broad shoulders and when he reaches forward and his shirt falls away from his body, you can see the ridge of his hip where his oblique sits. Then there is the sandwich shop on the first floor. The guy working behind the counter, though not immediately handsome, has something about him that just oozes sex appeal. Whenever he asks if he can get me anything else, it makes me blush.

The sexual influence Silas has on me is hard to describe. There is just something about a man who really knows his way around a woman's body. Once you experience it, there is no going back, no way to forget.

A skilled lover is surprisingly hard to find, and some women never experience one. With Silas, he knows more about how to hit my G-spot, or to engage my clit, or which angle creates the most friction—better than I know it for myself. He is so attentive and capable that I'm beginning to wonder if he is somewhat of a unicorn or jackalope; something we are all familiar with but no one ever really sees.

It's intoxicating, and due to my past ineffectual lovers, I'm seriously addicted to Silas' sex. Rough or tender, kinky or missionary, it all has morphed my normal thinking. Now I have regular thoughts, dipped in sex and then sprinkled with more sex.

***

There were a surprising number of naughty maid outfits at the lingerie store. Everything from corsets to bikini tops, latex to satin, and all with short fluffy skirts or tight, painted-on ones. I settled on a black and white satin corset; beautifully laced up the front, a frilly little skirt, and a wispy apron. After, perhaps too much thought, I had added a feather duster to my purchase and hurried out the door as a tiny bell chimed in protest of my departure.

Now, finally at Silas' with the real cleaners gone, I'm in black stiletto heels, thigh highs, and the newly purchased outfit. The corset laces are loosened at the top in a scandalous manner, exposing more skin than any self-respecting housekeeper would ever dream of.

I teeter around the loft dimming lights, setting up candles and chilling wine. My hair is in somewhat of a bun, with wisps of hair framing my face.

As I'm attempting to operate the sound system remote, I hear the key in the door, so I drop the remote on the couch and run like an injured daddy long leg spider to the den, trying not to twist an ankle as I whip around the corner.

Silas closes the door behind him and calls out, "Jessie, are you here?"

I falter up three rungs of the rolling ladder affixed to a bar above the wall of books.

Silas calls out again, "Jessie?" Cautiously, he peeks his head into the den after not finding me in the kitchen or the bedroom. I'm dutifully dusting the bookshelves as his face splits into a covetous grin.

"I'm so sorry, Sir, I'm not quite finished cleaning yet." I stretch my reach so the flowing hem of the skirt rises up, exposing my ass cheeks. Then I push my naked butt out a little, just to really look slutty.

"Stick your ass out anymore, and I'll spank it," he threatens, as he starts unbuttoning his starched, white shirt.

I do, and I wave it a bit for good measure.

Smack.

"Oh no, is my work not to your satisfaction, Sir?" I pout.

"No, it's not. You missed a spot there, up high," he points to the higher books.

I take another cautious step to the next rung. Now my feet are on different rungs, which opens me to his scrutiny. My bare ass is almost at his eye level.

"You will need to brace yourself with your foot on this shelf, so the ladder does not slide," he says as he points to a shelf much further to my right.

I timidly move my foot to where he had indicated. Now, my legs are open, extending between the ladder rung and the shelf. My desire displayed prominently before him as I pop out my ass.

"You are really going to have to reach if you're going to dust that spot you missed," he says, leaning into me as I reach up and attempt to dust the out-of-reach shelf.

His tongue is on me in an instant. His hands are spreading my cheeks while his nose and warm breath brush against my crack.

The leg anchoring me in place against the bookshelf begins to shake from the strain and from the exquisite pleasure of his mouth. I have to abandon the feather duster to grip the ledge.

Usually, when his tongue is this intimate, he focuses almost exclusively on my clit, but this time he probes in and out of my vagina, he licks and savors, then sucks tender flesh tightly into his mouth. He uses his thumbs to spread me for his tongue, and I almost howl with pleasure as he flutters against me. Then, with a firmer touch, the tip of his tongue begins flicking at my clitoris.

He spends a long time coaxing me toward orgasm then slowing down, but when he reaches his fingers between my shaking legs to fiddle with my clit, it only takes moments before I am coming in his mouth and groaning his name.

Once my orgasm has released its hold on me, Silas has to lift me down so I don't tip right off the ladder. Then, turning me toward him, he kisses me softly, then again.

***

I break our kiss, reaching for his hardness, and drag my palm up and down it.

He almost growls and then grabs my face with both hands, kissing me hungrily.

Breaking the kiss again, I ask, "Don't you want to inspect the bathroom... Sir?" As I back away, I'm tugging on the laces of my corset, loosening the top in a seductive manner.

I back into his bedroom while he stalks me like a jaguar. Playfully, I entice him into the bathroom and then sit on the edge of his enormous tub. I'm teasing the top of my corset more and more open with each fiddle of the laces, and Silas is coming unhinged.

"Fucking hell, Jessie, I'm going to tear you up." He tugs his shirt over his head and advances on me.

When he is within my reach, I stop his forward movement by reaching my hand to his belt buckle. He hesitates, possibly considering my next move, yet he's not totally derailed from his initial intent. Based on the look in his eyes, his initial intent was to lift me to the vanity and fuck me right into the white Carrara marble.

I loosen his belt, never breaking eye contact, and then unbutton his dress pants. My boldness is conflicting for him. He always wants to be in control sexually, but I can tell he is intrigued by my bold objective. I lower his white boxer briefs, leaving his unrestricted erection swaying free.

He kicks both pants and boxers to the side and wraps one hand around his impressive cock. He steps forward as I lean in to swirl my tongue around his head, the pre-cum already oozing against my tongue in slippery anticipation.

Letting go of his dick, he entwines his fingers in my hair while I take him deeply in, then slowly out. He is standing with his legs spread shoulder-width apart and his head craned back in exaltation.

I lengthen my hold on him with my hand, sucking and sliding him in and out. I reach between his legs and cradle his balls, caressing and tugging on them as he tightens his grip on my hair.

He groans, "Fuuuck, Jesssssssie."

I release his sack after an extra little squeeze and then reach back further to press on his perineum.

"Ohhhh, Jessie. Jesus, that's good," he moans as he tightens his fists in my hair, yanking it and driving me on.

Suddenly he pulls out of my mouth, grabs my waist, and flips me over the edge of the tub. His patience for me in the driver's seat has fully evaporated. He yanks the corset open and bends me in half, pressing my chest against the inside of the tub.

My nipples are throbbing with need and the sudden chill of the acrylic tub. While bent over the side of his huge tub with my ass in the air, he presses inside me, inch by delicious inch. Once he is buried deep, he grinds and rolls his hips until he is satisfied with the placement of his cock, and its ability to hit just the right spot for me. Then he begins with a slow grinding that readies me for his less gallant thrusts.

My position is both a blessing and a curse because Silas is able to achieve desperately deep penetration. I can accommodate his size, but still, Silas is a big man, so it's a lot to take. Nevertheless, his rhythmic plunges are poetic, and the sensation is indescribable.

Once he begins to fuck me in earnest, I feel like if I open my mouth, his cock head will emerge. My nipples are tingling against the cool acrylic as they rub against the inside of the tub, massaged by the chilliness as he roars into me, coaxing me toward an epic orgasm.

My hips are painfully gnashing against the tub, and they will definitely bruise, but I don't want Silas to stop. I want him to take me harder and harder until we both disintegrate.

I'm nearing my summit when he spanks me, hard. Needles prickle against my pink cheek, and endorphins flood my body. He does it again and again while raking the ridge of his head against my G-spot. Moments later, he pushes me over the edge of my orgasm.

He grabs both of my ass cheeks, gripping me hard while I shudder against the tub. A second later, he unloads into me with straining thrusts and a jaw-clenching finish.

Chapter Twenty-One

Silas'

We are snuggled on the couch watching a travel show about Santorini, Greece. The bestial atmosphere has dissipated and mostly returned to normal by the time Analise and Ruby return.

I expected Ruby to be sleeping or at least drowsy at this late hour, but when she careens into the room, it's with the force of detonating C4.

She runs to us and dives onto, not Silas, but me.

"Jessie! Are we having another sleepover? Oh, Please!" she squeals. She is squirming her way under the covers and smells as though she has been rolled in spun sugar.

"Yes Jessie, that would make this the best day Ev-er!" Silas says, with the same excited crescendo to his voice as Ruby. "I'll even make sure you get to work on time in the morning."

Analise tiredly walks to her lock-off condo, giving an exhausted over the shoulder wave. "Goodnight you all. Mornings come early around here," she says, with a pointed glance at Silas. As if he needs to be reminded that Ruby will undoubtedly be giving us our wake-up call.

"Ana, thank you for taking Ruby to the show. It looks like she had a great time," Silas says, scooping Ruby out of my lap and balling her up

179

against his chest. "You know Rubes, Jessie might not want to stay because she doesn't have any of her things here." He winks at me, as Ruby plays right into his plan.

"Why doesn't Jessie bring some stuff over so she can have sleepovers?" she asks, as Silas gently begins to undo the braids from her hair.

"I think that's a great idea! What a clever girl you are," he says, with a coy smile on his lips. "She will have to borrow some of my jammies for tonight though. As for you…" he gathers her in his arms as he stands up, "You need to brush your teeth and get into some Pj's too."

**

Silas closes the bedroom door behind him then withdraws some white and navy plaid pajama bottoms from a drawer. "Here you go," he says, with a wicked smile, "Your jammies, as promised."

I shrug and undress slowly, like a well-practiced stripper, while he lies diagonally across the bed with his ankles crossed and hands behind his head. I step into the pajama bottoms and cinch the drawstring, but they are laughably gigantic as I stand bolted to the floor, naked on top.

"They're too big," I say, my eyes sparkling as I take a step forward, the bottoms swallowing my feet entirely.

"I disagree, they are perfect," he says as he launches forward, grabbing and tumbling me to the bed, his mouth already on my nipple. "Not too big at all," he reiterates as if we were speaking about my breast size the whole time.

When he grazes his palm across my hip, I wince in pain, the bathtub having left its resounding mark.

"What's the matter?" he asks. His eyebrows are furrowed with concern as he sits up on an elbow.

"My hips are just really tender from the tub you tried to put me through." I smile to take away the accusatory statement and to let him know I was a very willing participant.

"Damn. I'm sorry. I actually injured you. I feel like such a clumsy asshole." The look on his face is one of inward admonishment and also a little bit perplexed at how he could let such a thing happen.

"A few battle wounds aren't so bad," I say, cupping his face in my hands and kissing him.

Tentatively he says, "I'm going to give your body a break, but these still have to go." He speaks as he unties the gigantic pajama bottoms.

I squirm out of the pajama pants, and once I'm naked against him, I find it hard not to initiate round two. His chest is so firm, his leg hair so raspy against my smooth skin, his arms so powerful.

He uses the remote to fog the windows to darkness and dims the light to a faint glow. Now, settled in the cocoon of his massive bed, my head on his chest and my body pressed against his naked frame, I cautiously say, "I want to talk to you about something."

I feel him freeze, as if expecting something he doesn't want to hear. He tightens his arm around me, "What is it?"

"It's about me getting pregnant," I start, but it comes out all wrong.

"Jessie! You're pregnant?" he exclaims, excitement bursting forth like a supernova. He rolls me onto my back and kisses me soundly.

"No, no," I say, muffled by his kiss.

"You are not pregnant?" he clarifies with some cautious disappointment, as he lifts his face from mine.

"No, but it makes me really happy that you would have been excited," I say slowly, quietly. I'm still tentative about sharing what's on my mind.

"Pipes, if you want to get pregnant, I'm all for it. I want to fill you with my babies," he says with excitement rejoining his voice. I know he means it too. The fact that he skipped the condom tonight had not escaped my notice and, if he is being truthful, I'm the only woman he's ever had sex with without using one. He even used a rubber when Amber got pregnant with Ruby. It broke, but still.

I pause for a minute to think of how to say what I need to say. I certainly can't simply announce, '*I'm not ready to be a mom,*' because that directly impacts Ruby, and Silas would escort me to the front door and lock it behind me.

I can't think of a good way to say it, so I just blurt out, "Devin wants me to have a baby for him."

There is a long silence while Silas' dream of filling me with his babies shatters into a million pieces and skitters across the floor.

"Jessie, I know you feel obligated to do this for him, but how do you *really* feel about it?" he asks quietly. He hasn't loosened his hold on me, doesn't appear to be forming an exit strategy, so I relax a fraction.

"Some days I want to, and some days I don't. I mean, I want them to have a family, and their options are limited. I don't think an adoption agency will place a baby with two gay men, will they?" My question seems frantic, an indication of my own state of mind on the matter.

"I don't know, babe," his voice is steady, controlled. Then I feel his chest rise with a deep breath in preparation for his undoubted resistance.

"Jessie, I love you. I can't imagine my life without you. In a few short months, you have managed to completely and utterly claim my heart. I feel bound to you on such a deeper level than I have ever experienced before. I am in this for the long haul, so I will support you in whatever you decide," he says, and it surprises me entirely.

"What did you say?" I whisper, finally looking up into his face.

"Jessie, I don't like it, but I want you to decide. If it's in your heart to do that for them, I will walk the coals with you. You mean that much to me."

"Do you mean that?" I ask cautiously, it sounds way too good to be true.

"Yes, I do... especially the first part," he chuckles. "But seriously, I want you in my life—pregnant with another man's child or not." He laughs at the irony of his words, but when he raises my chin and kisses me, I know he means what he says.

"Thank you," I smile through the growing lump in my throat. "I haven't decided yet, but it feels good to share it with you. It doesn't feel like such a horrendous burden now." My relief is palpable. I would never have guessed Silas would react like this. In my heart, I thought I would have to choose between Devin and Silas, so to be released from that feels like true deliverance from perdition.

"But, just so we're clear, one day, I *will* fill you full of my babies."

Chapter Twenty-Two

Saturday

It's Saturday, and for once, I don't have anything to do. I'm not used to having a ton of free time, so I can hardly find ways to fill the endless minutes ticking by. The thought of going to the gym feels like a chore, a shower seems tedious, making breakfast, too redundant, and laundry…beyond abhorrent.

I attempted to sleep in, in fact, I had been excited by the prospect. But, unfortunately, I found it impossible to avoid my wretched internal clock and by seven o'clock was staring at the ceiling, grumpily unable to fall back to sleep.

Devin and Corey decided a last minute road trip was in order, so they headed out early this morning with Devin's Bronco filled with camping gear and mountain bikes.

Silas is with a developer, and he thought that would take him most of the day. Ruby is at a friend's birthday party, and if all goes according to plan, she will spend the night there. She had been so excited by the prospect of going to a "big girl" sleepover, she hardly spared a thought for the fact that she would be away from home and most likely too afraid to stay all night.

Analise is off for the weekend, so Silas planned to make Mojitos and hang his new webbed sex swing tonight. With both Analise and Ruby gone, I figure it might be a good night to surprise him with the Zorro body harness too.

I have grown accustomed to the dynamics of Analise having a lock-off condo next to Silas. At first, it was weird, and her presence felt parental, but the convenience of a live-in nanny *and* the ability to banish her to her own place has proven to be incredibly convenient. The lock-off really is her own apartment, it's just right next door.

Often times the door remains not only unlocked but wide open. Like when Silas is at the club working late, and Ruby is in bed. However, with Analise formally off the clock for the weekend, we will lock that door, and not miss her presence.

The thought of Silas and I alone with a sex swing…no Ruby, no Analise, sounds amazing, but for right now, here I sit, alone and bored out of my mind.

I make my way to the couch and fumble through hundreds of channels before landing on a cooking competition that holds at least some of my attention. How there can literally be hundreds of channels and hardly a thing to watch is beyond me. However, once invested in the show, I find myself listlessly drawn into one cooking show after another.

After a while, I mute the TV and reach for the book Devin left on the coffee table. It's about an ill-fated Everest climb but has to be better than watching someone else cook.

I used to read voraciously. I would burn through books like potato chips, but in the last couple of years, I haven't had the time. Some of my girlfriends and I even had a book club that, if I'm honest, was really more of a wine club. Although, with all of our careers advancing and boyfriends in some cases blooming into husbands and families, even once a month get-togethers have fallen away with the demands of babies and small children. It's just as well, I don't have time for book clubs anymore.

I open the book, but before I start reading, I ponder cleaning the condo. Saturdays are my days to deal with the mundane—washing sheets, scrubbing bathrooms and floors, grocery shopping, and all the rest. My ambition to clean is short-lived, though. Whatever small amount of momentum I'd had is now gone, so I flop onto my back and begin reading.

In fairly short order, I am engrossed in the story and settle in. I love when a book immediately grabs you, and you lose an entire afternoon with the characters. However, a few hours into the story, I come to where the climbers start dying. When my favorite Mountaineer succumbs to a particularly disturbing death, I toss the book in the direction of Devin's room. I am unwilling to finish the horribly depressing story and curse myself for not reading between the lines about the *ill-fated* expedition.

I can't do depressing books *or* movies because I hold on to the sadness too long. I just can't seem to shake it. Years ago, when Devin and I watched the movie *Titanic*, I was depressed for a week—and that was hardly a surprise ending.

Disgusted with the resounding sadness left from the book, I turn my attention back to the cooking show and un-mute the sound. I become captivated by the chocolate, cappuccino cheesecake before me. The hypnotic trance it has over me makes it clear what I need to do to ease my boredom.

After a quick shower, I run some smoothing cream through my wet hair to ensure silky waves instead of the mane of anarchy I embraced all morning. Then I apply my makeup and slip on a navy blue cotton sundress that buttons all the way up the front.

On my way to the grocery store, I call Silas and tell him to brace himself for the chocolate cappuccino cheesecake that will be waiting for him at home.

When his response comes back with a tame, "Great, I'm looking forward to it." I know his client is right there. Normally he would have at least mentioned licking it off me.

***

At Silas', I deposit the cheesecake ingredients on the kitchen island and rummage through the cabinets for bowls, a mixer, measuring spoons and a round pan. I'm inspired by the baking show, and besides, once Devin and Corey get married and move in together, the gourmet home cooked meals are over for me, so I better figure it out.

I pull the iPad out of my overnight bag and turn on Pandora. It's easier this way because I know Silas' home audio system looks like NASA's launch headquarters, and I stand zero chance of figuring it out.

Then I quickly tap the screen and pull up the guided recipe. I'm excited to get to work and stop only to tug my hair into a high ponytail.

***

It doesn't take long for me to decide; maybe I won't take up baking after all. The kitchen is a mess, ingredients and dirty dishes are everywhere, and I'm only about halfway done. It looked so easy on the show. There wasn't powdered sugar everywhere, the butter had softened on the show—not scorched, and full disclosure, the term *soft peaks* in the whipping cream really is a wildly discretionary term.

188

I decide from now on, any baking I tackle will have eight or fewer steps, maybe even five. My standard of baking usually consists of breaking squares of cookie dough off a frozen plank of it and placing them on a pan. Truth be told, I don't even always preheat the oven. So really, my speed of baking is back in the minor leagues. This endeavor was clearly too ambitious for me.

All of a sudden, a gloved hand is placed aggressively over my mouth, and white-hot panic overtakes me.

"Don't you fucking scream," a man growls into my ear, barely allowing me to breathe, let alone scream. He is strong and completely subdues me with one arm around my chest and the other roughly over my mouth.

The terror I feel is all-encompassing, and my eyes are bulging from my face with electric fear. I try to nod, try to tell him I won't scream. I even try to beg him not to hurt me, but I can't move, not even a fraction of an inch.

My heart rate goes through the roof, and my fight or flight response is detonating inside me, begging me to fight my way out of his iron grip, to bite him so I can scream, to flail, to kick, but I am so terrified, all I can do is comply with whatever he asks of me.

It's crazy how everyone thinks they will turn into a ninja if put in this situation. They believe they would stomp on a foot, knee him in the balls or gouge his eyes out and run away, but the truth is, the terror is paralyzing, and the desire not to anger him is incredibly pervasive.

I whimper in response to his order.

He covered his face with a ski mask. I can feel the raspy wool scrape against the skin at my temple as he crushes me against him. "Scream, and I will fucking end you," he growls, he is angry, and I don't question for a second that he is serious.

My mouth is still covered with his gloved hand, but I nod my head in meek supplication. There is no chance I will scream. I'm not even sure I could if I wanted to.

He must know my intention to do as he says because he removes his hand slowly from my mouth. "Are you going to behave? This is what you asked for," he says. His voice is low and deep. He is delusional, who asks to be attacked?

I nod again just as hot tears spill down my cheeks. I can feel his erection against my back, and this is the point I realize he is going to rape me. I know it in my bones, and there is nothing I can do to stop him. If his intent had been robbery, with his mask and gloves, he had certainly adapted his plan, and it most assuredly involves me now.

He slips a hand down the front of my dress, tearing a button away from the fabric and ruthlessly cupping and squeezing my breast. I've never been touched against my will, and the helplessness to stop it is unyielding. This sudden loss of control is unconscionable.

My body is frozen as he yanks his arm down, ripping through the other button enclosures and opening my dress like a split open shank of beef.

He manhandles my breasts out of my bra, groping them roughly and slapping at my nipples before shoving me forward. He bends me over the island and presses the side of my face into the instant coffee granules, and confectioner's sugar covered Carrara marble.

He wrenches my arms back while shoving the remnants of my dress up to expose my panties.

I'm silently crying into the baker's dust beneath me, creating a sticky veneer for my cheek. My breaths are coming fast, first blowing the powder away then sucking it into my lungs to sear the tiny alveoli.

With one hand gripping my wrists against my back, he shoves down my panties and steps on them, pushing them the rest of the way to the floor. With an impatient slap to my thigh, he directs me to step out of them.

Without warning, he kicks my legs apart, opening me to his lecherous intent. After tearing a condom wrapper with his teeth and spitting out the torn casing, he fumbles with his pants. All I can do is squeeze my eyes shut. The thought that his DNA is now on the wrapper and that he must be on camera entering the building, does nothing to calm my frantic synapses. None of that will help me now.

I alternate wanting Silas to come home and save me, with needing him to stay safely away. When the stranger presses his latexed tip against my dry opening, I whimper in anticipation of being savagely ripped open.

When he cruelly shoves in, I can feel my tender channel snag against the parched latex. It's a brutal entry, forced and remorseless.

He pulls out to spit on his hand, callously swiping his saliva into my folds before again plowing into me.

I whimper, "Please don't do this…don't hurt me."

He pays me no heed as he continues to tunnel into my dry flesh, stretching me with the force of a barrel auger. In another attempt to moisten his entry, he spreads my ass cheeks and spits onto my crack, the thick saliva oozing down to fuse with the assault of his rigid penis.

I am gritting my teeth against his aggression, his violation so cruel. My hatred for him builds with each stroke of his penis. The rage at war with the inescapable shame I'm feeling.

I'm praying for him to finish, to end his heinous reign and leave, so I find I am unwilling to resist him.

"Do you like this? Is this what you had in mind?" he grinds out. He's trying in vain to remain hard in the inhospitable, arid environment of my violation. "Do you like this? Is this what you want?" He grunts again with his attempt, almost like he is doing this horrific thing *for* me. What an arrogant sadist, to rape me then ask if I like it.

I have heard that stranger rape is not usually about sexual gratification but the need to exert one's power over another. He definitely has power over me, and he is definitely penetrating me sexually, but his inability to maintain his erection starts a new wave of panic deep within me. Am I too complacent? Does he require a struggle to feel powerful? Does he need further violence in order to finish? I can feel him softening inside me, so in response to my thoughts, I panic and start to struggle against him, the effort weak and ineffectual.

"Move again, and I will take your ass," he says coldly, "Is that what you want, you dirty little girl, for me to take you in the ass?"

His response cuts me short, my galloping heartbeat starting a contentious sprint as I feel him slide limply out.

"Get on your knees," he demands, in frustration with his impotent penis, then yanks me up off the island.

I crumple to the floor nauseous and fearful, my face stained from the coffee grounds and sugar. Now he is going to force me to take him in my mouth. I'm sobbing now, my tears thick with the realization that I have just been raped. I am a sexual assault victim, and it's not over.

Do I have the spirit left to bite him? Hurt him and try to get away? I can hardly hold myself upright, so I don't think I could run fast enough even if I could bring myself to bite him. Not to mention, I lack the conviction to bite down hard enough to do damage. It would come off timid and unsure, and then he would really hurt me, but only after sodomizing me first.

Tears are falling onto my chest and dissolving into my torn dress. After a moment, I raise my head, but he is gone. I stay frozen for long minutes listening intently. I'm terrified he will return and find me on the phone or holding a weapon of some sort, so I stay on my knees obediently as my whole body trembles uncontrollably.

That sick fuck actually acted like I wanted that, and his rampant delusions have had a devastating effect on my body.

Chapter Twenty-Three

Aftermath

"Jessie? Are you home?" Silas calls out.

I want to scream for him to come and help me, but I can't find my voice. It's buried beneath hours of hoarse sobs and fruitless retching.

I'm lying on the floor next to his bed, an empty vessel. When he finds me, he hastily gathers me into his arms.

"Oh my God, Jessie!" I can feel him trembling as he steadies my face in his hands, trying to engage my vacant eyes. "Jessie."

"Someone raped me," I whisper. My lips are dry, and they crack with the movement of my jaw.

"No, No, No! Honey, it was me." His voice cracks before he hides his face in my hair and begins to cry.

His answer puzzles me. He is not thirsty for vengeance, not concerned with a break-in, not worried for our safety, or hauling me off to the hospital. *It was me.* What does that even mean?

"I thought you wanted that. Parker told me about your conversation with Devin. Baby, that was me. She told me about your rape fantasy." His voice is pleading, hoping he wasn't wrong but seeing that he clearly was.

The name Parker slaps me in the face. I think, but don't voice my confusion, *what did you just say?*

"I thought you knew. Oh my God, Jessie, I'm so sorry! I thought you knew it was me. Oh, my God. Why didn't you say RED?" He is frantic, unsure how to take the whole thing back. He's overcome with self-revulsion as he squeezes me to him and sobs openly with bitter contrition.

"*Red?*" The thought of using a safe word had never occurred to me, not once during the whole thing. "I didn't know rapists abide by hard limits," I say. My voice is hardly audible as a new level of realization sinks in. He did it because Parker told him I had a rape fantasy.

"Did you say, Parker?" My stupefaction is beginning to manifest into a raw, erratic, and unhinged rage. Silas didn't like doing that to me. He couldn't even stay hard...he was doing it because Parker told him I wanted it.

He wipes his face, still wet from his tears, then scoops me up and carries me to the bathroom. He awkwardly turns on the shower and steps in, both of us fully clothed. He shields me from the water until it warms enough to turn me toward the cascading flow. Setting me down, he pulls me into him as he sobs into the top of my head.

"I'm so sorry, Jessie, I thought you knew. I would never hurt you, never. I hated doing that, I just...I thought." He trembles with self-loathing and can't even finish his statement due to his level of disgust.

"There was no conversation with Devin about a rape fantasy," my voice is deadpan, and it shatters Silas. "Not to mention, I think rape fantasies are different...one should know it's part of a role-play. No one really wants to be raped, Silas." I'm angry at him for not knowing better, isn't he supposed to be the BDSM expert? Shouldn't he know that rape is

196

different from a fantasy? Rape by definition is non-consensual. Fantasies—even BDSM ones are *consensual non-consent*, there is a massive difference between the two.

I'm also angry at Parker. Who knows what she fed Silas as far as what I wanted in a rape fantasy. Her ax to grind with me has now gone way too far. My little Champagne stunt pales in comparison to this. Apparently, I brought a slingshot to a gunfight. This was too much, and it clearly demonstrates her unscrupulous character.

"I'm so sorry. When I saw you crumpled on the floor, I knew you thought it was real. I'm so, so sorry, baby. I wish I could take it back, I would do anything to take it back."

I feel the dried, sugary paste begin to moisten on my face as the humidity loosens the tight, crepe paper feel of it. The steam and spray from the shower sluice over me as if from another dimension, where water is as thick as honey and time has slowed to a crawl.

Knowing that Silas was my rapist somehow doesn't alter the trauma still ripe on my skin. I have to fight the urge to pull away from his embrace because his touch feels rancid and self-indulgent.

I hold my stiff pose against him, not because it comforts me but because he is suffering, and for some reason, I feel a responsibility to him. My guilt over my rape and how it might be affecting him is irrational, I know—but I feel it nonetheless.

Shame and guilt are the parasitic remnants of rape, and I feel them to an exponential degree. Why should I have to worry about how *he* is affected? All the while wearing the mask of a martyr and ignoring my own struggle.

His white dress shirt is completely see-through now that it is soaked from the shower. The sight of his muscled chest reminds me of how it felt when he forced himself into my unwilling body.

He tenderly washes and undresses me while I fight the urge to cringe at his every touch. I feel myself close up to him. How could he have listened to her? How could he not have known better? How will I ever forgive him? My feelings are so complicated, so contradictory. How can I love him so much and still cringe with revulsion at his caress?

I want to go home, but my sense of security has been shattered, and I can't stomach being alone. With Devin and Corey away camping, it is outside the realm of possibilities for me to go home to a dark condo alone. In fact, I'm worried I may never feel safe alone again.

As Silas begins to unbutton his sopping wet shirt, my heart starts to beat faster. His body, both rapturous and menacing at the same time, has a cataclysmic effect on me. All of a sudden, I have to get away from him. I open the shower door and step out onto the mat, grab a towel and slink into his bedroom, clutching it to my chest. A trail of water marks my path, as I wrap myself up and climb into his bed.

Silas hurries with the rest of his clothes, dropping them into a sopping puddle on the shower floor. Then he follows me into the bedroom, towel haphazardly hanging from his hips and water streaming down his body.

"Sweetie, what can I do? I know you are still feeling...um. I want to do anything I can, please. Let me help you."

"I'm really tired," I say, as I settle deeper into his bed, still clutching the towel to my body.

"May I join you? Or are you too..." He speaks with a pained look on his face.

"You can join me, I guess."

"We need to talk, don't you agree?" He is bashful and afraid to approach me. I almost don't recognize him.

"Silas, there was no rape fantasy. No conversation with Devin," I say, closing my eyes and just wanting the day to be over.

"She was so specific, why would she make that up?" he asks, trying to understand where exactly the wheels fell off. "I don't mean why would she do that, because she clearly did, I just mean why would someone do that to another person? It's so, so...evil. I've never known her to be like that, you have to believe me. She was so contrite about overhearing the *conversation* because she didn't want me to think she was eavesdropping. The whole focus of our chat wasn't even about what she claimed she heard. It was about her being nosy. I didn't believe her at first. It just didn't sound like you, but she had this whole story...you didn't want to know when, wanted it rough—almost brutal..." he trails off, realizing how horrible it sounds.

I roll away from him. I can't possibly defend my desire not to be raped if he can't recognize that Parker orchestrated the whole thing out of vengefulness and jealousy.

"Talk to me," he says while laying a hand on my hip, causing me to flinch. He pulls his hand back, surprised by my response.

"Jessie?"

"Silas, you can't just...take it back. I wish you could, but you can't," I reason quietly, with my back to him. "I was viciously raped. Knowing my lover did it doesn't change the emotions I'm feeling. But what's worse, is knowing you doubted your intuition about me...in place of Parker's bullshit story. It really is a new level of betrayal."

"I would never betray you, ever. I know I can't take it back...do you, need to be away from me?" he asks.

"I don't want to be alone," I say, and then add, "But I don't want to be touched either."

"Oh, Jessie, what have I done?"

Chapter Twenty-Four

Announcement

I'm sitting cross-legged on the couch, playing solitaire on my phone when Devin and Corey burst through the door, elated and sunburned. They drop armfuls of campfire permeated gear to the floor and rush me like two overgrown, smelly linebackers.

Caught off guard, I can only scream, "NO!" before they grab me and wrestle me to the floor. They kiss and hug me like I'm back from the dead instead of merely absent from their lives for a three-day span.

"Stop, let me go!" I demand, as the hysteria builds inside and floods me with irrational fear. When they don't stop, I begin kicking and flailing against them. I land a punch against Devin's jaw before he sits up, shocked and affronted.

"What the hell, Jessie!" he says, as he rubs his scruff covered jaw.

"I don't like being pinned down, you big oaf!" I exclaim, still trying to calm down. Then I scream, "I'm not your doll to manhandle as you wish!" My heart is pounding out of my chest, and I realize I have never screamed at Devin before.

He is unsure what to make of it as he slows his hand against his jaw and eyes me with malice.

Corey jumps in to steady the sails, "We are just so excited to tell you something. I know we smell like two hothouse plague victims, but listen—"

"NO," Devin says, still regarding me with a suspicious eye. "Not like this." With that, he gets up from his knees and walks to his room, tugging his shirt over his head, presumably to go shower.

Corey sits back against the base of the couch, his legs stretched out before him. "Want to tell me what's going on?"

I'm still in the posture of a startled cat on the floor, so I try to calm my body language and act normal. "What do you mean?" I attempt, brushing the hair off my face with both palms and then settling them more calmly against my knees.

"What was that all about?" he coaxes, his warm brown eyes beseeching.

"Nothing, I just couldn't breathe that's all," I lie. There is no way I can admit what happened. Devin would never forgive Silas, and he is just starting to warm up to him— if you can even call it that.

"I don't believe you, and Devin, most certainly knows something is up," he says, calling my bluff.

"Seriously, nothing is up. I'm fine, you guys just stink like a campfire and freaked me out when you bum-rushed me. That's all."

"Are you sure?" Again he invites me to unburden my soul.

"Absolutely," I smile and nod, a bit too fervently perhaps.

"K, well, I'm going to go shower," Corey says, and I can tell he is humoring me for now. Once Devin comes out, the sanction will be lifted, though, so I need to get my shit together. If I act like a wounded animal, they will never let up, and they are nothing if not persistent.

There is blame to be placed, but I've decided it's not on Silas. In his kinky world, a rape fantasy is par for the course. It's no more contemptuous than, say, age play or pony play. If Silas is to blame for anything, it's trusting someone who he knows, at least on some level, has it out for me. He can no longer deny or play dumb about Parker, but how he handles the situation remains to be seen.

***

I disappear into the kitchen to cook a welcome home dinner and down half a bottle of chilled Chardonnay in an attempt to appear breezy and unaffected.

After chopping a myriad of vegetables, I begin sawing through a frozen chicken breast, still debating if we should just stick with a veggie stir-fry.

"Let me help," Devin says, freshly showered and uncharacteristically stoic.

I move aside and hand him the knife. "How was your trip?" I begin rifling through a stack of pots and pans in the cabinet so he can't see the strain of keeping something from him, on my face.

"It was great. Are you going to ignore the fact that you just decked me in the face?" he asks, setting down the knife and backing into the counter with his arms crossed.

"I'm sorry, Dev. You guys caught me off guard," I say, and then hide my face in my wine glass, gulping, not sipping.

"Um-Hum," he says, waiting for me to come out with it. He knows I'm lying, just like Corey did, but I have to stick with the lie. The repercussions of the truth are way too damaging. In fact, they are unrecoverable.

Lately, Ruby has been a bridge between Devin and Silas because Devin and Corey have been spending a lot of time with her lately, adoring *uncles* that they are, but the fragile peace treaty would end if Devin knew the truth.

I change tactics, "Is your big news that you guys are engaged?" I ask this as if I didn't already see the rings on their fingers.

"No," he says simply, and then just waits, knowing if he gives me enough rope, I will hang myself. Devin has a way of looking at you, that makes you think he knows everything you are thinking and can read every emotion you feel. Contrary to my nature, I hold the silence.

This is the awkward moment when Corey enters the kitchen. "Ok, now that we don't smell like we work in a rendering plant, I'm happy to announce we are now Mr. and Mr." He delivers the news like he's announcing that it's Taco Tuesday instead of the life-changing event it is.

His words take a minute to saturate my befuddled brain. When I realize they are married, I squeal and throw my arms around them both, knocking our heads together. The very real joy I feel for them is perfectly genuine, so I'm able to distract them from my *own* very real issues.

With the focus successfully shifted, I swat away the little birdie in my head saying, *and a baby makes three*. "Congratulations! Oh my goodness, I'm so excited for you! Wait. Does this mean I don't need to wear a horrendous bride's maid dress?" They both back up smiling, the tension forgotten.

"Where's the Champagne? This is fucking fantastic!"

Chapter Twenty-Five

Breakdown

I'm sitting at my desk with thirty-two unanswered emails staging a coup against me. I'm cognizant of the need to answer them, but I feel ill-equipped and ineffectual at the moment. Well, not really at the moment, more like, from here on out.

There is a melee of emotions inside me, and until I can sort them out, I feel like I have no energy or focus for anything else. The first and foremost is Silas. Although I don't blame him for what he did to me, he can't take away the effect it has had. I have nightmares where I wake up hoarse from screaming in my sleep. I feel disconnected when he touches me. The same things that used to make me melt into him, now cause anxiety and a certain detachment on my part. I try to keep these feelings from him, but he is so good at tuning in to me, especially sexually, that it's no use trying to hide them.

I can't talk to Devin and Corey, and it's a second job keeping anything from them, not to mention a huge burden to carry alone. My subconscious is working overtime to purge the repressed feelings that I know I need to deal with, and the fact that my sleep is now invaded makes me that much more anxious. What if Devin and Corey hear me screaming? I have been lucky thus far that they have been spending so much time at Corey's place, but before too long, they will inevitably hear my nighttime sufferings.

Twice I have had nightmares at Silas,' and twice I have paralyzed him with the knowledge that he has done this to me. The nightmares are not specific, and for the most part, I don't remember them, but I always wake up screaming, covered in sweat, with my heart pounding outside of my chest. When I'm with Silas, he holds me when they happen, and I can feel him shuddering in the dark with his own tears of torment.

Another thing I am struggling with is the fact that Parker has driven this wedge between Silas and me. I *never* would have thought she had the power, but she did, and she swung it like a medieval war hammer.

The fact that she is part owner of the club muddies the water that much more. I don't want her to see the damage she has done, but pretending it's not there mires me even deeper in my anxiety. I frankly cannot feel comfortable at the club—not sexually, not as her prey, and not with the business relationship between her and Silas. Simply put, I feel vulnerable, and that is not a feeling I'm used to having. It presses down on my shoulders and feels like a barbell is resting on them—always.

Yet another insurmountable obstacle I can't deal with, is becoming Devin and Corey's incubator. Now that they are married and Corey's re-enlistment plans have been thwarted, it is only a matter of time until they start tightening the screws. Here I feel helpless. How do I say no to them? How do I say yes? Neither answer feels right, yet neither answer feels completely wrong either.

In a moment of complete and utter hopelessness, I lay my head down and start to cry. These aren't the tears of polite society. They are the tears of anguish, the runny nose, swollen eyes, and hick-up tears. Once they start, I can't stem the flow. It's as if my life depends on their release to simply trudge through what is fast becoming the quicksand of my life.

***

"Jessie, are you ok?" Salinger whispers into my exposed ear. He speaks gently, not to startle me.

I don't respond right away because the first thing I'm aware of is the puddle of tears, saliva, and snot cradled beneath my arms and face.

"JB, it's me, Salinger." Again soft, gentle, like he is waking a baby. I wipe my face with the back of my arm and sit up.

"No," I start to cry again, "Salinger, I am not ok." I'm exhausted and not sure how long I have been here, but for the first time in over a week, I feel a glimmer of hope. Just voicing that I am *not ok* is almost cathartic. I'm not hiding, not pretending, not suffering all by myself—it's so freeing.

He pulls me to him and holds me soundly while I cry, the reservoir not yet depleted. He is on his knees behind my desk, holding me while I sit hunched in my office chair. He smooths my hair and rubs my back. Never slackening his hold, never uncomfortable with my crying, only helping to shoulder my burden.

Once I'm all cried out, I pull back a fraction, and he loosens his grip on me. I look like a prizefighter with my eyes swollen almost shut. Salinger cradles my face in his hands and wipes my cheeks with his thumbs.

"Get your purse," he says while helping me up and wiping the hair from my tear-stained cheek.

He hurries me out of the office, chattering about meaningless reports and clients, as though to act normal and not attract any notice.

My face is all but stuffed in his armpit, as he delivers me safely through the maze of offices and cubicles and into the elevator.

When a man tries to join us, Salinger holds up a hand and says, "I'm not feeling well, you should grab the next one." The man steps back in complete agreement. Alone on the elevator, we don't speak. He holds me, and I sniffle against the side of his chest with his chin protectively resting on my head.

Once in the parking garage, Salinger speaks to me for the first time since telling me to grab my purse. "It's going to be ok, JB." Coming from a war-hardened marine, you would think his words prophetic and from raw experience, but the weight of them goes unnoticed.

"I don't know about that, Salinger."

"What do you need more right now, booze or ice cream?"

I laugh at his attempt to right the world's wrongs, wishing it was that easy. "I don't know what I need." The truth of my statement couldn't have been more obvious.

"Alright then, get in the car, and we'll figure it out." He opens the door to his silver SUV, and I climb in. The black leather and the subtle smell of the air freshener plugged into his vent swallow me whole.

***

Salinger's house is nothing like I remember. Back when he was still married, the house was outfitted like a model home, plush and over accessorized to the point where not even a candle was out of place. Back then, I never felt comfortable hanging out because I might un-crease that little karate chop to the top of the accent pillows.

Now that his cheating wife moved out, she has evidently taken all the pretense too. Now there is a comfortable, masculine feel to the minimalistic furniture and clean lines. In a word, it's monochromatic. The walls are gray, the furniture is black, the crown molding and accent pieces are white, and there are sight-lines into the stainless steel kitchen.

I feel very much like I'm in the home of a tidy bachelor. The only real color in the room is a giant lime-green dog bed in the corner.

"You have a dog?" I ask, as I take in the hand-scraped wood floors I know he installed last year.

"Depends on your perspective, some people call him a horse," he says while nodding toward the French doors. An enormous Great Dane sits on the deck. His head cocked in puzzlement as to why he has not been let in yet. His breath is fogging the glass, and his undocked ears are piqued.

"He was kind of an impulse buy. I decided I needed a companion," he says, with a bashful shrug. "I'm going to let him in, but ignore him until he is calm and bump him away with your leg if he approaches you without being invited. His name is Nash." With that, Salinger opens the back door, and a puppy with the body of a pony and the grace of a water buffalo comes charging in, his tail flapping with unchecked joy.

He sniffs me once, in a sort of fly by, then goes and sits next to Salinger's leg. Nash is clearly bursting with excitement but just as clearly, trained to wait for an invitation.

"That's a lot of dog," I say with raised eyebrows. Then hesitantly, "Come here, Nash." He bolts over to me, nuzzles my hand then flops onto his back at my feet, waiting for me to scratch his belly.

"Not much of a watchdog, are you?" I tease as I squat down to rub his silver belly. "You're pretty, though," I add, marveling at his blue—or maybe gray eyes.

"Want to sit outside?" Salinger calls out, as he tugs open the refrigerator door and retrieves two beers.

I don't answer, but I make my way to the impressive deck with Nash trailing behind me. I'm a little surprised to see pots of flowers and an umbrella covered patio table with thick, geometric patterned cushions on the chairs. He obviously has an affinity for the outdoors. His yard is a huge, lush oasis, nothing like the bachelor pad simplicity inside his house.

There is a hammock stretched between two shade trees further out in the yard, and I can imagine myself sitting there for hours reading. His yard is well manicured, and I notice he has paid attention to details out here that he has skipped inside. For example, the neatly weeded raised garden beds and the flowers around the parameter of the yard. The yard is bursting with life and ablaze with color. There are Day Lilies, Columbine's, Delphinium's, and Gladiola's peppered in amongst vibrant hues of every color and every type of bloom. There are fresh herbs, a bountiful vegetable garden, and even a small pumpkin patch where pumpkins are beginning to emerge in time for autumn. It's beautiful and really, quite domestic.

He hands me a beer then turns to light the grill. He has yet to mention my office breakdown and seems as though he won't, but it's the reason for our mid-day, impromptu BBQ, so I decide to tackle it head-on.

"So, about earlier, I guess I owe you an explanation." I sink into one of the patio chairs as Nash trots off to a shady spot by the hammock.

"You don't owe me anything, Jessie. I just want you to know I'm here for you if you need me. If you want to talk about something, I'm willing, but I know enough about stress and trauma not to push you."

I'm caught off guard and just stare into his hazel eyes for a minute, trying to collect myself. Oddly, his demeanor makes me *want* to confide in him.

After a bit, he sits back and takes a swig of his beer, lessening the pressure even more.

"I was raped," I blurt out, never thinking I would ever mention those words to anyone.

He stills the rocking of his chair, but otherwise carefully masks his face and waits for me to go on.

"It was a misunderstanding, but I'm having trouble shaking it," I say, as I pick at the label on my beer bottle.

"How exactly does someone rape you under the pretense of misunderstanding? Did they mistakenly shove their dick in you? Maybe it was meant for someone else?" His careful mask is chipping, and he is showing his anger with small, incremental changes to his body language.

I can see fury behind his eyes, I can even sense him vibrating with rage, but he is careful not to burden me with it. His anger is mostly silent to not spook me, but I can see his jaw tighten into a compressed knot.

"I told you Parker wants Silas. That she hates me."

He jumps in, unable to hold his silence any longer. "A woman raped you?" His disgust is apparent, but he tries to relax his face anyway.

"No, she told Silas she overheard me talking to Devin on the phone. She told him I said... I have a rape fantasy." My voice is calm and collected, with no inflection at all, but my label picking divulges my true state of mind.

"I see," he takes another swig of beer, "Clearly, you didn't get the memo, and now you are saddled with the aftermath of rape trauma, am I right?" I nod, happy I don't have to spell it out, and not even sure I could have.

"I'm having nightmares. I feel weak and vulnerable, but I'm also on high alert all the time. I have no idea how to handle Parker, or Silas for that matter. I have to keep the whole thing from Devin because he hates Silas. Poor Silas is destroyed. And now Devin and Corey are married, so it won't be long before they bring up having a kid." It comes out like word vomit. I can't even stop my ranting long enough to breathe. I just open my mouth, and all my troubles barge out all at once.

After finally taking a deep breath, I feel a thousand times better. Now that I have everything out there instead of simmering in my belly like an ulcer, I feel renewed. It feels like I've finally flipped the nozzle to let the steam out of a pressure cooker.

"First of all, I think you should know a little about PTSD. I have some experience with it, and it might help you." He is so diplomatic. Obviously, he wants no details about my rape but wants to help me nonetheless.

"Salinger, you were in active combat. You lost what, seven of your closest friends? You witnessed untold atrocities. Not to mention you were blown up and almost killed! You can't minimize that by comparing it to the crap I'm going through." I'm astonished he would even correlate the two, and I feel guilty for dumping all this on him. My face falls with indistinct shame. I have never in my life been through anything close to what he has. This perspective makes my issues seem shallow.

"I'm not minimizing anything, but I've come to understand a few things, and I think my familiarity can help you. I've spent a lot of years in therapy trying to muddle through my own traumatic events. If the condensed version of what I've learned can help you, I want to try." He sits forward and laces his fingers together on the table, his eyes are confident.

"First of all, you need to understand that trauma changes you. It's impossible to go through something horrific and not be affected by it. So go easy on yourself, your feelings are exactly what they should be."

"Ok," is all I find to say, but I stop picking at the beer label. What he is saying makes a lot of sense. Of course, I have changed. I should expect nothing less.

He continues, "When our experiences lock us in a state of danger or unpredictability, it's natural to act out in anger. Anger feels powerful, and that is preferable to feeling weak or vulnerable." He lets that sink in a minute and then goes on. "I feel like that rage is the basis for your nightmares. You are angry at Parker for instigating such a thing, at Silas for not knowing better and for making himself a victim of his own guilt, and at Devin for asking you to do something you feel like you can't say no to. You're angry, and you should be. You just haven't given yourself permission to feel that anger, so it's manifesting in your nightmares. They are giving your brain and body an outlet, a release for the incredibly powerful emotion of just being really fucking pissed off." His look is beseeching, his words compelling.

"You're probably right," I'm impressed that he has it all neatly figured out. "But, what do I do now?" He is so insightful. Now that he has worked through understanding my issues, I want him to fix them or tell me how to. I feel like I'm talking to Confucius or Buddha.

"First of all, be angry! Honor your struggle. I can't tell you how many times I hiked into the middle of nowhere just to roar my wrath and indignation to the universe. After what I've seen and lost, I have enough rage inside me for ten lifetimes." His fingers are laced together, eyes still penetrating mine. I nod, and tears prickle the backs of my eyes.

"Then, realize your true self is still in there, it's just hidden for now by your coping self, and that's ok." He must know how much I need to hear that—that I'm still myself and that my feelings are normal. It's a profound realization and intensely validating.

"Next, it's important to understand that there are powerful chemicals in your brain that reinforce traumatic memories. You will never simply get over them, not even with time. They are a part of you, but they don't have to define you. They can be a part of your story without infesting the whole book."

I nod again. He is speaking to my soul.

"And lastly, Jessie, know that you are capable of recovery and that you will get past this," he says while placing his hand on mine. It's warm and comforting and helps me absorb what he said. Just being told I will recover is something to cling to, and I love him for his words.

I trust him implicitly because he mastered the subject matter by walking through fire and brimstone.

"That was really powerful, Salinger." I want to thank him, but it sounds so trite. I'm not even sure how to spring back after his insightful discourse. He doesn't seem to need a response, though no accolade would do him justice.

After a long moment, letting everything he said sink in, I ask, "Can we go sit in the hammock?"

Salinger just smiles, but he knows what he has done for me. I think the change in my demeanor is obvious. It's nice that through his own struggle with PTSD, he is able to help others with his words of understanding and recognition. Someone should put his statements on a plaque, or tattoo them on their forehead. They are *that* encouraging. *Honor your struggle*, pure genius.

***

We sit facing each other in the hammock, my feet by his shoulder and one of his legs at my side. His other leg is dangling off the hammock, pushing us casually. We both have fresh beers, and there are two chicken breasts and some bacon-wrapped asparagus spears on the grill.

"Thank you, Salinger," I say, and it sounds wispy. I'm watching the sun peek through the leaves above, the light playing off his face with flecks of sunshine.

He smiles and then takes a sip of beer while squinting his eyes against the light. "What are you going to do about Parker? Shank her at the club? Have a blanket party in the parking lot?"

"No," I laugh, "Probably just take some diabolical spin classes at the gym. I'm not really cut out for her kind of vengeance."

"No, you're not. That's why you are so much better than her. Silas knows it too." Now *he* sounds wistful, almost dejected even.

"You are a really great friend, you know? I'm not sure I deserve you," I say honestly, then take a cold sip of my beer.

"Of course you do. You have always been there for me. Remember when my ex bought a Lexus and seven thousand dollars' worth of designer clothes on the same day?"

I laugh at the memory, "What am I, some sort of heartless bitch? I wasn't just going to let you wallow in self-pity—you had credit cards to freeze."

"But you were the one who pointed out that she was probably seeing someone else and padding her lifestyle for when I would have to assume our marital debt. Do you remember how you sugar coated that observation?"

"If I remember correctly, it was with a paintball gun held to the side of your neck."

"Yep, you got the jump on a career marine and snuck up behind me. Imagine my surprise!" The grin on his face is infectious.

"What was I supposed to do, take you for high tea at the Emporium?" I say, and my smile mirrors his.

"My point is you've picked me up a thousand times. You've always been the one who was there for me."

"Do you ever miss your wife? Or miss being married?" I ask.

"I don't miss her because she wasn't good for me, but I miss having someone to share my life with."

"Salinger, you're crazy. You could have anyone you want, do you not see that?" I say, stunned.

"That's not true, and besides, I'm a tough guy to be with."

I cough on my sip of beer, "I spend all kinds of time with you, and you're not hard to be with *at all*. Any woman would be so God damn lucky, Salinger."

"Are you so sure about that?" he asks, with his eyebrows raised.

"Yeah, I'm sure. Anyway, what about Bradley?" Her name gets stuck in my throat, and my eyes dart to his crotch then back to his eyes. It's like my brain has fused the memory of them together with thoughts of his dick.

"She's alright. I'm having fun, but I don't want to end up with a club girl. I've never been that guy, I don't want to control someone, and I certainly don't want to be controlled. I don't need to have a *scene*. I just want to find a good woman that I can love for the next fifty years…and fuck raw, for forty-nine of them." He smiles into his beer bottle.

I feel a shiver at his statement, I've seen him fuck, and it's magic. "I don't think the kink scene is always about controlling someone, but if you need to settle down with a nice wholesome girl, that's fine too."

"What I want is irrelevant. Besides, like I said, I'm having fun for now," he is dismissive in a flighty way. Then he changes the subject. "I wish I could help you with the Devin situation though. I personally think that's an awful lot to ask of someone," he says, as he strokes the top of his dog's head.

Nash doesn't seem to mind the rope of the hammock edge rhythmically bumping up against his chest as we sway back and forth—he's just happy to be included in whatever we are doing.

"They would make such great parents. I wish it wasn't so hard for them; they have faced resistance their whole lives. I would like to see them finally not have to fight for something." As I speak, I reach over Salinger's leg to scratch Nash's sleek, silver head.

"Um, your boob is touching my leg," he says with mock disapproval.

Taking a line from his book, I say, "You're welcome," and we both laugh.

"I think I'm going to do it," I say, again surprised to have voiced my innermost thoughts.

"That would be the most selfless thing I've ever heard of. Would it surprise you to know that I knew you would all along?"

"Not really, I think I knew it all along too."

Chapter Twenty-Six

Reckoning

It's nearly seven o'clock by the time Salinger drops me off at my car. There are only a handful of vehicles left in the parking garage, and I find I am edgy and suspicious of each one. I'm worried about what might be lurking behind them in the near solitude of parking level 5.

Dutifully, Salinger waits until I am safely in my car before he waves and heads toward the winding exit ramp on his way out.

It feels good to be understood, it's somehow validating, and it makes me feel like I'm normal for feeling this way, not crazy or irrational…or weak.

Armed with my new perspective, I call Silas and let him know I am heading to the club but will stop by after because we need to talk. What I have to say will be hard for him to hear, but I can't worry right now about his journey. It's mine that I need to heal from and that knowledge feels powerful in itself. It's like I have permission to only worry about my own shit, instead of packing up everyone else's and hauling it around with me.

***

Silas must have dropped everything he was doing and hauled ass to 1462, because when I storm through the door, he is poised and ready to receive me, afraid of what I am planning to do.

"Jessie, let me handle her. I promise I am taking care of it. Please, I don't want you going to jail." He is hurriedly walking in my wake but knows better than to physically restrain me.

In the end, he concedes and just follows me to the office—as moral support or bodyguard, I'm not sure. I do appreciate that we look like a united front, though, as we storm the castle.

I don't bother knocking, just push the door open. Parker is sitting at the desk. Her brow furrows with conceit when she lays eyes on me.

"Hi Parker, I just wanted to give you the opportunity to explain yourself to both Silas and me," I say, as I round the desk at a very aggressive pace.

Not one to back down, she pushes away from the desk and stands up, facing me nearly toe to toe, "And just what the hell do I need to explain?"

"Ok. You had your chance," I say, as I pause briefly and then deck her square in the face. My brother would be proud of me because as kids, he told me to always follow a punch all the way through. I do, almost instinctively, then I hear and simultaneously feel her nose crumble beneath my rage. Her face explodes with blood as tears flood her eyes.

"Silas?" she pleads as if she expects him to jump in.

"Don't you fucking look to me! I just wish I could have done that myself." He is grinning, with pride maybe?

"Get your shit, and get out of here." He stands with his feet planted and arms crossed.

"I'm calling the police, look at me!" She lowers her hands and spits into the trash can. Her face, hands, and rhinestone tank top are scarlet red with blood, and it's still flowing.

"She broke my nose and knocked out my teeth!" she seethes, while placing her tongue gingerly against her gums where the top two front teeth used to be, then spits more blood into the trash can.

"No, Parker, you will not be calling the police," Silas simmers. "You had worse coming, and we both know it. Now get the fuck out of this club." He raises his voice this time. She obeys with her face stuffed into her open hands and streaks of blood trickling down both of her forearms.

When she is gone, he shuts the door and faces my panting frame. My fists are still balled up as though ready for round two.

"Do you feel better?" his voice is calm.

My breathing slows marginally, "Actually, yes." I realize I do feel better, and it's not from hitting Parker, but because he finally stood up for me. If only he had done that from the beginning, we wouldn't be in this predicament now.

"Good. I was working on buying her out, but that wasn't as efficient as knocking her stupid." He smiles and looks down at my fist, cradling it in his hands.

When I realize he *has* been doing something to get rid of her, relief washes over me. I finally don't feel so alone in dealing with my feelings toward her. I walk into his arms, and it feels good for the first time in over a week to have him wrapped around me.

"If I had known you were doing something about her, I wouldn't have felt like I needed to handle it by myself," I say, and it's muffled by his chest.

"Jessie, *of course*, I was doing something about her. What am I, some oblivious asshole? My solution was better long term, but I guess you needed something a little more direct." He kisses my head and asks, "How is your hand?"

"It's fine. Will you still be able to buy her out now?"

"I would prefer she not have the satisfaction of knowing that she got to you and just go quietly away. Now it's probably going to cost me more, but I can work with that too. How could you have thought I would let her get away with that? Don't you trust me to take care of you?"

"I didn't feel like you *were* taking care of me. I didn't know you were doing anything about her at all. Anyway, it's fine, Salinger helped me realize that I need to acknowledge my anger and honor my struggle. So I did."

"Yes, Pipes, you certainly did. Like a champ." He raises my hand and kisses my knuckles.

"So, in the interest of honoring my struggle and allowing myself to be angry, it's your turn to get your ass kicked."

"Wha—"

"That's right, let's go."

***

When we walk into the gym Silas is unconcerned, but when I take him to the mixed martial arts room and close the glass door, he asks, "So you are literally going to kick my ass?"

"Yes. Take your shoes off before stepping on the mat," I say over my shoulder as I walk toward the pads.

He takes in the room for a minute, the walls of mirrors, the hanging heavy bags, the life-sized body torsos, and the speed bags. Then tugs his athletic pants up to mid-calf and pulls his t-shirt off over his head.

"Oh, it's on!" He looks sexy again, now that I don't think he's a pussy that was ignoring the fact that Parker had me raped.

I approach him with two hand target pads and toss them over to him. He immediately slides his hands into the mitts and holds them up to me, crouching to show me he is ready.

I slip on some fingerless grappling gloves, and then cringe as my hands meet with the sweaty, muggy insides of the gloves. Clearly, someone used them recently and abundantly. I resist the urge to fling them to the mat in favor of the much too big ones and settle into their damp nastiness. My right hand is very sore, and my knuckles are incredibly tender but not enough to stop me.

Bouncing back and forth between the balls of my feet, squeezing my hands into fists, and punching the soggy gloves into my palms, I advance on him.

"Silas, I am pissed because you left me to suffer all Parker's bullshit and never stood up for me, whereby silently giving her your blessing to treat me however she wished." Then I swing at him, fast— two jabs and a right hook.

His utter surprise at my intensity allows me to land my hook. Stupidly, he challenges me, "*Whereby?*—" cross, cross, elbow strike, cross, cross.

He barely gets his pads up in time, but he does. "Jessie, I—" cross, cross, jab, jab, cross, elbow strike.

"I thought she would get over her jealousy. I *also* thought if I stepped in, it would get worse for you."

"You tolerated her saying things to me you would never let anyone say to someone else." cross, cross, jab...jab, jab, "You left me blowing in the wind! No fucking support whatsoever!" jab, jab, uppercut, "Essentially giving her the green light to behave however she wished." cross, hook, jab, jab, "You put her before me! And then you trusted something she said," cross, cross, cross, "about me!" I turn away for a second, and then come at him full force, jab, jab, upper cut, cross, cross, right hook, cross, cross, right hook. Now *I'm* surprised at my intensity.

"I'm sorry! You're right."

"You can't fucking stay neutral in that situation!" cross, cross, jab, "Or your girlfriend will think you're a pussy!" jab, jab, jab. Sweat is dripping into my eyes, so I wipe the bridge of my nose with the knuckles of the grappling gloves and then land a huge right hook.

"Are you done?" he asks, re-assuming his guard.

"Not even close!" cross, uppercut, jabjabjab, "You *assaulted* me on her word! Then make me feel bad about—," jabjabjab, "how *you* feel!" cross, cross, pant, pant, "Well, you can choke on your guilt! That should have never happened!" jab, jab, pant, jab, jab, jab.

"Jessie, I will never forgive myself for what I did to you." Then he surprises me by dropping his guard.

I stop mid-jab, "Get your guard up, Silas." Pant, pant, pant.

"No," he says, as he drops his pads to the mat.

I approach him with my arm cocked, but at the last second, I put my foot behind his and ram into his chest, knocking him backward to the mat.

"Get your fucking guard up, Silas!" I growl, now I'm really angry. He flings me onto my back and holds me down in the mount position, straddling my body and pinning my fists to the mat above my head.

"Now it's *my* turn." He leans down and speaks into my face, "I have been working on buying out Parker for weeks, long before this fucking nightmare! I have not told her off because I didn't want to take away YOUR power! In no way was I just sitting by, letting things unfold! I just didn't advertise what I was doing! As for my guilt, I *have* choked on it, almost constantly, in fact! I feel you cringe every time I touch you, and I know that's my doing! I hold you in the night when you are screaming, and I know you feel vulnerable and weak because that's *all* my doing! Blacklisting Parker from the club scene would have had a lasting effect—which is what I was going for! I didn't want to fight your battles and undermine *you*; I wanted to end them from behind the scenes to protect *your* honor! So if you think I don't *have your back*, if you don't believe I started talking to my lawyer after the *very first time* she talked down to you, and if you think I'm going to *let someone* disrespect my girl or me in *MY* club, then you go right ahead and unleash your anger on me! **Do it, Jessie! DO IT!**" He is shouting now, his eyes blazing and only six inches from my face.

I'm still panting hard, my chest rising and falling between his knees. Weirdly, I don't feel vulnerable or trapped beneath him. Actually, I'm happy he has a little fight in him—it redeems him a little bit.

The fight drains out of me, though, "I needed to honor my struggle. Validating my anger is important." I'm panting and feel like my right grappling glove is full of blood and little bits of random finger bones. This is going to hurt tomorrow.

"Then get *the fuck up* and let's do this," he says. A smile flutters against his lips as he helps me to my feet. "Because when you finish, I am going to take you home with me, and you will **never** question my loyalties again. Do you hear me? I am in this *with* you, as long as it takes for you to feel good again. Now, let's go."

I assume a fighting stance, and he finally raises his guard.

"I might regret saying this, but let's pretend I'm your attacker…the one who you didn't know, that is."

I shrug, "Ok, but you better grab a cup and some headgear from over there." I point to the supply shelf and then look back at him unapologetically.

Chapter Twenty-Seven

Recovering

Back at Silas' loft, after stopping for frozen yogurt on the way home, I realize I feel a little better. Anger *is* powerful, and letting it out was tremendously cathartic. I think about Salinger hiking into the woods just to be alone and screaming his lungs out. Yes, releasing anger is good. Society is chock full of anger and discontent. I am hardly alone in that, but acknowledging the pent-up rage is critical in moving forward. Realizing it's ok to be mad is a huge step forward for me on my path to healing.

Silas walks back into the living room after checking on Ruby and kissing her sleeping head goodnight. "You know I'm going to have a black eye, right?"

"Oh, for sure," I cock my head and smile. Indirectly I think the whole boxing session helped him too. Not only to add outward appearance to his inward strife but to defend himself against all the resentments I had built up. It turns out, he *was* taking care of me. I just didn't know it. I also think it gave me some control back, and that's good for him to see too.

I'm done feeling bad about his guilt, I've set that down. I'm done being angry at his complacency with Parker—now that I know he wasn't,

I've set that down too. The extent of boxing probably wasn't necessary, maybe an open conversation would have served, but I needed the chance to funnel all that turmoil and then purge it from my system. It was healing for both of us.

"Do you think Parker filed a report?" I ask, as he drops on the couch next to me, shirtless again.

"No way. She knows better, thanks to your little reminder, not to bite the hand that feeds her. It was a hard lesson for her to learn, though," he chuckles. "I'm proud of you," he says, then tugs my chin to pull me in for a kiss.

"I'm only proud of finally taking ownership of some of the shit that was weighing me down," I say, scrunching down further into the couch.

"I know, babe. How are the knuckles feeling now?" he raises my right hand to inspect them, "You need some ice. This doesn't look good."

"My knuckles will be fine. They hurt, though." I back away, lying down and resting my head on the arm of the couch. I had intended to put my feet in his lap, but he surprises me by shifting his weight and crawling up my body. He stops at my lips and kisses me soundly.

Presumably, Analise is asleep just like Ruby and in her condo next door, but I still feel like a teenager getting felt up on her parent's couch. I don't cringe, and I don't panic right away, but after a bit, my nervous system begins to sound the alarm.

"Silas, stop. Let's try me on top, so I feel less trapped." It seems like a reasonable idea, and evidently, he agrees because he relinquishes his position with a fairly smooth rotation of his body.

With hardly a pause, I sit up on his hips, straddling his body where *his* head now rests on the leather arm of the couch. On top, I do feel better, and I suppose it's high time I test my limits. I pull off my shirt and present myself and my black sports bra to him.

He lets out a lengthy exhale; it's been a long time since we have been intimate. He has been patient but diligent in his quest. I rock slightly against his erection and reach up to peel my sports bra over my head.

He helps remove the sweat-soaked bra and moans when my breasts are displayed for him. He bites down on the corner of his full bottom lip and swipes his fingers gently over my nipples, then down my stomach where they stop. He is so afraid to press his luck that he gives me control, and with that, a sense of authority over myself.

I'm no longer having things done to me, I'm in charge of what happens, or I'm the one doing them. I inch down his hips, allowing his hard on to tent against his workout pants. I look to his hardness, then to his eyes and back again, contemplating if I want to push myself.

Finally, I work his elastic waist down, freeing his straining penis. I back down his legs to give myself some room, and then suck him into my mouth, right to the back of my throat. I have hardly even begun when he stops me with a hoarse sounding voice.

"Jessie, I'm not going to last if you keep doing that." I move a few more times up and down his length, then release my wet hold on him. I stand up to shimmy down my workout shorts and panties, then straddle his frame again.

His cock juts up from between us like it was my own. It's engorged and slippery from my mouth. I reach back to support my leaning body with one hand on his shin while caressing his satiny cock and pressing the shaft of it against my core with the other.

I drop my head back and begin to lose myself in the sensation of his smoothness between the folds of my skin. I stroke my hand slowly up and down his length. When a drop oozes from the tip, I rub it over his head with my thumb, then lean forward with my breasts not quite touching his chest.

"Kiss me," I say in a whisper, and he immediately complies. I reach down and guide him into me, hesitating slightly before swallowing it deep within my body. The sensation is drawn out, yet hungry, and my own groan follows his two quick inhales.

"Fuck me, Pipes," he commands in a strained whisper. So I begin sliding up and down methodically while cupping my breasts in my hands.

He hesitates to touch me, but my nipples are aching for him to stroke them. Finally, he does reach out, but it's my ass he grabs. He spreads my cheeks as he grinds me against him. I lean forward, lowering my mouth back to his.

My nipples are sensitive and ticklish as they brush against his smooth chest. I'm riding him sensually and squeezing his hardness inside my body. Before too long, the slow ministrations of my rocking hips grinding against his pelvis brings me closer to my climax.

"I'm gonna come, Silas."

"Do it, Pipes. I need you…all over me." His throaty, dirty talk pushes me over the edge as the deep muscle spasms take my breath. I orgasm quietly, mewling by his shoulder in an attempt to not wake Ruby or roust Analise from her condo.

His release comes in much the same way, holding his breath and grinding his teeth as the veins in his neck strain against the confines of his skin. I collapse the rest of the way against his spent frame, with my knees still drawn up next to his sides and our sweat fusing us together.

My pose is downright obscene, tucked up against him like a tree frog. I yawn and then sit up, so I don't inadvertently fall asleep in this position and give Analise or Ruby the opportunity to walk in on my vulgar position.

"It's bedtime, Silas."

"I know, it's been a long day. You will have to thank Salinger for me. I think he made quite a breakthrough with you, and I am grateful for that," he smiles.

"Truly, you will be able to see it all over my face tomorrow," he adds sardonically.

***

Silas comfortably tucks me against his naked body, and the bedroom is as quiet as a buried coffin. I silently wonder if I have broken through my issues with touch. Could it possibly be that easy? Honor my struggle, then lay down the heavy load and just walk away?

Then I start thinking, am I all that comfortable confined like this? Held against his sleeping frame? In fact, I'm concentrating so hard about it that I begin to obsess over his proximity. Anxiety starts to trickle in. Is his hold on me a little too tight? Maybe I would feel better if I had more space, just an inch...or twenty. I'm starting to feel really hot. Maybe if I wasn't facing him I would be more comfortable. Maybe if he wasn't breathing on me.

Nope, it's too much. I can't breathe very well. I am really feeling trapped. His one arm around me feels like a vice. Is that even possible? The relaxed, easy nature of his one arm...it's not even holding me, it's resting on me, yet the weight of it feels like a fallen tree. What the hell? Why am I breathing so fast? Why is my heart pounding like this?

I feel safe. I do. Salinger said when our experiences lock us in a *state of danger or unpredictability, it's natural to feel like this*, but I'm not in danger, and Silas' sleeping body is hardly unpredictable. So, what is my problem? I'm sweating, though the air conditioning is set to a frigid sixty-seven. I have to get out of his iron grip, or I am going to come out of my skin.

I roll to the side, and his arm slips easily off of me. Then I scoot further away toward the edge of the bed, my migration toward a safe refuge. As I bail out, Silas casually rolls onto his stomach. It's his go-to sleeping position—on his stomach, arms under his pillow, very unassuming and undemanding of me, so why can't I relax? Why is the air so heavy to breathe?

"You ok, Pipes?" he mumbles, not even lifting his half-asleep face from the pillow.

"Yeah, sure, why wouldn't I be ok?" I ask.

"Then why are you talking so fast...and loud?" he chuckles and then leans up on an elbow. "You look like a cornered animal. I can sleep on the couch if you would feel better," he says. It's sincere, although a little too accommodating.

"Silas, I'm fine," I say, affecting a more casual position. "I just can't sleep."

"Do you want to talk? I could talk about capital expenditures or differential cash flows, or maybe, accumulated cost recovery. That should put you to sleep." I can hear the smile in his voice more than I can see it on his face, with the room being mostly dark.

"I don't want to talk about that stuff," I say, and it's like I missed his sarcasm entirely.

"What about your future in mixed martial arts?" more sarcasm.

"No," sigh.

"Drilling rigs? Permeability Factors?"

"Ewww no, I certainly don't want to talk about *my* job," I say dryly.

"Then what, what's on your mind?" he asks.

"I just feel squirrelly, that's all."

"Alright, well in case it's me, I'm just going to stay over here on my side of the bed…don't even think about coming over here. I mean it, Pipes. Consider this space between us the Iron Curtain—you be the Soviet Union. And just let me know if you change your mind about differential cash flows. I could go on for hours."

I do smile at his wit, but I don't respond, and before a solid minute goes by, his breathing has slowed to that of a sound asleep man.

I still can't fall asleep, so for a long time, I just stare at the darkened, shadowy chandelier that hangs above the bed. It runs together and morphs into strange shapes as my tired eyes try to make sense of the rusty thing. If you want the truth, I think I'm afraid to fall asleep. If I have a nightmare, it will prove that acknowledging my anger was too easy of a fix.

Silas and I had sex for the first time since the rape, and I hadn't cringed at his touch. I no longer feel resentful of him or guilty about how he is taking the whole thing. On top of all that, Parker will be out of the picture soon. I should be able to sleep, but there is still some anxiety ruminating within. Maybe it's my throbbing hand. It feels like it has its own sledgehammer heartbeat. I probably should have put some ice on it.

I glance over at Silas' half-covered body and remember how he couldn't keep his dick hard while he was assaulting me. The idea of him not staying hard makes me giggle to myself because if there is one thing I can count on, it's Silas' penis being hard. I'm glad he didn't enjoy it. The thought soothes me enough to snuggle up next to him and eventually fall asleep breathing in his warm scent.

Chapter Twenty-Eight

Condo

"So, I was thinking. Now that Corey is almost out of his apartment and has his mom settled, we should get a house. You know, me and him." Devin says this as if he's testing the piranha-filled water and only looks up to me when he finishes his appraisal and hasn't lost a limb.

I have just taken a bite of my avocado chicken sandwich, so my nodding and aggressive chewing hang in the air for a bit before I respond, having swallowed most of the bite.

"Devin, I think that's great," I say as I swallow the last bit. "Really, it's time we venture out on our own." I recognize the truth in my statement, but inwardly I panic. I knew this was coming, but I'm still not ready for it.

"Do you mean that? I mean, you could come with us," he says, and I think he really means it, as he loosens his perch on the barstool.

"Devin, I'm a big girl," I say as I crane my neck, looking for the waitress. I'm in desperate need of more iced tea.

"Would you move in with Silas?" he asks and then takes a cautious bite of his jalapeno-topped burger.

"No, it's too soon for that. I *am* gainfully employed, you know. I could buy my own place." The thought sprouts out of nowhere but kind of makes sense. I might even like my very own space, my own food, my own mess.

He looks at me as he slow-motion chews his burger, his wheels turning. Then he swallows the bite, slaps the table, and announces, "You could buy the condo." I can almost see the lightbulb above his head as the thought strikes him.

"What? No. Do you know how much those places are going for now? It's insane." I'm right, he bought our place when it was a brand new build, and only about twenty percent of the units had sold. Now, the two bedrooms, especially those with deeded parking spaces—of which ours has two, are going for nearly triple what he paid. It's crazy.

"Jessie, do you know how much money I've saved by you paying me rent all along? I think you should buy it. I'll sell it to you at my special friends and family rate." He winks and shoves a few sweet potato fries into his mouth. To him, the topic is settled.

"I don't know, Devin."

"How many places in this part of town have deeded parking *and* laundry facilities in the unit? Not to mention all my upgrades…granite, stainless steel, extended deck space, bay window, *two* master suites, AC…there is a doorman, and storage, I mean, seriously. 720 Linden Street, unit 1140 could be all yours. What do you think?" He is excited by the prospect, and I know Devin. He doesn't want to bother with listing his condo and having random people all through it while we still live there.

"I'll think about it, maybe see what I qualify for," I say to pacify him until I give it some serious thought.

He barely pauses before a whole new thought spills out of his mouth. "I'm thinking about taking Corey home to meet my folks. You know, a little, *Surprise! Your queer son has married another man, and here he is!* What do you think?"

I'm surprised he is even considering it, his parents are appalled by his homosexuality, and still, he seeks the approval from them that will never come.

"Devin, I don't know. Are you sure you want to subject yourself to that? I mean, I know you crave their acceptance—however masochistic that seems, but—"

"It's more than that. I want them to know I turned out just fine *despite* my upbringing...*despite* their lack of approval. Besides, who doesn't like Corey?" The way he is making his way through his burger is further evidence of his discomfort, though he tries to pass it off as a non-issue.

"Do you need a support crew?" I ask, secretly hoping he does not. His parents provide a very poisonous, toxic environment and not just for Devin. It really is shocking how closed minded and hate mongering they are. They are judgmental to the highest degree, despite touting their Christianity. I always thought Christianity by definition is, loving acceptance, lack of judgment and service to others, but the Bachman's play by a different set of *religious* rules.

"I might, are you offering?" he asks, his eyes lighting up at the suggestion.

"Devin, it'll take a village," I say with a resigned sigh. I wish we had stayed on the uncomfortable topic of buying his condo.

Chapter Twenty-Nine

Village

In the end, Devin, Corey, Silas, Ruby, and I all book flights back to the town where Devin and I grew up. On one hand, I'm excited to introduce my parents to Silas and Ruby, but on the other hand, I'm not looking forward to exposing them to Devin's lifelong tormentors.

In a strategic move, we book hotel rooms and rental cars so as to not trap ourselves in the inescapable tar awaiting us. That is, the tar of my parents being so happy to see us, they would smother us with their joy, and the diametrically opposed tar of Devin's family's glaring disappointment in his life *choices*.

I truly think Devin's parents thought he was just being difficult as a kid and that he would grow out of his need to displease them. You know, his disappointing gayness. They thought, with their staunch condemnation, he would snap out of his tiresome *phase*. When he did not, they took it as a personal affront on their parenting capabilities.

Their concern about how they would be viewed in society with a *'troubled'* or *'confused'* son completely overwhelmed their desire to nurture or accept Devin. To their loss, if you ask me.

My mom, on the other hand, was despondent that Silas, Ruby and I would not be staying with her and my dad. However, truth be told, she would have guarded my (*ahem, cough*) virtue…and put us up in different rooms.

Needless to say, I have not discussed Silas' BDSM club with her. Only that he works in commercial real estate and is raising his daughter on his own. The honor my mother sees in a man raising a child on his own luckily trumps the fact that he does, in fact, have a daughter…out of wedlock.

***

Almost upon touchdown of the plane's landing gear, Devin's agitation ratchets up to a dangerous threat level of, off the charts RED. This level of anxiety is reached even though Corey has already slipped him a Xanax before the flight and is about to repeat the dose.

Devin fumbles with his seatbelt, and when it doesn't immediately disengage, he shakes it and tries to yank it apart with the force of his temper tantrum instead of simply lifting the clasp.

After Corey gently reaches over and lifts the lever, freeing Devin from his own bluster, Devin stands too quickly and whacks his head on the overhead luggage compartment.

Corey raises both hands in the gentling posture of one trying to convince a wild boar not to charge. Devin calms, or pretends to, while standing awkwardly with his head bent to the side and the gale of the cabin fan blowing down his shirt.

Once he finally begins the long, indolent walk down the aisle, he stops to help an elderly man retrieve his luggage from the overhead bin. The man's wife smacks his hand with her cane—as if he were going to steal their carry-on instead of graciously assisting with the heft of it.

Devin pauses, slowly turning his head to the woman, and says, "I'm sorry…did you just *rap* me with your cane?" But before his inner pit viper can strike, Corey bulldozes him down the aisle like a linebacker, to deliver him safely off the plane without the flight attendants having to involve TSA.

***

Devin's hackles are still up at the way Corey manhandled him off the plane. So Corey knows enough to keep a safe distance behind while remaining vigilant for the next provocation.

Not surprisingly, Devin's calming influence is Ruby. Once off the plane, she slips her hand in his, as we all make our way to baggage claim. His shoulders loosen immediately.

She drags her rolling flower backpack, full of activities for bored little girls, behind her. The two of them walk ahead of us, jabbering away like reunited twins separated since birth.

In the last few months, ever since Devin first met Ruby, they have formed a really sweet bond. He and Corey take her places I would never have thought of for a six-year-old, like a fashion show where all the designs were made of paper, or the Art Museum or parkour gym where they pretend to be American Ninja Warriors. And when they talk on the phone, they whisper and giggle like little teenage girls.

"So level with me, Jessie, what do I have in store when we get there? Devin is so dramatic about them, are they really that bad?" Corey asks. His face is so warm and kind, it's hard to imagine someone disliking him on principle alone. His parents were fine when he came out, saying they had known all along, but he *did* face huge closeted obstacles in the military, so he is not naive about such things. I wonder if Corey's loving acceptance from his parents has anything to do with

241

what a kind person and gentle soul he is. I know Devin's past has been with him like a parasite, and I'm *sure* it contributes to his thorny personality.

"Corey, just be yourself. They tend to be more passive aggressive because they care so much about outward appearances. Their scorn will come more from snarky comments and leading questions. The good news is that they *love* me, so I will be able to deflect a lot of their shit. If that doesn't work, we will slip them some Roofies and raid their liquor cabinet on our way out," I laugh, but I'm not too sure I'm kidding.

"Thanks for coming, everyone. This is very important to Devin, and it will help having Y'all here." Corey says, with ten times more hospitality than we stand to receive at the Bachman's home.

"I'm not so sure Ruby will *let* them mistreat him." Silas grins and points to Ruby, who sits perched on Devin's shoulders. She is carrying her rolling backpack on her back now. "It's too bad she isn't going over there with us."

"They are little kindred spirits, aren't they?" Corey chuckles. "Is it still ok if we take her swimming at the hotel later tonight, after you see your folks?"

"Absolutely. She has a sense of him that is really touching; it will do him some good," Silas states as he takes my hand in his. "In fact, she is starting to want to be with you two more than with us."

"What kind of uncles would we be if we didn't spoil her? Plus, it was just Build-a-Bear, and the Aquarium…and the paper fashion show," Corey says, almost blushing.

"The fashion show was a little heavy-handed, don't you think? How can Silas and I compete with that?" I say, even though I love the relationship they have formed with her. It's the bond between them that has softened Devin toward Silas. Devin would never admit he was wrong about Silas, but I can see his guard is down. He will actually laugh at Silas' jokes now instead of eying him blankly.

"I'm taking Devin on a long hike later today. I need to keep him active, keep those endorphins flowing, or this trip will be the death of me. I guess the plan is dinner tomorrow night in the lion's den." Corey says.

"Yes, let's leave the hotel at the same time tomorrow and show up as a united front," I say. "Text me if you need anything, we will just be at my parents' house for the rest of the day."

"All right, but if I need anything, it will be an elephant tranquilizer," Corey says, as he hitches his military issue backpack higher on his shoulders and quickens his pace to catch up to Devin and Ruby.

"What about me? What do I have in store with your parents? Everything I have ever heard about them has been really touching. Like how they reacted when you left high school to replant Devin in better soil," Silas says, and I'm impressed he remembered the story I told him on our very first date.

"Well, my mom was starting to think I would die a very successful old maid, so she will be thrilled. My dad is harder to impress. If anything, he is skeptical about me finding anyone who would be willing to put up with my shit." I wink at Silas.

"We all have our crosses to bear," he laughs. "Actually, I kind of like putting up with your shit. It makes me feel a real sense of accomplishment."

"Oh stop, you've had it pretty easy."

"Yeah, I have. I just have never put up with it before—not from *anyone*," he shrugs but is still smiling.

"Nobody ever stood up to you before? Or gave you any shit?"

"No. Never."

"Why do you let me?"

"I guess because it's in your nature too. You know? Not to put up with anything less than you deserve."

***

My mom flings the door open and envelops me in her arms, crushing me against her as she utters, "Jessie, my girl. I'm so glad you are home." Ever since my parents have been empty nested, they seem to pine for the commotion of the past. Jonathan's cleats on the floor. My screeching violin practice. Alyssa's brooding music. The piles of laundry. And the bottomless pits of adolescent appetites that prompted my dad to offer to put a trough in the kitchen.

The house is too quiet now. Too serene with their cross-stitching and reading old history books. It's like they need the pulse back in the house again—need someone to drink straight out of the milk carton, or scream about who cleared the table last night or used all the hot water for their shower.

My dad pats Ruby on the head and then extends his hand to Silas. "Welcome, welcome it's so great to finally meet you. I'm Jessie's dad, Stewart. Come in, please. Anna, give the girl some breathing room we do have a few days you know."

My mom releases me but takes hold of my hands as she looks me over, then turns to Silas. She gives me a nod of approval before I notice a dampening behind her eyes. She really did think I would never find a man. Not because I couldn't, but because I have been so focused on my career. A fact she couldn't totally embrace with her old-school values and hunger for grandchildren.

If my mom is hungry for grandchildren, my dad is *starving* for them. I think he missed out on a lot of our childhoods working so much, and now he desperately wants to spoil some grandkids. It's like his noble act of atonement.

Silas shakes hands with my dad, nods at my mom—who hasn't let go of me just yet, and says, "It's great to meet you both, Jessie has told me so much about you." My mom blushes beneath his good looks and quickly looks away, smiling shyly.

As we enter the house, my dad smiles at Ruby and says, "My, my, aren't you sweet, I think I'll just dunk you in my coffee."

Ruby squeals with delight, "Noooo, not your coffee!"

My dad gives her a mock, threatening look then hugs me, kissing me on the temple. "Good to see you, Jessie."

I hug him tightly, taking in the familiar Old Spice aftershave scent from my childhood. He must have crates of the stuff. Every Christmas, birthday, or father's day, he received a lighthouse decanter or a glass lantern or ship's wheel full of it. The thought of the fancy glass bottles of aftershave makes me nostalgic

"Let's all head out to the patio. I've made lemonade, and we can sit and visit out there. Where is Devin?" my mom asks. I think she is hesitant to start without him. He has been such a part of our family, always with me like a fun new branch to our family tree.

"He will be here later, they are going for a hike." I glance around at the unchanged foyer, same slate floor, same lowboy, and mirror...same brass candle sconces. Thankfully they finally updated the old wood paneling in the family room a few years back, replacing it with a very sensible beige color. For the most part, though, my childhood home is pretty much the same—unless, of course, you go upstairs.

There my old bedroom, the one with gold flocked wallpaper, is now used as a room to store a treadmill and stationary bike—used maybe five times a year. Jonathan's room is designated as the guest bedroom. Alyssa's the craft room, for when my mom goes on her creativity jags and decoupages everything, or scrapbooks like a shut-in Martha Stewart.

I see my family a few times a year, usually for holidays but once you start to factor in everyone's work schedules, significant others and diverging agendas, it is becoming harder and harder to pull off trips home. Often, my parents do the traveling, and we converge on one of my sibling's homes. Or, like the past three Thanksgivings, at mine and Devin's condo.

"Silas, excuse my manners, I'm very pleased to meet you," my mom states formally. She extends her hand, appalled at her breach in propriety and as if just now realizing she never responded to his charming introduction. Silas shakes her hand then gives her a chaste hug.

"It's very nice to meet you too, Anna." My mom blushes, again taken by his handsomeness, but she recovers quickly.

"Shall we?" she says, as she leads the group to the flagstone patio. It's now covered by a wooden gabled roof, complete with skylights and a ceiling fan.

"I love the addition to the patio, I still remember the brown and cream striped canvas cover," I say, a little sentimental about the change.

"Yes well, it's been what…three years now since we covered the patio. Is that right, Stewart? Has it been that long already?"

"Yes, it has my Dear."

"Anyway, tell us, Silas, how did you and Jessie meet?" she says with a polite hostess smile, as she pours everyone a chilled glass of lemonade.

"We met at a young professionals meeting," he smiles warmly. I relax at his easiness with my mom, though he tells her an outright lie. I blush with the memory of his mouth on my nipple and my arms tied behind my back with my own panties.

"She was there with Devin, helping him to meet potential fabricators, and I was looking for business collaborators."

"How nice, and what is it you do?"

"Anna, give the man a minute to get comfortable, he has only just sat down," my dad says, playfully scolding her.

"Ok then, Miss Ruby, what do you like to do?" my mom asks in a conciliatory tone, hands placed properly in her lap.

"I like fashion. I'm going to be a fashion designer when I get big." She speaks while sliding off Silas' lap and running back into the house to retrieve her backpack.

"I'll show you!" she yells over her shoulder, not even slowing down.

"How nice," my mom says, unsure how to respond to a six-year-old's explosive energy.

When she returns with her backpack, my dad says, "Ruby, you come show me your designs. You wouldn't know it to look at me, but I'm very into fashion. Just look at how my shoes match my belt. You might think that's Anna's doing, but I'm the one who knows a thing or two about dressing well. I'm a real fashionista you know," he says, winking at my mom as Ruby climbs up next to him on the wicker couch, clutching her portfolio.

My dad's sarcasm is so similar to Silas,' she is used to the teasing tone. She gazes up at him with a knowing look and a very mature nod as if to say, *You and I both know that's not true.*

"Anna, the lemonade is delicious, thank you for taking the time to freshly squeeze it," Silas says to my mother.

Flattered, my mom smooths her hair and replies, "Oh, it's really nothing."

"Har!" my dad says over the top of Ruby's head, "She's been fluttering around here for days. You would have thought the Pope was coming to visit."

"Stewart, that's quite enough. Is it so bad to want everything to be perfect when our daughter finally brings a man home for us to meet?" My mom asks, in order to justify every pillow fluff and counter wipe down that preceded our visit.

"Am I the first man she has brought home for you to meet?" Silas asks, a smile curling his lips.

"Easy, you two," I say.

"Yes, well, except that boy who picked you up for prom in a convertible. Remember Jessie, after all that time spent on your hair?"

"Yep, that was a prom for the record books." I'm a little embarrassed by the memory, but happy my mom is finally starting to loosen up.

"She never dated anyone long enough to get serious. Her sister, Alyssa would always tease her about the flavor of the week. You know, lots of dates but no one special."

I groan, "Someone special in high school, Mom, Really?"

Silas laughs and sits forward, utterly engaged in my mother's account of my dating history.

"Is that right? I bet that was hard for you, I already feel like I'll be accompanying Ruby on all her dates."

"That's the truth of it, isn't it, Silas?" my dad pipes in. "I used to tell Jessie I would be introducing myself to her dates with a shotgun in my hand."

"Never mind the shotgun, I'll be in the front seat with them," Silas says, and I'm pretty sure he is serious.

"It's shocking that I never brought anyone home, right?" I ask sardonically, as I sit back and cross my legs. My embarrassment is, however, tempered by Silas' easy banter.

"In fact, Anna go get my shotgun, I would like to know Silas' intentions with our daughter," my dad says, grinning from ear to ear.

"Daddy is going to marry Jessie. Right, Daddy?" Ruby blurts out.

"We are working on that, aren't we, Rubes? Someday we'll reel her in," Silas says. He's totally comfortable with the awkward announcement and the sharp intake of breaths.

One of Silas' many talents is not rattling too easily. He has a certain grace about him that allows him to roll with the punches. He probably learned this trick long ago as a coping mechanism, considering all the outrageous things he has seen in the world of BDSM. He simply can't be easily shocked or surprised.

"Yes, Jessie is going to be my mom and you—" she points to my dad, "Are going to be my Grandpa," Ruby states this as a matter of fact, and my dad melts with her declaration, then raises a hand to his Izod covered heart.

"I think that would make me the happiest man on earth, but only if you like to go fishing," my dad says, and then pokes her in the belly. As Ruby is jumping for joy at the idea of fishing with a new Grandpa, Devin and Corey step out onto the patio.

"You really should lock the front door. Never know what might creep in," Devin says. My mom stands up and rushes to him, his welcome only slightly less than mine.

"Oh Devin, look at you! So handsome and rugged." She kisses his cheek, and they hug for a long time. Devin is absolutely basking in the maternal love he never knew inside of his own family. The smile on his face is the one that belonged there since birth, and would have been, had his circumstances been different.

"And you must be Corey! I'm so pleased to make your acquaintance," she says, while she shakes his hand and then decides, what the hell, and pulls him into a warm hug too.

My mom knows Devin had a hard time growing up, so she tends to lay it on really thick when it comes to him. She genuinely adores him, but she likes to make it *really* clear that she loves and accepts him. It's sweet, but sometimes it makes me wince a tiny little bit.

Devin loves my family, thinks of my parents as his own and Jonathan and Alyssa as his siblings. In fact, I can't even remember a Christmas or an Easter where he didn't have gifts or an Easter basket from my mom. Actually, since middle school he has spent every holiday with us, he has always been a fixture, and he fits like a glove.

Forgetting Silas and me entirely, my mom gushes over Devin and Corey and every detail of their wedding, though the details are terribly few.

My dad and Ruby set off to explore the property and probably to collect grasshoppers they can skewer with fish hooks at the lake.

Silas and I move to the porch swing to enjoy some quiet time alone before everyone reconvenes for lunch.

"I'm sorry if Ruby made you uncomfortable with the whole marriage thing," he says, leaning his head closer to mine. My legs are draped across his lap, as he rocks us absentmindedly with one foot.

"Are you kidding? If she didn't say it, my mom would have," I say, and we both laugh.

Chapter Thirty

Bachman's

We aren't headed to dinner at the Bachman's until six, but Devin is already as agitated as a wet cat, and it's only 11:30. Corey has dutifully planned a day of exertion in hopes of taming the shrew. What circuit sprints up and down the bleacher stairs at our high school and paddle boarding at the lake don't temper; we will surely deal with later.

Oddly, I think dinner might actually go well. If time has shown the Bachman's anything, it's that life is short. They only have one child, and he is all but lost to them. So I hope they see this little parlay as an olive branch and not a shot across the bow.

They have already missed out on so much of his life. I'm hoping they have softened over the years and have realized their *only* choice in the matter is to accept and love him or lose him forever.

There *is* a part of me that thinks Devin might just want to say, '*Fuck you. I turned out great no thanks to you fools, now piss off and die.*' But there is another part of me that knows he craves their acceptance, more of a, '*Hey Mom and Dad, look at me, I'm a good person.*'

Devin is amazing, smart, and successful, but he seems to need their love in order to understand his own value in the world. It's hard for me to understand because I have always had the love and support of my family, but I suppose lacking such a basic need *would* impact how someone perceives their own value.

Either way, tonight there will be somewhat of a reckoning. I'm just not quite sure for whom.

I feel strongly that this is Devin's last-ditch effort. If his parents don't get on board, he's done. In a way, the closure would be good. However, if it doesn't go in his favor, the damage would be hugely catastrophic. To not be good enough for your own flesh and blood would be incredibly damaging.

Up until now, avoidance has been Devin's shield, but once he faces the firing squad, he can't go back to avoiding. He will have to face the truth of it. I just hope they are finally able to see him as worthy and begin to rebuild their shattered relationship. Because if they don't accept him as he is, it will sever their relationship forever.

Silas, Ruby, and I are on our way to have lunch with my parents. After that, Ruby has her eyes set on the hotel pool, with the vision searing fog of chlorine and suffocating humidity among its many charms.

We decided from the beginning not to expose Ruby to this evening's dogfight, so she will happily stay with my parents. Watching her search for snakes in the field with my dad last night had settled it. It's a noble decision and better for all of us.

My parents have found an adventurous type of bliss with Ruby and are already treating her like their spoiled granddaughter. On the agenda tonight is popcorn, movies, and fort building.

When they asked what movie she wanted to watch, she didn't skip a beat when she said, The Greatest Showman. Little do they know, thanks to Analise's hearty obsession with musicals, Ruby knows every word and will belt out every song.

Chapter Thirty One

Family

As we approach the stately entrance to Devin's affluent childhood home, he turns and says, "Listen, if this goes sideways, none of you are under any obligation to stay." His hair is combed back in a preppy fashion that he would never wear at home, I suspect in an attempt to appease his high society, nose in the air parents.

"Got it, now take a deep breath and try to relax," Corey soothes, as he straightens the starched collar of Devin's dress shirt and gives him a peck on the lips. Corey's good nature is such a strong character trait; its influence soothes us all. It also reminds Devin that there is all the family he needs standing right behind him.

Devin runs his fingers through his hair, clears his throat, and knocks on the regal door. You would think we were at the Palace of Versailles with the showiness of the gaudy thing. No one would ever guess there's a staunch reformatory hidden within.

Devin's back is rigid as a plank while he waits. To an outsider, he looks haughty and brazen, but we all know the truth.

After an inordinate amount of time and two watch checks later, the door opens timidly but only partway.

"Hi, Mom," comes Devin's voice, it's strong though I know he doesn't feel it. The door opens the rest of the way while she stands planted to the ground, looking him over. It's been many years since she has laid eyes on him, so I wonder what she could be thinking.

Devin is a stunner. So handsome and put together. His hair is never tame, but always perfect, and his hazel eyes are currently glowing in the sunlight.

Next to him is Corey, with his strong chiseled frame, melted chocolate eyes, and military haircut. He is confidence personified, and dressed impeccably.

Each one of them on their own is enough to stop traffic, but together, *together*... they really should have their own solar system. What's a mother to think?

"Hi, Devin," her eyes dart around, taking in each one of us. She used to have the most beautiful brown hair. It was so soft and shiny it looked like it was spun from shimmering mink. Now, it's dyed too dark for her sallow skin, and it has the plastic look of a cheap wig.

"Come in everyone," she says.

I still can't get a read on what she is feeling. Does she want to embrace him and cry for all the lost time, or slap him for bringing a lover into her home and send him on his way? It's hard to tell because her countenance is so timid, almost frail, like something has drained out of her, life maybe.

The four of us crowd into the travertine entryway. An enormous vase of dusty silk flowers holds its ground in the middle of the foyer, causing us to feel cramped and unwelcome. The awkward clump of us, crammed in like a pack of trick-or-treaters coming in from the cold, all because Margret has yet to back up more than a few steps.

Uncomfortable to the highest degree, I charge forward, shimmying between Devin and Corey. "Margret, it's been so long," I say, as I tug her forward into a hasty yet firm embrace.

She startles at first but then returns the hug with a few quick taps to my back. Once the ice breaks, Devin steps forward to hug her, and the lump in my throat almost explodes. It's heart-wrenching to see the loss between them.

To her credit, she does welcome him into her arms, and she rests her head on his shoulder for quite a tender embrace.

While clustered in the foyer, Devin says, "Mom, I'd like you to meet Corey." Corey steps forward, shaking her hand and lightly kissing her cheek." None of us miss the fact that Devin has chosen not to introduce him as his husband.

"Hello, Corey." She is wringing her hands but is able to look him in the eyes.

"Mam," Corey nods.

"Supper's ready, would you all like to come in?" Margret asks as her voice incrementally gains strength.

As we make our way around the towering vase of flowers, I introduce Margret to Silas. Her cool expression and darkly dyed hair give her a sharp, aggressive appearance that she clearly doesn't mimic on the inside.

Silas smiles warmly, "It's a pleasure to meet you. This must be very overwhelming for you after all these years. We all certainly appreciate you opening your home to us."

Devin's mom smiles, I think with gratitude at his frank acknowledgment, but one can never tell with her. It could just as easily be a token of her self-sacrificing martyrdom.

"Where is Dad?" Devin asks, put off that his father hasn't bothered to greet us yet.

"I'm right here, Son," comes a deep voice from the library. His dad is standing right next to a brass liquor cart, leaning on it as if it hurts him to stand on his own.

The room is dim and lined with taxidermy sporting a dozen sets of vacant eyes. There is cherry wood Wainscoting and a large burgundy-toned Oriental rug that dominates the space. Books line the ponderous bookshelves making the space feel stuffy and overcrowded, though the room is dreadfully large.

"Oh, good. I'm parched. We all drinking Scotch?" I blurt out, crossing the room toward him at a fast clip. The tension in the air is so thick I feel like we all might drown in it.

"Hank, it's been a long time, how are you?" My discomfort shows itself with my restless impulse to simply get on with it. I tug him into a stiff hug, and you would think the man had never been hugged before, based on the rigidity in which he receives me.

"I'm well, Jessie," he says, as he turns toward the liquor and blessedly begins to pour three fingers of scotch for all six of us. He's dressed in head to toe tweed, so the herringbone pattern plays tricks on my eyes if I look too long at one spot.

The room is stuffy, he is stuffy, and no one is speaking, so I charge ahead with tragic compulsiveness and a complete inability to keep my mouth shut.

"Great, well this is my boyfriend, Silas, this is Corey—he's a Marine, fought for our country, spent nearly eight years overseas, you know, securing our freedom, aannnnnd... you've met Devin, he is a successful business owner, amazing cook and loves the outdoors." I throw back my entire glass of scotch as Silas grimaces and shakes his head slowly at me.

The amber liquid scorches my throat and sits in my belly like it was the whole cask instead of a huge swallow. Silas looks down, still shaking his head at my major breach in etiquette, and then draws everyone's attention to himself.

"Hank, I see you are a hunter." He graciously tries to save me from myself, while noting all the dead animal heads protruding from the walls. "Rifle or bow?"

Relieved by the shift in the room, I hazard a look at Devin, his stance is rigid, and his own glass is empty. Corey stands supportively right next to him. He radiates dignity and complete unflappability, ready and able to take on the dreaded Basilisk should the need arise.

"Well, Silas, I'll use a rifle, but I prefer a muzzleloader. Never had much use for a bow, them fancy things don't sit quite right in my hand," Hank says, enamored at the thought of another hunter in the room. Hank loosens up, seemingly thankful to engage in a manly conversation.

"Ah, a traditionalist. My father prefers a muzzleloader as well. I'm a thirty ought six Springfield guy myself. Did you and Devin ever do much hunting together?" Silas asks, innocently enough though I know better.

"No, Devin wasn't much of a hunter. Never could quite bring himself to pull the trigger. Said he wasn't comfortable taking a life," Hank says, his overgrown hair combed neatly back in damp salt and pepper rows.

"Ah, the gun range then?" Silas presses, though he doesn't want to monopolize the attention that should be squarely on Devin, *and* I think to draw some awareness to Hank's own shortcomings as a father.

"No, you never were much into guns, were you Devin?" his dad asks, with disappointment thick in his tone.

"Who had the time? What, with all the disappointing—"

Cough, Cough, Cough... "Oh goodness! I just choked on my own spit." *Coughcoughcough.* "Margret, may I have a glass of water?" I plead. *Cough...cough.* "I must have sipped my drink a little too quickly." *Cough.*

"Of course, Jessie. In fact, how about we all move to the formal dining room?" Margret directs us with a sweep of her arm and a bit of derision in her voice.

We all follow dutifully behind her, Silas cupping my butt and kissing my ear as he whispers, "You are quite the wrecking ball, aren't you, my love?" We follow the procession through two marble columns and into the formal dining room. Crisis averted...for now.

***

The dining room is heavy, like the air. It consists of bulky, oppressive brocade curtains, a cumbersome dining set—much too big for the room, chairs upholstered in stubbly worn velvet, and a massive mirror that sits above the sideboard. The layer of dust on the mirror makes the room feel even smaller, rather than more open and spacious.

"Dinner smells delicious, Margret," Corey says as he slips into his dusty, velvet, too big chair.

"Thank you, Corey. It's pot roast, one of Devin's favorites." She speaks as though she has always been motherly and attentive to Devin's needs, which we all know to be far from the truth.

"Sorry, Mom, I'm a vegetarian," Devin says, his face flat with smugness. She drops her arms to her sides in complete befuddlement, as if there's no length he won't go to in order to disappoint them.

"Just kidding, but see? It *could* get worse." He says this with ill-timed humor, or cynicism—depending on how you look at it. He has so much resentment inside him, it just bubbles out. He was quiet for so long, a victim of his own *indiscretions* and chiding parents, that it seems he is unable to hold his tongue now.

This time, it's Corey who comes to Devin's aid. "So, has Devin shared much with you about his business?" He looks amiably at Margret and then directs a heavier gaze on Hank.

"Oh, does he have his own business?" Hank inquires, eyes mildly interested. Apparently, business ownership is of small consequence when compared to tromping through the woods, preparing to lay siege against a grazing deer.

"Yes, he does. He's a lighting designer, with an extensive waitlist for his designs. His work is exhibited all over the country. He was even featured in *Architectural Digest* and *Dwell* magazine. You should be very proud. Your son is incredibly talented and highly regarded."

"That's fantastic," Margret says proudly, as though she had a hand in his success.

"Who are your clients, Devin?" Hank asks. His face is puffy and his nose rosy with broken capillaries that are now visible, thanks to the antique candelabra hanging above us, cobwebs and all.

"All kinds of people, Dad," and just when I think he is going to mention that he does work for heterosexuals as well, he adds, "Art galleries, lofts, restaurants, clubs, salons, private homes, country clubs, resorts, hotels, bars—really the list is endless... if they can afford me." He says this lightly, as he places his napkin in his lap.

He really has accomplished a tremendous amount and is incredibly successful. Now, he only takes on extremely high-end clients and only for obscene design fees. He *should* be proud of himself. He has more money in the bank than his stately childhood home is worth, yet he remains humble and down to earth. His parent's pretentiousness outshines his, and their house isn't even clean for his homecoming.

"And what about you, Corey, what is it that you do?" Hank asks, and it's a challenge. I now have decided he has the swollen, tired look of a lifelong alcoholic, and his eyes and skin look jaundiced and fragile.

"Well, Sir, as Jessie mentioned before, I'm a Marine, specifically an explosive ordnance disposal technician. So, I identify, neutralize and dispose of various hazards."

"Mm-Hmm," is Hank's only reply, and it's dull at that.

"In my field, I deal mostly with conventional devices, like high yield explosives and improvised explosive devices." Corey talks amiably while spooning out some pot roast and over-cooked vegetables onto his china plate, then passes the pot to Devin.

"What kind of training is involved with all that?" Hank asks as he scoops a huge dollop of lumpy mashed potatoes onto his own delicate plate of fine china.

"Well, Sir, I have a master's degree in computer science and a bachelor's degree in mechanical engineering," Corey says this completely conversationally, though Hank takes it as though Corey is trying to show him up.

Hank doesn't respond and instead turns his capricious eyes to me. "What about you, Jessie? What have you done with your life? I see your dad now and then down at the hardware store, doesn't talk much though."

I don't mention that my father despises him, or that he's lucky to get more than an obligatory wave out of my dad. "I work in oil and gas." I keep it short—no need to try and impress these two.

"You do all that fracking?" he grunts through a mouthful of mashed potatoes and shriveled up green beans.

"Not personally, no…" I pause, wondering if I should even bother, then dive right in. "You know it's perfectly safe, we've been hydraulic fracturing for over sixty years."

"I like my water clean," Margret says, her jaw stern as if she knows anything about fracking besides the recent trend toward renewable energy.

"There are thousands of feet of impermeable rock between the horizontal wells and any aquifers," I say, defending an argument that I have had countless times.

Devin surprisingly comes to *my* aid, fed up with his parent's perceived superiority. "Allow me to clarify a few things," Devin says, and we all brace ourselves. He clears his throat, "I am successful. Corey is smart. Fracking is safe. And I am gay." He puts both hands on the table beside his plate, evidently waiting for the figurative dust to settle.

"I just needed to get that out there, so we can all stop pretending. Mom, Dad, this is my husband, Corey. He is an amazing person if you choose to get to know him." His hands are still on the table, steady as can be.

"You're married?" Margret asks, stunned into the wide-eyed look of an owl. She wipes her mouth and places the lipstick stained napkin back on her lap, while Hank pours another glass of wine—nearly to the top of the crystal goblet.

"Yes, and I am happier than I have ever been. Are you at least relieved that I'm happy? Or do you prefer me angsty and withdrawn?" Devin spits out, his glaring eyes only *hinting* at the rage bottled inside of him.

"I, I, all I've ever wanted was for you to be happy," Margret says in a soft voice, looking to her lap as if even she knows this is a lie.

"You want me happy on *your* terms, with *your* convictions. Can you really say you want me to be happy *how I am?*"

"Yes," even smaller voice, she can hardly push the word out.

"Devin," Hank pipes in, "You come from a long line of Bachman's. We are a proud family, worked hard for our place in the world. Do you even know what your grandfather had to endure just to secure a better life for us? For you? Huh? All those struggles, all those years just barely squeaking by, and look how far we've come." He sweeps his hand around as if to establish the prosperity, while ignoring the neglect.

"Well, son, you're it, the last one. The name dies with you if you don't have children. And just how do you hope to carry on the family name without a proper wife and family?" Hank challenges, with his face reddening before he slams down his fist. I'd say he had lost his appetite, but he didn't, which is evidenced by the gnawing mouthful of roast he shoves past his teeth.

"Is that all you want? For me to carry on the family name? Even if family doesn't mean shit to you?" Devin shouts. This fight was a long time coming, but if Devin truly lets go, the bridge will burn to cinders because Hank clearly isn't backing down from his generations-old convictions.

"Devin," Corey puts a hand on his lap to stop him. "What I think Devin means is tha—" Corey attempts to smooth the raging waters but is interrupted.

"I know exactly what he means!" Hank roars, red as a beet now.

Silas looks to me, probably waiting for me to throw myself off the chair in a fake choking incident, but he just raises his eyebrows, unsure of what to do. The candid look in his eyes says he's not too far off from decking Hank himself.

"Actually, Devin will be able to carry on whatever name he chooses to," I say. It's like my mouth has a motor that I can't shut off. All eyes are on me as I trudge on, through the murkiness. "Devin and

Corey are two of the greatest people I know. They will be the parents you could never be." *Stop talking, Jessie*!

Again Silas tries to deflect the attention from me, "You know Hank, these guys have been absolutely wonderful with my daughter. She adores them, and they love her. You really should consider that there are all types of families nowadays."

"And how exactly is that? We will die old and gray before we ever have any grandchildren," Hank laments.

Devin erupts, "You don't deserve grandchildren! You had *one* kid, and you fucked that up! And now you want the one you ruined to give you grandchildren?" Devin shouts while standing up, his chest heaving.

"You *will* be grandparents, but you will have to earn the right to be involved in their lives," I say, and it cuts through the room like a broadsword.

All eyes are on me, the simmering, rage-filled ones, the meek, holding back tears ones, the cautious, protective ones, and Silas'... with knowing acquiescence.

Devin turns back to glare at his dad, his mom is quietly weeping into her napkin. Silas looks at me and knows what is about to happen. In solidarity, he places a hand on top of mine and curls his fingers around my shaking hand.

"I am going to carry their baby," I announce. "Now, can you please pass the gravy?"

Chapter Thirty Two

Pool

There is a resounding echo around the indoor hotel pool. Splashing water, muted voices, and unrestrained little girl giggles, all sound as if they are coming from under a dome. As I lie on the inadequately inflated raft—drinking wine straight from the bottle, I realize the echo is coming from inside my head. *I'm going to carry their baby.*

The responses were varied. Corey genuinely had choked on his wine, Devin looked at me like I was crazy, and the Bachman's, with their mouths gaping open and faces ashen, looked as if they had seen a ghost.

Silas kept things moving tidily along by actually passing me the gravy I had asked for and then saying, "Won't that be wonderful? A baby in the family. What do you think, Margaret, a girl, to wrap her daddies around her little finger? Or a little boy for them to throw the football with?"

When she didn't respond, or even close her mouth, Corey had added, "Well, there is certainly a lot to discuss first." He had widened his eyes to a ridiculous degree at me, in complete shock, then turned and continued directly to the Bachman's. "I hope you know, we would cherish a child. I understand your reservations, but truly, our child would never be hurt by our lifestyle, only loved to the ends of the earth. Your grandchild would be so blessed, so adored."

Hank's response had been despondent and had preceded our sudden and immediate departure. He had simply asked, *"How could you do that to a child?"*

My ruminations are interrupted by Silas' stealthy, underwater advance, and Ruby's chant, "Get her, Daddy!" When he surfaces next to my hip, I say, "If you dilute my wine with this pool water, we're done."

He laughs before disappearing like a Navy Seal back under the water, heading back to grab at Ruby's vulnerable, swimming legs.

Devin and Corey had taken off after our abrupt departure from dinner, and I don't expect to see them for a while, maybe not even until we get back home.

Devin's way of dealing with disappointment is usually to run away from it, but this latest blow, he will never be able to outrun. Frankly, I'm glad Corey is tending to him instead of me because I have my own crap swirling around in my head.

In fact, *swirling* is a good word because I'm plastered. If I hadn't been on this raft all along, I would have already drowned. I can't believe my big mouth. I had wanted to shut his parents up in a big way, but this feels too real now. It's out there, in the universe, and I can't take it back. My declaration, my sacrifice. My big fucking mouth.

I can't even begin to think about everything involved with getting pregnant with someone else's baby. What will my family think? Or Silas' family, especially Ruby? What about my job? And my body, I will be lactating for Christ's sake.

I start ineffectually paddling to the side and tell Silas and Ruby that I need to go to bed. My drunkenness is pervasive and thick, and if I can actually make it up to our room, I'll probably pass out face down on the bed.

Silas helpfully guides my raft to the edge of the pool and stabilizes it while I kind of jelly-roll off the side onto the packed pebble pool deck.

"Need a hand, Pipes? We can come up too," Silas offers. It's sweet, but I want to be alone…or invisible, one of the two, maybe both.

"No, I got this."

***

Once on the hotel elevator, it's that final lurch when stopping at my floor that brings the vomit. Luckily, Providence has provided a trash can between the two elevators.

I throw up with such force that it hits the far side of the can liner and slides down into a vat of regret and images of my own looming stretch marks.

After far too long with my face in the trash can, I straighten up. I can't say the receptacle will ever be the same, but my body feels almost purged from the night's disasters. I am, however, reminded of said disasters, due in part to the lingering taste of scotch on my tongue.

If I could just wad up the evening and stuff it in the trash can with my puke, I would. Everything, the scotch, the pot roast, the Bachman's, the dusty furniture, the closet alcoholic father, the pretentiousness, all of it…especially my declaration.

***

"How do you feel?" Silas' words are delivered delicately, but they still sound like they're coming from a blow horn. I cringe and try to crack my eyes open. My mouth is sticky and disgusting, and it feels like it's been soldered shut.

"Like hammered shit," I groan. The headache comes on in waves, one second feeling almost like it's not there and the next like it's trying to bulge my eyes right out of my head.

"Shut the curtains," I whisper.

"Sit up and drink some water, then Rubes and I will leave you alone and go get breakfast," he says. I can smell hotel soap and the herbal, camphorous scent of his shaving cream.

"Is there any chance last night was a dream?" I mumble against the pillow.

"I'm afraid not. Why, are you having a bit of buyer's remorse?" he asks, as he runs an ice cube across my parched lips.

"Would I be a bad person if I said, yes?"

"No, Jessie, you would be human."

Chapter Thirty Three

Cage

Once the proverbial dust from our trip has settled a bit, and Devin is speaking in full sentences again—instead of badly tempered grunts and clipped remarks, he throws himself into house hunting with the strength of a gale force wind. Ruby is his designated interior design expert and has been assisting him in his search whenever she can.

The fact that she demands a window seat or reading nook in a home before she will grant her consideration is of little consequence to Devin. In fact, I have heard him discuss the houses with her as if her opinion were paramount to his decision-making ability.

He has said, "Ruby, what did you think about that wine cellar? The one with exposed rock." She had scrunched her nose, so he went on, "You're absolutely right, in fact, I think Fortunato is still looking for the Cask of Amontillado... Never mind, it's a little too early for Poe references. What about the one with the huge farmhouse sink?" Ruby's answer was that she didn't like the floor plan. To which Devin replied, "You're right. I'm glad you're here as my design consultant. Floor plans are *obviously* of the utmost importance."

Devin does not want to talk about the implosion at his parent's house and bats away anything that hints in that direction. I swear, if

Salinger could have just five minutes with him, the axial tilt of the earth would right itself.

Unfortunately, Devin is not one to expel his anger. He would rather repress it and pretend it's not there—simply letting it seep out of his every pore.

He and Corey are talking about backpacking through Europe for a few weeks. And you will never convince me that the whole idea is not his attempt at running away. As if the expanse of the ocean is enough to nullify his pain.

Truth be told, I'm on board with the extended trip because it's hard for me not to absorb all his shit right along with him. Streamlining my stressors right now is important because I'm already on the razor's edge of my own psychotic break.

I hear the front door slam, announcing Devin's arrival home, so I cautiously make my way into the living room. Lately, I'm not sure what to expect when I see him, poison darts, or gushing stories about his house hunt.

"Sup, Sugar?" he is amenable, thank God.

"Nothing much. How was the showing?"

"The design aesthetic was a little too Coastal for me. Ruby loved it, sea grass on the walls and all," he shrugs.

"Devin, you can change the interior decorating of the home. You should be looking at the structure of it, the location, stuff like that—not the paint on the walls or the cheap furniture."

"Indeed. But there was coral everywhere. I'd never be able to wipe it from my memory," he says, as he steps out of his shoes and falls onto the couch.

"You're going to gut anything you find and put your own spin on it anyway. Maybe you're just not ready."

"Speaking of not being ready. Are you about there—with regard to the condo? Seriously, make me an offer, and it's yours."

"Devin—"

"Say a number."

"I haven't even talked to a lender yet."

"A number Jessie. You know you want it...a doorman, laundry, central location...*two parking spaces.*"

"I haven't even thought about it yet, Dev."

"How about what I paid for it?"

"Are you insane?"

"That's not really up for debate, is it? Because, as you well know, I have been insane since birth."

"I wouldn't feel comfortable... I mean, it's appreciated so much in value since you bought it."

"Then what I paid, plus fifty."

"Fifty grand?"

"Or dollars, either way," he shrugs, and it's obvious he really doesn't care. Money means very little to Devin, which is ironic because he is rolling in it.

"Besides, you have been here paying rent the whole time. So the equity is yours too." I pause for a moment and then realize I *do* want to stay here.

"Ok, what you paid, plus fifty grand." His face splits into a huge smile, a genuine smile for the first time in a while.

"Deal!"

***

When I woke up this morning, I realized two things right away. One, I had slept through the night, no nightmares. In truth, the strength and frequency of my nightmares have been steadily dwindling in the last few weeks, but to actually sleep through the night and not wake up anxious every few hours just to think, and worry about life, is downright liberating.

The other thing I realized is that I'm super excited to buy Devin's condo. It will be the first time in my life that I live by myself, and I'm looking forward to being a grown-up. I will paint the walls and buy new furniture, really make it my own.

Now that I have made a decision about where to live after Devin buys a house with Corey *and* the fact that my uterus has been granted an extended reprieve, I can take deep breaths again. Corey and Devin's indefinite trek through Europe has me feeling almost calm for the first time in ages.

"What's that dopey grin for?" Salinger asks while peering across the desk at me through his dark-rimmed glasses.

"Nothing, I'm just relaxed, that's all." I spark to attention and refocus on the leasehold transaction glaring at me from Salinger's turned laptop. He shifts uncomfortably in his seat again and begins chewing on the end of his pen.

"You seem fidgety, you got ants in your pants?"

"I wish it were ants, JB." Now he stands and pushes down the legs of his slacks as if they are bunching or crowding his impressive package. Then he sits back down, no more comfortable than he was before.

"Did you get crabs from Bradley?"

He scoffs.

"Gonorrhea?"

"No."

"Chlamydia?"

"No, Jessie, just leave it alone, will you?" He looks away from me as if that will stop my questions.

"Salinger, what's wrong?" I reach my hand across the desk and lay it on his. "I'm done teasing. What's bothering you?" My demeanor has immediately shifted into caring, protective mode.

"It's not a big deal. Can you just look over the lease?" Now he seems in a hurry to leave, and I want to stop him from dashing back to his office.

"You can tell me anything, you know. Nothing you say will damage how I feel about you." I want him to feel comfortable talking to me even if he did pick up something nasty. He surprises me by laughing.

"I don't have any STD's Jessie, but thanks for your show of support." He squirms in his seat again but doesn't take his hand away from underneath mine.

"Why are you so edgy? Something is clearly bothering you." I close his laptop and scoot it to the side of my desk.

"You really want to know?" he challenges. Then he stands up and knocks three times on his dick. It makes a solid thunking sound with each rap. Then he quickly sits back down.

"Ok? Can we drop it now?"

"You are wearing a cock cage?" I ask. I'm a little stunned, and then a smile creeps across my face.

"Yes, and mark my words, Jessie, this is the last time. My dick is trying to get hard right now, just from that little jostle. I can't stand it anymore." He looks too sincere for me to tease anymore, but the questions abound.

"How long?"

"This is only my second day…out of four. Although I'm seriously thinking about slamming my penis in the car door just to break the damn thing off."

Just as I am forming a response, my cell phone rings. It's my college roommate.

"Hi Tori, long time no see. Wait, you're pregnant again, right?"

"Hell no! Ryan's only eight months old. I told Tyler he needed to get snipped before I'd let him touch me again. The little shit thought about it for three months before he finally did it!"

"Three months? Wow. Well, if you're not pregnant, we should meet for a drink."

"That's exactly why I'm calling; Krissy is back in town for the weekend, so I sent emails out to the whole crew for a girl's night out this weekend."

"Oh, nice! I could use a girl's night out."

"K, check your email, and we'll catch up Saturday."

"Great, I'm looking forward to it." I glance at Salinger as I push end. He is sitting back in his chair and smiling at me.

"What?"

"Girl's night out, huh? Any hot, single friends I should know about?" He widens his eyes with curiosity.

"No, they are mostly married with little kids. They hardly ever go out anymore. But yes, every one of them is hot." I wink at him before I open his laptop again.

"As if I would ever set you up with one of my girlfriends. Pshh, I'm keeping you for myself."

"You just let me know when you're ready, JB."

Chapter Thirty Four

Girls Night

"Why can't I come? Them my Bitches too," Devin says as he flops down on my bed.

"Because you have a penis," I say while stepping into my skirt and wiggling my hips to help shimmy it up.

"Thank Christ for that."

"And because you told Silas you would hang out with Ruby tonight. He *still* has to work late, and Analise *still* has weekends off."

"You would hardly notice us," he says, as he rolls onto his belly then cradles his face in his palms. "What's the kid count up to these days anyway?" His comment about kids makes me pause, but when I realize he has no hidden agenda, I resume breathing.

"Tori has two, Vanessa and Paige each have one, and Krissy has none. Her job is way too demanding."

"Ah, the trials of life as an executive."

"She has a fantastic job, Devin. Not all women pine to be mothers." I regret saying it as soon as it's out of my mouth, but Devin seems dutifully unaffected.

"Are these thigh-high socks?" he asks, in a completely random departure from the topic.

"Yes, Devin, they go under my knee-high boots. Hasn't Ruby taught you anything? They show at the top of the boot. It's cute." I snatch them from his hand and sit on the edge of the bed to tug them on.

He sighs dramatically, "Alright, I guess Ruby and I will hit the red light district instead, see if we can pick up some drugs and hookers," he says as he rises from my bed.

"Make sure you wear sensible shoes," I call out to his retreating back.

***

I'm meeting the girls at a Mexican restaurant that's famous for its insanely strong margaritas. It seems fitting because tequila, tortilla chips, and salsa were some of our main food staples back in college.

When I approach the front door of the restaurant, the outdoor speakers are blaring festive Mexican music, which is swallowed up by the rambunctious crowd as soon as I step through the door.

I have to fight through the horde of tipsy patrons and manage to have not one, but *two* people slosh their too full margaritas on me, a baptism of sorts, I guess.

When I finally see my friends, they are standing around a tall bar table with a foamy pitcher of margaritas in front of them. They hoot and holler, drawing all kinds of attention to themselves as they wave me over.

After a round of hugs and an aggressive kiss on the cheek from Krissy, she asks, "What's on your shoulder, Jessie?" She lives in Los

Angeles now, and of all my friends, it's been the longest since I have seen her.

"It's tequila, of course. My neck too. I always like to feel a little sticky when I'm out with my girls. Where is Tori?"

As if in answer to my question, Tori arrives with a tray of shots. Each one has an edge dipped in salt and a lime perched on the rim. Her short dark hair is styled in the most perfect artistic curls. She looks exotic in an edgy way. Her eyebrow is still pierced from when we went to the tattoo/piercing studio together years ago—her brow, my upper ear, or as she insists—my Helix piercing.

Vanessa pours me a margarita from the pitcher and asks, "Tequila shots already?" Her tone is not one of disappointment or even weariness, but of pure amusement.

"Yes, Ma'am, Mama finally has a night off!" Tori says. Then we all pluck a shot glass from the tray.

"Cheers to the people who love us, the losers who lost us, and the lucky bastards who get to meet us," Tori calls out, as we all lick the salt, slam the tequila and bite the lime in well-practiced synchronicity.

***

We have burned through three pitchers of margaritas, reminisced about old times, and caught up with everyone's hectic lives—minus my kink and incubator status for now, when a group of well-dressed guys approaches us, carrying another round of shots.

"Hello there, ladies. We thought you looked lonely, so we brought tequila." They introduce themselves as Justin, James, Tom, and Douglas before I hold up my hand and speak.

"Hold it. Are there…or are there not…Roofies in these shots?" and if I'm being honest, my speech is a tiny bit slurred.

The tall, sandy-haired one, Justin I think, turns to me and says, "No Roofies, I promise, but you do look very pensive. What can I do to put a smile on your beautiful face?"

My tequila-soaked brain is too muddy to come up with a snarky remark, but Vanessa is quick to the gate, "You could try a pants-down-handstand. That might put a smile on her face." The entire table erupts with laughter, then Tom…or James, whichever one has the shaved head and green eyes, proposes that if Justin can make me laugh, then we all take the shots. We agree, and I look to Justin with my eyebrows raised, challenge accepted.

Justin slides closer to me and with a very intent look on his face, he begins. "A man named Seamus is sitting at the bar one night. He is depressed with his head down on the bar when the bartender approaches and asks him what is wrong. The man replies (insert heavy Scottish accent) 'Do you see that bridge over there?' The bartender answers, 'Aye, Seamus. That's a verra fine bridge.' 'I built that bridge with my own two hands, ' Seamus says, 'but do they call me *Seamus the bridge builder?* No, they don't. Do you see that house over there?' Seamus asks the bartender. 'Aye that's a verra fine house,' the bartender replies. 'I built that house for my family, but do they call me *Seamus the house builder?* No, they don't. Do you see that wagon over there?' Seamus asks. 'Aye that's a verra fine wagon,' the bartender replies. 'I built that wagon with my bare hands; does anybody call me *Seamus the wagon builder?* No, they don't…But you fuck *one* goat…'"

I laugh in spite of myself, the guys high five, and my friends all accept their shots with drunken compliance.

Our table is loud and obnoxious with cheers of "Salud" and howling laughter, not at the story of Seamus but at Justin's boisterous telling of it.

After my nasty shot of warm tequila, I excuse myself to go to the bathroom, and Krissy and Tori do the same. Krissy bushwhacks us through the lively crowd, and the three of us stumble into the bathroom, snorting and giggling like it was our first time drinking alcohol.

Tori is clinging to me in an effort to stay upright. "Fuck, it's been a long time since I have had a drink. I've been pregnant or nursing for like three years straight!" she says, as the door to a bathroom stall opens, and she careens forward, nearly plowing through the women exiting the stall.

This is funny in and of itself because Tori has completely ignored the two empty stalls right next to the one the woman was in.

"You should have paced yourself," the woman says, in a superior tone that Tori takes exception to.

"And you should have burned that sweater, but I guess hindsight is 20/20, right?" Tori spits out, while the sour-faced woman hastily washes her hands and snatches a few paper towels on her way out.

As soon as the humorless woman leaves the bathroom, the three of us whoop with unrestrained laughter. Tori has always been a spitfire, I'm happy to see being a wife and mother hasn't changed that.

"We need Ubers and our beds. We are so out of practice that we blew our wads at the first bar," Krissy says, while holding on to the paper towel dispenser like a life raft, only partly due to her seriously high heels.

I step into the next stall while Tori muses to herself, "It's not like we drank all that much. They were just really fucking strong."

As I'm awkwardly trying to hover above the toilet seat while peeing like a trained racehorse, I clumsily pull my phone from my purse and tap Silas' number. When it rings through to voicemail, I press end.

Tori, Vanessa, and Paige all live on the north side of town, and Krissy lives in L.A but is staying with Tori, so they will all get a cab or Uber together tonight. I happen to be just sober enough to know that I'm too drunk to get in anyone's car by myself, and Silas isn't answering his phone, so I do the next best thing.

"Jessie, are you ok?" Salinger answers, he sounds groggy.

"Oh, I'm jus fi-ne," I say. "Wanna come meet my friends?" I give up on hovering and sit down on the toilet seat, which is now splashed with my own urine and toilet water.

"You're drunk, where are you?" He is more alert now.

"I'm in the bathroom, but I gotta get back to my girls, we left them alone with a group of w-wolves."

"What bar?" I can tell he is rushing to get dressed with all the scuffling in the background, and I can picture him hopping on one foot while holding the phone with his shoulder and shoving his foot into the leg of his jeans.

"Ah, it's…it's La Cantina. On 14th. But Saling-er…don't flirt with my friends, Ok?"

***

The night is brisk, and that fact along with the blaring speakers outside of La Cantina helps to revive us from the tequila haze that has settled around each one of us. Paige is exchanging numbers with, I think James. But that isn't that scandalous because she admitted earlier that she and her husband have been separated for three months and are filing for divorce. So, good for her. Way to get right back up on the horse, Paige.

We are all clustered together under the squawk of Mariachi horns, laughing because Vanessa has just belted out, "But you fuck *one* goat!"

284

This is the moment when Salinger marches up, hands shoved into the front pockets of his jeans. "Hey ladies, you all get a little tuned up tonight?" He is wearing beat up old jeans, a white t-shirt, his sexy glasses, and a stubbly-faced smile. I watch as all my friend's mouths drop open, and he steps through our little group toward me.

"Salinger! Hi!" I fling my arms around his neck as he lifts me off the ground, almost crushing me with his huge hug.

"You a little ripped, JB?" he mumbles into my ear, then kisses my cheek before setting me down. He still has me tucked under his wing, and it's cute and protective, so I loop my arm around his waist. The truth is, I can use the support; his attractiveness is just a bonus.

"Hi sexy, who might you be?" Vanessa asks while looking him up and down.

"Salinger, this is Vanessa, Krissy, and Tori. And that over there, kissing that perfect stranger, is Paige. Girls, this is my friend, Salinger."

"You ladies smell like Margaritas," Salinger says as he sniffs my hair.

"It's Jessie, she dumped a little marg down the side of her neck," Tori says, and then blows a perfect corkscrew curl out of her vision.

"She was saving it for you—little salt, little tequila, little lime..." Krissy adds.

"Is that right?" Salinger eyes me playfully.

"Go ahead, Salinger...take your shot," Tori again.

I'm just drunk enough to tip my head back and present my neck to him. He surprises me by licking my skin from collarbone to ear, raising goosebumps down my neck, and making my nipples pulse.

"Mmmmm, I just found my new favorite drink," Salinger says, as he smiles at Tori in that panty-dropping way that comes so naturally to him.

She fans herself and says, "I might have spilled a little down here too." She motions to her cleavage and wags her eyebrows. She is kidding, but I'm not sure she would stop him if he went for it.

"One's my limit, I'm driving tonight," he says, with a shy smile.

"Jessie didn't tell us she has a hotty on the side," Vanessa says, her caramel-colored eyes both questioning and impressed, as she taps the toe of one suede slingback heel.

"He's not my hotty. He is seeing a little nympho that makes him wear a cock cage!" As I say this, and with complete reckless, drunken abandon, I drop my hand to his package expecting to feel the same hard plastic he had thumped in my office. Instead, I feel him freeze, suck in a quick breath and begin to harden in my hand.

I yank my hand away just as Krissy exclaims, "No fucking way! A cock cage?" Her statement blessedly redirects the focus away from my major breach and allows Salinger and me a moment to recover.

"I don't actually recommend it," he says, and I can feel the tension in his body. It's almost like he is holding his breath.

"It would be a shame to cage such a majestic beast," Tori says, just as her phone vibrates in her hand. She glances at the screen and announces, "Our Uber is here. Paige, rein it in, it's time to go."

After hasty goodbyes and promises to do this more often, the girls pile into their waiting Uber, and within minutes, Salinger and I are alone.

I look sheepishly up into Salinger's face, "I'm sorry I grabbed your cock. I wasn't thinking."

"Fuck…don't apologize, all I can think about is you doing it again." His face is ashen, like he is fighting a battle within himself. He removes his arm from around my shoulder and turns me to face him.

My heart is thrashing in my chest, every nerve impulse in my body is firing all at once, and within the tiny pause between us, I can imagine myself kissing him. It would be tender and sweet, yet hungry and determined, and I would melt into him. I would never want him to stop.

"I need to get you home. Do you want to grab anything from your car?" he asks, and he is completely composed again. He must not realize the horrendous turmoil I'm in. I'm in so deep, I'm suffocating.

I lean into him, burying my face in his chest as he wraps his arms around me. I don't know how long we stand like this, but for long minutes all I can do is breathe. Breathe in the muffled air, breathe in his warm scent, and breathe in the *what could have been*. It's excruciating, and I can't bring myself to move.

Finally, Salinger says, "Come on, let's get you home."

Chapter Thirty Five

Implosion

I'm just returning from Salinger's office with a batch of files. It's Monday morning, and I'm not surprised to find that he has completely moved on from Saturday night. He is acting as though nothing out of the ordinary happened.

Strictly speaking, nothing did happen. He simply drove me home, accompanied me safely to my door, told me to have a good night, and left me burning with the memory of his tongue on my neck.

Thankfully, Sunday morning Silas and Ruby arrived with coffee and breakfast burritos, so my hangover was successfully thwarted.

Silas and I made love in the shower while Ruby watched TV. The sex was slow and passionate, harmonious in a way that was new for us. I found myself clinging to him, afraid if I didn't hold him tight enough, he would disappear forever.

Now, after mostly recovering from my weekend, I have a lot of work to do. Nearly three-quarters of the files retrieved from Salinger are records that I need to audit so I can report the acreage to the investors. The rest of the stack requires paying out royalties to mineral owners.

This is one of those days where I send all my calls to voicemail, and my emails go mostly unanswered.

I hear my office door open, but I'm in the middle of calculating a hefty royalty, so I don't immediately look up. When I hear my receptionist say, "Can I help you, Sir?" The harsh tone of her voice catches my attention, and I look up to see Silas standing just inside my office.

"Hey, babe—" I start, but right away, I see that something is wrong. Silas is angry. His face looks hardened with pure contempt. He closes the door and stalks up to my desk. He has a look in his eyes that I don't recognize; it's a blackness or a rage that doesn't fit him.

I stand and open my mouth to speak, but he silences me by tossing a manila envelope onto my desk. It slides across a suddenly meaningless file and comes to a winding stop.

My receptionist Adelaide pokes her head in and asks if I want her to call security.

"No. No, of course not," I stammer. "Everything is fine." Then I repeat it, "Everything is fine," while hoping to convince myself that everything is not about to implode.

Silas crosses his arms across his chest and sets his jaw for battle. His nostrils are flaring, and I can see how heavy he is breathing.

"What is this?" I ask, my voice is pensive, and my mouth is suddenly dry.

"I was hoping you could tell me that," he grinds out, holding his aggressive stance.

Afraid to sit back down, I reach for the manila envelope and turn it over in my hands. It has Silas' name and address on it but no return address. I tip it over, and a small stack of 8x10 photos slips out.

The one on top is a close-up of me with my head tipped back. I'm smiling in what looks like ecstasy while Salinger has his face and tongue buried in the side of my neck. The photo is deceiving and looks incredibly intimate the way he is holding my face and passionately *kissing* my neck. Ironically, the image captures the necklace Silas gave to me, the one claiming me as his.

I slide the photo off the stack and try to lick my lips, but my tongue feels like carpet. Someone took the next photo when I had leaped into Salinger's arms in greeting. It looks like he is a soldier returning from war, and I look every bit like his doting wife welcoming him home.

Both pictures look as if we were completely alone, instead of among a crowd of my friends. I push it aside.

Someone snapped the next one during our long embrace before he took me home. There is no question about it, we look like lovers. I don't even want to see the rest. I'm sure they all misrepresent what was really happening.

I know I'm tempted by Salinger...a ton, but I am utterly, dizzyingly, in love with Silas.

"It's not what it looks like, Silas." My voice is impassioned, but it doesn't make a dent in his armor.

"Oh no? I think it's *exactly* what it looks like. There are not a whole lot of ways to interpret these, Jessie!" I have never seen him so angry. His reaction to the photo book pales in comparison. The repetitive tick in his jaw even seems ferocious.

"You had me followed?"

"No, I didn't fucking have you followed! You see, the funny thing is, I actually trusted you!"

"Let me explain."

"No. There is no explanation necessary." He turns and storms out of my office before I can even form words.

Adelaide rushes into my office, asking if I'm ok. She makes quick darting glances back and forth between Silas' retreating frame and my bloodless face.

"Nope. I am most assuredly, not ok."

Keep Reading for a Sneak

Peek of Book 3,

1700 Grant Street

Dedication:

This book is dedicated to everyone who has jumped into this series with both feet. What started as me wondering if I could actually write a book, blossomed into so much more. I could never have done justice to Devin, Corey, and Salinger without continuing the series, and they are so much more than secondary characters to me. Books 3 and 4 dive even deeper into each character and weave them together beautifully. I can't wait for you to see what happens next!

—KC

Also by KC Decker:

Standalone Books

Little Dove

My name is Etta Freeman.

There is something special about me.

Not special in a good way, though, more like special in a way that will get me killed one day.

It's not something I talk about with anyone, but that doesn't stop me from trying to snare my neighbor in my devious web.

He is angsty and brooding and completely sexy in a scrappy, bloody knuckle kind of way.

I should also mention that he's a scheming, felonious drug dealer and I'm drawn to him like flies on shit.

The problem is, he doesn't yet know his role in my narrative, but he will fall in line.

They always do.

Trigger Warning: Little Dove contains content that some readers may find distressing.

Of Ash and Angels

** Silver Medal Winner of the International Reader's Favorite Book Awards*

Justin:

I've never had a therapist I didn't want to punch in the face. As a collective group, they all say there is no way around grief, only through it, but for me, grief has become who I am. The idea of shedding it is as ludicrous as stepping outside of my own skin.

The fact is, some things can break you. I mean, shatter your soul and cast it into the wind in a billion tiny pieces. To think you might one day be able to find all those infinite pieces of yourself, patch everything back together, and move on with life—well, I don't even need to dignify that with a response.

Norah:

A few months ago, I shaved off a hundred and eighty-five-pound parasite. Then, once I was rid of him, I wondered why I didn't stick it out because the dating world is treacherous these days. Turns out, so is unemployment.

I suppose, to offset all the swiping left and streaming marathons in my life, I should take this job. There is a massive problem with the position, though.

The problem's name is Justin Abernathy.

Gradation

Friends. Ride or die, right?
Always have your back.
Know all your dirty little secrets.
Love the shiny parts of you, and embrace the crappy ones.
Yeah? Well, I don't know about all that nonsense because my friends are a bunch of assholes.
They're taking over.
They're commandeering my love life.
They're constructing a dating profile for me, and it's bad…
Because I don't even have the *password* for it,

and I have to do *exactly* what they say.

Mercy

**INTERNATIONAL BOOK AWARDS FINALIST and
KIRKUS FEATURED REVIEW RECIPIENT!**

My parents abandoned me a decade ago to the walls of this institution. They believed my troubled childhood mind was something sinister instead of homegrown or explainable. The truth is that my condition is complicated. It's messy and often misunderstood.

I've worn all types of labels over the years: Non-believer, pariah, deranged, *orphan*... It's all in my file if you care to understand me better. However, the label that implanted the deepest and garnered the most attention is the one I wear, like a Scarlet Letter. It precedes me when I enter a room and gets whispered about like a schoolyard crush.

Paranoid Schizophrenic.

Dr. Sutton has some lofty ideas about my condition and claims mental illness is only one aspect of hundreds that make me who I am. Not one to shy away from a challenge, he thinks he can help me. His confidence is legendary, but I've carried this burden for a long time. Despite what he thinks, I can't be fixed.

He doesn't realize I'm falling for him or that I have some lofty ideas of my own. He should know better because people like me deserve a hero, too.

The Jessie Hayes 4 Book Series

(Must be Read in Order)

1462 South Broadway (Book 1)
*Winner of the National Excellence in Romance Fiction Award)

It's said that a bird never has to doubt the stability of her branch because her trust is in her own wings.

I myself, am trying to grow some wings of my own, but I'm kind of mired in place right now.

My roommate fondly calls my situation *a rut* and seems to think he knows how I can climb out of it.

The problem with his solution is that he's stone-cold crazy.

There is no way in hell I'm going to a *sex club*.

A scorching, witty, and unexpectedly tender story about finding courage in the unlikeliest places—and discovering the kind of freedom that doesn't come from a stable branch, but from daring to fly.

720 Linden Street (Book 2)

My kinky introduction to BDSM has been less about dipping my toe and more about being tossed into the deep end…bound.

That simple fact has required me to make some pretty hefty leaps outside of my comfort zone.

Turns out, there is a whole lot more to the BDSM scene than I initially thought.
There's a staggering array of possibilities, all wide open for me to see and experience.

You see, my boyfriend owns a sex club.

And I have a lot to learn.

Trigger Warning: 720 Linden Street contains content that some readers may find distressing.

1700 Grant Street (Book 3)

Have you ever found yourself at a crossroads on your journey, with your entire future depending on tiny little decisions here and there?

Do you resist temptation and stick with your current choice? Or will you always wonder how life *could have been*?

When you get to this branching of your life's path, it's not enough to merely choose one direction. You must distance yourself from the rejected road. Because dancing between the two will slowly unravel you.

And it will start with your fickle heart.

945 Cedar Avenue (Book 4, Salinger's Story)

A wedding engagement is a joyous occasion, right?

Well, I suppose that depends on your perspective.

If you happen to be on the side of the path that branches to the left, when the love of your life chooses to go right, you may have a different opinion.

So, what do you do when someone else's choice annihilates the future you counted on?

The answer to that may depend on your membership status at a certain sex club.

Namely, 1462 South Broadway.

COMING SOON!

<u>The Space Between</u>

<u>Midnight Sun</u>

JOIN KC DECKER:

Mailing List: www.KCDeckerBooks.com

Instagram: www.instagram.com/author_kc_decker

X: www.X.com/KCDeckerBooks

Facebook: www.facebook.com/kc.decker.79

Bookbub: www.bookbub.com/profile/kc-decker

www.KCDeckerBooks.com

Chapter One
Trouble

"Do you need some water?" Adelaide asks, as she pensively makes her way toward me. She has a crazed look in her eyes, while ironically, her hands are motioning for me to stay calm. She can sense the devastation in the air. It resonates in my office—thick, like Silas' disgust and my own reckless folly.

I laugh stiffly at her approach, it's like she needs to disarm a bomb strapped to my chest. Her tall, lanky frame is stubborn in its advance, but I can see her outstretched fingers trembling. Her hair is pulled into a sleek bun that gives the illusion, or not, of her forehead and temples being pulled tightly back, which only adds to her look of alarm.

"Adelaide, relax. That was my boyfriend." As shocking to me as it is to her, my voice quavers and hardly makes it past my teeth.

"Oh...ok, well then....perhaps some coffee then?" She lowers her hands and begins to back out of my office. She's pensive, like she wants to believe me but Silas' wrath is still too oppressive, it has not yet dissipated.

"Nothing for me, thank you. This is all just a big misunderstanding. I'll get it figured out. Nothing to worry about. Everything will be just fine." I realize I'm rambling, mostly to myself and then drop succinctly into my chair. Alone in the metaphorical rubble of my office, the air I suck into my lungs feels stale.

Adelaide resumes her post at the reception desk, but the wild look on her face has not yet diminished. She uses what must be sweaty palms to smooth her already slicked back hair, then busies herself tidying up her desk.

I grab my desk phone and punch in Salinger's extension.

"Yes?" his answer is preoccupied, and I know he's busy with the same end of month deadlines I have looming over me. I'm certain I only have about forty percent of his attention, but what I have to say requires all of it.

"Get in here." I slam the phone down before he can make one of his usual witty remarks. Then I begin seething.

***

Salinger takes his sweet time getting to my office. By the time he struts in, the vehemence I feel has soaked the walls.

"What the fuck?" he asks, seeing I am in no mood to play. He crosses his arms and widens his eyes at me as if annoyed I'm disrupting his productivity. When he cocks his head sharply, prodding me to answer, I snap.

"What is the matter with you?" He further narrows his eyes in confusion.

"What are you talking about, Jessie? I don't have time for this," he motions with his hand, indicating he doesn't have time for me and all my crazy.

"How could you do this to me?" my voice is softer now. "I mean, don't you care about me at all?"

"JB, land the plane. I have no idea what you're getting at."

"This." I hold out the rumpled stack of photos. He walks forward and then takes them from my hand. I watch his face as he looks through the pictures one by one. His expression doesn't change beyond his initial, interested eyebrow lift.

After far too long, I say, "Well?"

"Well what?" he asks, innocently looking up from the pictures.

"Well, did you get your money's worth?" I spit out. He's stunned by the abhorrence in my voice.

"What? You think I did this?" his question dangles in clumsy silence.

"Who else Salinger? Who else would do this?" My ribs are tightening and squeezing the breath from my chest.

"Who else? How about Silas, for one? He clearly doesn't trust you," then, with self-satisfaction, "Looks like Mr. Perfect has a chink in his armor."

"He didn't do it. He actually does trust me... Well, he did, anyway."

"Clearly not! Oh, look, one for our Christmas card," he smiles and holds up the 8 x 10 of me grabbing his package. I remember it vividly. The photo was taken out of context, but still looks severely damaging for my relationship.

"Salinger, it wasn't him."

"Well, it wasn't me either," he steps forward and drops the stack on my desk, "I'm serious, Jessie, I had nothing to do with those."

"Who then? And why?" I start to shake, but it's from the inside, so Salinger doesn't notice. I can feel my relationship unraveling. It feels like in a cartoon, when a thread gets pulled and the person slowly starts to turn, and then ends up spinning around and around as the sweater disappears. I'm dizzy and suffocating, and the feeling won't stop.

"Easy, JB or you're going to hyperventilate. Do you need some water?"

"Why does everyone keep offering me water?" I ask, my breaths quick and shallow. "Is water supposed to save me from this personal hell?"

"Not exactly, but you are clearly on fire," he clears his throat, "Do you want me to talk to Silas? I will if you think that would help."

I scoff at the thought, "Only if you want a broken jaw. Tell me Salinger, would you like to eat your meals through a straw?"

"Don't be so dramatic. There is nothing in those photos that can't be explained. Well…maybe not the one with your hand on my dick." He assumes the posture of someone deep in thought as he slowly rubs his chin.

"Nope. Nothing to be done for that one."

"Salinger! This isn't funny."

"Honestly Jessie, aren't you more concerned that there is someone out there that has taken such an interest in you? Someone who is obviously following you and taking pictures of you?" he over-enunciates the last part like I'm a moron and completely missing the big picture.

"This is psychological warfare, Salinger. I'm not in any real danger. I don't think."

"Ok then, if it's psychological warfare, it's someone who wants Silas and hates you, or vice versa. It's obviously an attempt to cause friction in your relationship."

"I bet it's that bitch, Parker! She hates us both."

"Maybe. What about his ex-girlfriends? And what about Ruby's mother? Could she be stirring the pot?"

"There has been no sign of Ruby's mother for years, and what, now she decides she wants Silas and Ruby back? No. It can't be her."

"Ok, then. What if it is Parker?"

"I don't know. I need Devin for that," I crumple my brows while deep in thought, then ask, "How long does one really need to traipse the European countryside anyway?" I really do need to consult Devin, he thrives on this shit.

"Devin's trip must be very inconvenient for you."

"I know, Right?"

Salinger delivered his last statement with a healthy dose of sarcasm. Unfortunately, it didn't dawn on me until after he had already left my office.

End of Chapter One
1700 Grant Street